"Violent, funny, beautiful, intelligent."
—Jane Rule

"*Lover* is that rare thing, an authentic classic, with passages so lyrical they beg to be read out loud. I have two copies of the 1976 edition, one I have reread until it is frayed and soft with use, the other pristine and locked away, just in case some desperate lover were to steal the first—which they have. Quite a few copies have gone missing since 1976. Thank god someone has finally had the wisdom to reprint Bertha Harris's opus. Now I can give women copies instead of threatening them if they touch mine."
—Dorothy Allison
Author of *Bastard Out of Carolina*

"The re-issuing of *Lover* marks the return of one of our most brilliant novelistic talents. Bertha Harris's melancholy comic genius can now be appreciated by a new generation. And the lengthy introduction she has provided, telling the lugubrious story of Daughters Inc. in hilarious, poignant detail, is itself a stunning achievement with all the condensed complexity of a first-rate novella."
—Martin Duberman
Director of the Center for Lesbian
and Gay Studies (CLAGS) at the CUNY
Graduate School and the author of
Cures and *Stonewall*

"Harris, an American equivalent of Monique Wittig, . . . is ingenious, sardonic, parodic. [She] explores the various roles women have played: grandmother, mother, daughter, sister, wife and second wife, business-woman in man's clothing, prostitute, factory worker, movie star, muse and tutelary spirit, warrior, artist, fake saint, martyr."
—Catharine R. Stimpson

"*Lover* seduces the reader with its playful masquerading, its lyrical language, its entwined stories of women lovers who appear as debo-nair actors, precarious beam-walkers, languishing beauties—sexual outlaws all, pursuing, teasing, embracing, birthing each other. The in-troduction, by turns funny, sad, moving, and outrageous, is alone worth the price of the book. *Lover* is everything a seduction should be—smart, unpredictable, witty, provocative—and sexy."
—Carolyn Allen
University of Washington

The Cutting Edge:
Lesbian Life and Literature

Series Editor: Karla Jay

LOVER

Bertha Harris

with a new Introduction by the author

NEW YORK UNIVERSITY PRESS
NEW YORK AND LONDON

NEW YORK UNIVERSITY PRESS
New York and London

Library of Congress Cataloging-in-Publication Data
Harris, Bertha
Lover / Bertha Harris ; with a new introduction by the author.
p.   cm. — (The Cutting edge)
ISBN 0-8147-3504-5 (cloth)   — ISBN 0-8147-3505-3 (pbk.)
1. Lesbians—Fiction. I. Title. II. Series: Cutting edge
(NewYork, N.Y.)
PS3558.A6426L6 1993
813'.54—dc20   93-17716
CIP
New York University Press books are printed on acid-free paper,
and their binding materials are chosen for strength and durability.

Manufactured in the United States of America
10 9 8 7 6 5 4 3 2 1

Editorial Board

Lover is for Louise Fishman.

"Never lift a foot till you see the money in your hand."

—Advice from my father,
John Holmes Harris,
regarding the art of tap-dancing and survival.

Contents

Foreword

Despite the efforts of lesbian and feminist publishing houses and a few university presses, the bulk of the most important lesbian works has traditionally been available only from rare-book dealers, in a few university libraries, or in gay and lesbian archives. This series intends, in the first place, to make representative examples of this neglected and insufficiently known literature available to a broader audience by reissuing selected classics and by putting into print for the first time lesbian novels, diaries, letters, and memoirs that are of special interest and significance, but which have moldered in libraries and private collections for decades or even for centuries, known only to the few scholars who had the courage and financial wherewithal to track them down.

Their names have been known for a long time—Sappho, the Amazons of North Africa, the Beguines, Aphra Behn, Queen Christina, Emily Dickinson, the Ladies of Llangollen, Radclyffe Hall, Natalie Clifford Barney, H. D., and so many others from every nation, race, and era. But government and religious officials burned their writings, historians and literary scholars denied they were lesbians, powerful men kept their books out of print, and influential archivists locked up their ideas far from sympathetic eyes. Yet some dedicated scholars and readers still knew who they were, made pilgrimages to the cities and villages where they had lived and to the graveyards where they rested. They passed around tattered volumes of letters, diaries, and biographies, in which they had underlined what seemed to be telltale hints of a secret or different kind of life. Where no hard facts existed, legends were invented. The few precious and often available pre-Stonewall lesbian classics, such as *The Well of Loneliness* by Radclyffe Hall, *The Price of Salt* by Claire Morgan [Patricia Highsmith], and *Desert of the Heart* by Jane Rule, were cherished. Lesbian pulp was devoured. One of the primary goals of this series is to give the more neglected works, which constitute the vast majority of lesbian writing, the attention they deserve.

A second but no less important aim of this series is to present the "cutting edge" of contemporary lesbian scholarship and theory across a wide range of disciplines. Practitioners of lesbian studies have not adopted a uniform approach to literary theory, history, sociology, or any other discipline, nor should they. This series intends to present an array of voices that truly reflect the diversity of the lesbian community. To help me in this task, I am lucky enough to be assisted by a distinguished editorial board that reflects various professional, class, racial, ethnic, and religious backgrounds as well as a spectrum of interests and sexual preferences.

At present the field of lesbian studies occupies a small, precarious, and somewhat contested pied-à-terre between gay studies and women's studies. The former is still in its infancy, especially if one compares it to other disciplines that have been part of the core curriculum of every child and adolescent for several decades or even centuries. However, although it is one of the newest disciplines, gay studies may also be the fastest-growing one—at least in North America. Lesbian, gay, and bisexual studies conferences are doubling and tripling their attendance. Although only a handful of degree-granting programs currently exist, that number is also apt to multiply quickly during the next decade.

In comparison, women's studies is a well-established and burgeoning discipline with hundreds of minors, majors, and graduate programs throughout the United States. Lesbian Studies occupies a peripheral place in the discourse in such programs, characteristically restricted to one lesbian-centered course, usually literary or historical in nature. In the many women's studies series that are now offered by university presses, generally only one or two books on a lesbian subject or issue are included, and lesbian voices are restricted to writing on those topics considered of special interest to gay people. We are not called upon to offer opinions on motherhood, war, education, or on the lives of women not publicly identified as lesbians. As a result, lesbian experience is too often marginalized and restricted.

In contrast, this series will prioritize, centralize, and celebrate lesbian visions of literature, art, philosophy, love, religion, ethics, history, and a myriad of other topics. In "The Cutting Edge," readers can find authoritative versions of important lesbian texts that have been carefully prepared and introduced by scholars. Readers can also find the work of academics and independent scholars who write about other aspects of life from a distinctly lesbian viewpoint. These visions are not only various but intentionally contradictory, for lesbians speak from differing class, racial, ethnic, and religious perspectives. Each author also speaks from and about a certain moment of time, and few would argue that being a lesbian today is the same as it was for Sappho or Anne Lister. Thus no attempt has been made to homogenize that diversity, and no agenda exists to attempt to carve out a "politically correct" lesbian studies perspective at this juncture in history or to pinpoint the "real" lesbians in history. It seems more important for all the voices to be heard before those with the blessings of aftersight lay the mantle of authenticity on any one vision of the world, or on any particular set of women.

What each work in this series does share, however, is a common realization that gay women are the "Other" and that one's perception of culture and literature is filtered by sexual behaviors and preferences. Those perceptions are not the same as those of gay men or of nongay women, whether the writers speak of gay or feminist issues or whether the writers choose to look at nongay figures from a lesbian perspective. The role of this series is to create space and give a voice to those interested in lesbian studies. This series speaks to any person who is interested in gender studies, literary criticism, biography, or important literary works, whether she or he is a student, professor, or serious reader, for the series is neither for lesbians only nor even by lesbians only. Instead, "The Cutting Edge" attempts to share some of the best of lesbian literature and lesbian studies with anyone willing to look at the world through lesbians' eyes. The series is proactive in that it will help to formulate and foreground the very discipline on which it focuses. Finally, this series has answered the call to make lesbian theory, lesbian experience, lesbian lives, lesbian literature, and lesbian visions the heart and nucleus, the weighty planet around which for once other viewpoints will swirl as moons to our earth. We invite readers of all persuasions to join us by venturing into this and other books in the series.

When I queried the board of "The Cutting Edge" series about which books they thought worthy of reprinting, Bertha Harris' *Lover* was the title most often named. The novel's experimental form and panoply of fictional and historical characters who run the gamut from saint to poor white trash and who are by turns vulnerable and strong make *Lover* one of the finest examples of early post-Stonewall lesbian fiction when some writers, such as Bertha Harris, broke with patriarchal narrative structures as well as with traditional content. The rich language, which reflects that of Djuna Barnes, makes *Lover* the perfect sequel to *Ladies Almanack* in our reprint of lesbian classics.

Karla Jay
Pace University

Introduction

How Lover *Happened in the First Place: 1*

I grew up in an excessively hick town in the South where there was never anything to do, so when a big-time polio epidemic hit one summer there was suddenly even less to do than nothing. I was kept confined to the house and yard.

This happened before television. My family didn't own any books. I spent a couple of days outside trying to dig a swimming pool of my own with a teaspoon. Then I went inside and switched on the radio. The radio was encased in green Bakelite, its dial was hot orange with black numbers. It was perched on a cast-iron plant stand beside a red begonia. It had to warm up for a minute or so before it started broadcasting. What I wanted was the baseball game; that's what I believed I wanted.

It was Saturday. Vic Damone was singing over the radio. I gagged. I was a child aesthete. At nine, I had joined the Girl Scouts because the leader was an antiques dealer; instead of letting me touch her eighteenth-century chairs of "chewed paper" (some know it as *papier-mâché*), she'd led me and the rest of the troop deep into some piny woods to heat up beef stew over damp sticks: I turned in my uniform. Within the year, I would fail to construct a chandelier out of the only available materials—three wire coat hangers, a thoroughly smashed milk bottle, glue and thread. The polio epidemic had aborted my plan for the summer, which was to be kidnapped by a family with exquisite taste. I was a lonely, anxious, skinny child; on a daily basis my mother compellingly described to me how worthless I was. I had early on elected to love beauty rather than love or hate my mother.

I spun the radio dial. A man with a honey of a voice came in loud and clear, dispassionately reciting the events of the final scene of *Salomé* by Richard Strauss: Herod, who is enflamed by an unnatural lust for his daughter, Salome, promises her anything she desires if she will only dance for him. Salome, who is enflamed by an unnatural lust for the prophet Jokanaan—who has repulsed her advances— performs the dance of the seven veils, then tells her father that what she wants is the head of the prophet Jokanaan on a platter. Herod is horrified by his daughter's wish; his unnatural lust for his daughter turns to abhorrence. But he keeps his promise. When the executioner hands the head on a platter to Salome, she sates her unnatural lust for Jokanaan by kissing it passionately on its mouth. Her father orders his soldiers to crush Salome with their shields. They do so.

The honey of a voice belonged to the late, great Milton Cross whose career was spent telling the folks at home what was happening on the stage of New York City's Metropolitan Opera House during the Saturday afternoon performances.

Unnatural lust couched in sumptuous harmonics was my first experience of art. I lay on the floor next to the plant stand's bowed legs and let it convert me. I never missed a single broadcast. The kid across the street sneaked off to the movies one Saturday afternoon and wound up in an iron lung. Not me.

Lover should be absorbed as though it were a theatrical performance. Watch it. It is rife with the movie stars and movies of my childhood and adolescence. A perverted, effeminate *Hamlet,* and Strauss's *Der Rosenkavalier* have supporting roles. There's tap-dancing and singing, disguise, sleights of hand, mirror illusions, quick-change acts, and drag. In opera, when a soprano performs the role of a young man who is in love with the soprano who is the girl in love with the young man, the soprano who is the young man is singing a "trouser role."

Lover has a vaudeville atmosphere. My father did tap- and soft-shoe dancing in the waning days of vaudeville, and when vaudeville died, he consoled himself by recreating (or, twinning) the good old days with the means he had at hand. I was the means at hand. My father taught me his routines and we performed regularly for the lifers at the state asylum for the insane, and for the residents of the state home for the deaf and the blind: which was better than nothing; it was, in fact, much better than nothing. To tap-dance for people who cannot hear, and do soft shoe for people who cannot see, and to do both for people who are certain that the dancers are not at all who they say they are, but instead are Satan and the Holy Ghost, or a plate of fried chicken, or President Harry S Truman and Princess Margaret Rose—this gave my father a few essential horse laughs out there on the "death trail," which is what *very* small-time vaudeville was called, and engendered in me a taste for surrealism whose expression would eventually worm its way into *Lover.*

In my father's day, and before, vaudeville dancing was

done exclusively by men. In *Lover,* replications are perversions and effeminitizations of originals. Francis Bacon's example of *perversion,* in one usage, was governance of men by women. A lapsed definition of *effeminate* is addiction to women. One of the twins in *Lover,* Rose-lima, suggests that Metro-Goldwyn-Mayer plans to film an extravaganza based on *Lover.* It will be, says Rose-lima, a pastiche of every Hollywood film ever made before the end of its author's adolescence, with special appearances by gallons of menstrual blood and the Blessed Virgin Mary.

The character of Flynn thinks this: "That a thing, if performed, is its own duplicate."

Lover *Falls in Love with the Women's Movement: 2*

Women's liberation in New York was, at its onset, about sexual liberation; too many men were not interested in finding out what makes a woman come. Too many women had sedulously anaesthetized libidos. The women's liberation movement was about the American woman's American orgasm. It was that simple.

Every other thing that the women's liberation movement was about during the sixties and seventies in New York followed from that, including the fact that I looked out my window one morning and saw lesbians everywhere. It's easy to recognize lesbians; they look like you, only better.

The early days of the women's liberation movement in New York was as intimate as the boudoir scene which opens *Der Rosenkavalier.* The more intimate the women, the higher their consciousness, the greater their liberated displeasure in men, the greater their pleasure in one another. That's how liberation initially worked. But pleasure frightened many women; so did the displeasure of men.

Betty Friedan, a social reformer from Peoria and the author of *The Feminine Mystique*—a primitive analysis of sexism which immortalizes Ms. Friedan as the liberated housewife's liberated housewife—put the fear of pleasure into words; she accused lesbians of trying to subvert the women's liberation movement with orgasms. A sexual panic broke out.

When the dust cleared, the movement was roughly divided between the sexual subversives and the rest of the women's movement—women who feared both the displeasure of men and the pleasure they felt with one another.

Lover is the pleasure dome—which includes *fêtes champêtres* and excursions to bars, the movies, and Niagara Falls—I imagined for those sexual subversives. The twins, Rose and Rose-lima, tell their sister Flynn that at the end of the movie everyone ascends into Heaven. *Lover* "ends with Justice being done . . . true lovers united." It's a Renaissance heaven I had in mind, where there's sex.

Just as my father had invented an "alternate" existence for vaudeville dancing, with me, so I assumed the women's movement's sexual subversives (as if they were, en masse, a duplicate of the Blessed Virgin Mary) into the "heaven" of *Lover*. I wanted them to have a good time, unmolested by women who were afraid of pleasure.

Although *Lover* is presumed to be a "lesbian" novel, and it is, the sexual subversives I put in it are not always, nor necessarily, lesbian. I am no longer as certain as I used to be about the constituents of attraction and desire; the less certain I become, the more interesting, the more like art-making, the practice of love and lust seems to me: it becomes more like something I first grasped as a child.

Shortly after I was born, my mother moved in across the street with a beauty parlor operator. Their ordinary routines centered on hard work and the double bed they bought on layaway. Their "hobby" (but it was an obsession) was attending beauty pageants. They made notes— hair styles, approximate bust and hip sizes, legs, posture, gait. They thought that the talent category in the pageants was a waste of time, stuck in, they said, to distract people from the real issue at hand, which was the girls' bodies; to make it seem, they said (when it certainly wasn't!), that baton twirling or a ham-fisted performance of the first movement of "The Moonlight Sonata" was more important than an eighteen-inch waist. They almost always disagreed with the decision of the judges. My mother told me why she'd moved in with the beauty parlor operator: "Because I worship beauty."

Rather than love or hate me, my mother elected to become a confirmed aesthete; I became acquainted at Mother's knee, so to speak, with a way to overwhelm reality that has come to be called the gay sensibility.

Lover's central characters, my sexually subversive elite —Maryann, Grandview, Honor, Metro, Daisy, Flynn, Mary Theresa, and "the beloved" (who appears under other aliases too) are highly aestheticized, like contestants in a beauty pageant; they are not intended to remind readers of actual flesh and blood. As well, my characters are from time to time distorted or magnified or reduced, like the stars (Rita Hayworth, Lana Turner, Loretta Young) in the Hollywood movies of the forties and fifties. Or they are painstakingly romanticized into melodrama, like the artists (highly temperamental composers, ballet dancers, et al.) in the camp classic of my generation, the British film *The Red Shoes*.

Or they are very often like those saints of my Roman Catholic girlhood, every one of them a *femme fatale* like Salome, who single-mindedly pursued any extreme, the more implausible the better, to escape the destiny of their gender. At St. Patrick's Academy, holy cards were distributed as rewards for excellence in English grammar and composition, Latin and penmanship, and for keeping a straight spine up your back, especially during the elevation of the Holy Sacrament at Mass: girl-saint holy cards for the girls, boy saints for the boys. The saints I earned appeared to me against a robin's egg blue background in a state of ecstacy: a rapturous transport often accompanied by physical phenomena (swoons, trances, stigmata, speaking in tongues, agitation of the limbs), in which the soul is liberated from the body so that it may contemplate the nature of the divine more readily. The exempla of some saints preface *Lover*'s episodes to honor their acumen at ecstacy.

I deliberately mistook holy cards, which were intended as aids in meditation and prayer, as objects of art. Depicted in glowing colors, with blazing eyes and parted lips, the saints were all raving beauties. I mistook, I mean, raving beauties for objects of art: I was young and unworldly. I am no longer young.

Life affects *Lover*'s characters as if it were, instead, *Traviata* or *Norma*—just as it did the queen of art, Maria Callas. In my mid-thirties I threw a yard sale in front of my Greenwich Village building which I advertised as "The Maria Callas Memorial Yard Sale." Swarms of strangers approached, dropped some small change into my cigar box, and reverently bore away my mismatched kneesocks. No one charged me with falsifying my old clothes; everyone already knew that Maria Callas had never set foot in my socks. Together, the patrons of my "Maria Callas Memorial Yard Sale" and I were collaborating in a sort of workshop production of the gay sensibility, whose practice hinges, like the arts, very much on decisively choosing *as if* over *is*. I recall saying this to one devotee: "She was wearing those argyles the morning of the day she so tragically died in Paris. That's twenty cents, please." And he replied, "Too true. I'm going to keep them in a silver box on my coffee table."

But real flesh and blood does hover at a safe distance behind *Lover*'s unreal characters. As I wrote, I had in mind some of the most intellectually gifted, visionary, creative, and sexually subversive women of our time. I got to know nearly all of them within the women's liberation movement, and I was drawn to them in the first place because they were hot. Some appear in *Lover* as sexual subversives. Others are in place to sabotage how the vulgar think about love, lust, sex, intellectual activity and art. Ask them this: Are you a practicing homosexual? They will answer, I don't have to practice. I got perfect at that years ago.

The real women join with the fictional characters to commit *Lover*'s "style." All of them, like all good performers, are protean in their capacity to exchange one identity for another; they are so intrepid and ingenious they are able, when circumstances call for it, to shapechange to male. Other women I came across in the movement are responsible for the personal anecdotes and jokes in *Lover,* which are as much a part of its texture as anything I invented myself.

In no particular order, the real life lurking behind *Lover* was: Jill Johnston, Eve Leoff, Jenny Snider, Esther Newton, Jane O'Wyatt, Phillis Birkby, Carol Calhoun, Joanna Russ, Yvonne Rainer, Valerie Solanas, Smokey Eule, Mary Korechoff, Kate Millett, Louise Fishman, and myself. Books by Virginia Woolf, Gertrude Stein, Jane Ellen Harrison, and Valerie Solanas show up on a bookshelf in *Lover* as my own *objets de virtu.*

It does not flatter them to say so, but the work of Jill Johnston, Yvonne Rainer and Louise Fishman made the ultimate difference in how I imagined *Lover,* and determined, however obliquely, *Lover*'s expression.

Lover *Enjoys Postmodernism: 3*

In the 1960s, I saw Yvonne Rainer's dance, *The Mind Is a Muscle.* A virtuoso dancer, Yvonne Rainer, like many postmodernist dancers-choreographers of that era, was moving against technique, especially her own technique, to abolish choreographic meaning and narrative. She freed her work from social, political, and cultural associations, and from the familiar arguments of cause and effect. She turned the body's movement over to the play of randomness, coincidence, and chance. Her mentors were, of course, John Cage and Merce Cunningham whose music and choreography had also gone some distance in liberating me from the ordeals of purposefulness. My mind was a Zen blank as I absorbed *The Mind Is a Muscle.* After the performance, I thought of the noncontinuous writing of Gertrude Stein and of the ethereally discrete fiction of Ronald Firbank. *The Mind Is a Muscle* was a world unto itself. I wanted to make one of my own like it.

All allusions to the brain throughout *Lover* are emblematic of Rainer's *The Mind Is a Muscle*, which was my *donnée.* References to cancer of the brain are memento mori, the imagination as death's head when contaminated by exegeses. The blank spaces, the silences in *Lover,* where useful narrative is expected, indicate that *Lover* is meant to be an aesthetic rather than a useful entity. My subversive elite are recluses from usefulness and meaning: they are *objets d'art*.

When *Lover*'s character Veronica isn't writing the fiction I'm supplying her with, she's forging masterpieces and salting archaeological digs with fakes. Forgeries, I'm suggesting, are aesthetically at a further remove from usefulness and meaning than their originals. As mirror-images, duplicates, twins, of the originals, they are better art. Within the secluding perimeters of *Lover*, women are the originals, lesbians are the forgeries.

I would rather my character Flynn to have sprung full-grown from my brain (mine, not Zeus') than descend from a womb: but I don't write fantasy. The mothers in *Lover* must make themselves reproductively useful before they may enjoy ecstacy. Motherhood in *Lover* is the real worm in the bowl of wax fruit: which is *Lover*. Every biological reality in *Lover*, but especially motherhood, contaminates the aesthetic surround.

I abstracted the character of Maryann from the brilliant and complex personality of Jill Johnston who, during the sixties, had become my literary hero. Her writing had nerve. Much of *Lover*'s deliberate plotlessness, which I hoped would affect the reader as a delirious spin, spins around Maryann, my idea of the lesbian's lesbian.

Jill Johnston had already established herself as the most knowledgeble and sensitive critic of New York's avantgarde when, in the mid-sixties, she began to turn her *Village Voice* dance column—which was always about much more than dance—into a gorgeous performance of radical self-psychoanalysis, introspection, self-revelation. She began to apply the wit, erudition, comic turns, intellectual acuity, and artistic discernment, for which she was already famous, to an in-public exposure of her own life. Jill Johnston became her own subject: the "dance" of her column became Jill's illuminating dance through the details of her own life and mind.

Shortly after the Stonewall revolution in 1969, Jill came out in print like gangbusters and became my sex hero. Her *Voice* columns were collected under the titles *Marmalade Me* (1970), and *Lesbian Nation: The Feminist Solution* (1973).

Lover's *Stab at Manhating: 4*

I've read somewhere lately that what the real-life (the biblical) Salome wanted cut off from the body of John the Baptist ("Jokanaan" in the opera) was not his *head*.

In the late sixties, the women's liberation movement felt a rush of manhating. So did I. It was a heady, Dionysian sensation. We went up on the mountain and stomped. Sensation led to daring suggestion, which Valerie Solanas elegantly dealt with in her publication the *S.C.U.M Manifesto*; the acronym stands for Society for Cutting Up Men. I chose to deal with the daring suggestion with less than daring. In *Lover,* from time to time, I recount, sometimes word for word, stories women were telling me about what men, sometimes *their* men, had done to them. Toward the novel's conclusion, I wheel in the body of a murdered man. Think of the corpse as *Lover*'s revenge motif. The character of Veronica hides the corpse by hastily turning it into fiction. *Lover*'s author loves murder mysteries.

Life Before Lover: *5*

My pre-*Lover* fiction was still entrenched in the themes of Southern Gothic and Lesbian Gothick; they are not dissimilar, nor are they unlike Italian opera. Both genres tend to be soaked in booze, blood, and tears; both are thick with madness, violence, suicide, and love's tragic finales. I was perversely laboring to apply, perfected, my version of a literary technique that had died, already perfected, along with the Bloomsbury group, to booze, blood, tears, madness, violence, suicide, love's tragic finales.

When I asked Parke Bowman (who would publish *Lover*) why she was so eager to take my novel on, one of the things she told me was that she wanted her company, Daughters, to represent the work of a female avant-garde and that as far as she was concerned, I was it. She went on to say that she was disinterested in feminist and lesbian content or sensibility. Parke freed me from any sense of responsibility to force a direct figuring of the politics, ideals, or goals of feminism or lesbianism or lesbian-feminism in my writing. Nonetheless, my politics (such as they are) exist side by side with my DNA in *Lover*.

But I've never been much of a political animal, nor even a social one: it's the *rules,* the ordained procedures and ideologies. I like to be either alone or having a good time. A good time is an interval of passionate and intimate exchange followed almost immediately by seclusion; a night in a great gay bar followed immediately by seclusion; a big, lavish party musiked by wall-to-wall Motown, washed in gin, and dense with new breakups, new couplings, new networking, new gossip, and good dope—and when it's over, two days later, a month of seclusion.

At one of those parties, circa 1973, the funniest and smartest and straightest woman in New York, Eve Leoff (Keats scholar and Professor of English at Hunter College), told some bozo that she'd rather sit on my lap than dance with him. The bozo threw a sexist, heterosexist, and homophobic tantrum, after which Eve danced with me. Politics are where you find them.

I became, sort of, to the best of my ability, a political

animal in the early seventies because, most particularly, I didn't want to disappoint Kate Millett, whose first book, *Sexual Politics*, turned me instantly into a radical feminist. But mostly I became a political animal in order to have a good time. Feminism struck me as a good time, and it was. Back then, it still frightened the horses; it made most men foam at the mouth, and it got the best women horny. As such, feminism forcibly yanked my writing up from under the Bloomsbury tomb where it had been trying to pass as good but dead.

Some of the best times I had being political were with the artists, Jenny Snider and Louise Fishman; with Phyllis Birkby, the Yale-trained renegade architect; with Smokey Eule and Mary Korechoff, master carpenters who also kindly hammered some sense into me; with my highly significant attorney, Carol Calhoun; with the anthropologist Esther Newton, whose first book was *Mother Camp*, a study of heterosexual male transvestism; and with Jane O'Wyatt, mystic and graphics designer. Very often, the most political thing these friends and I did together was to tell one another the truth. Which made us fearless.

Lover *Regards Print:* 6

By the early seventies, the new political consciousness created by feminism and lesbian-feminism, and by the 1969 gay Stonewall revolt, was being met by a corresponding cultural consciousness out of which a new kind of highly politicized writing was born. Mainstream publishers, by and large, found this work either too inexpert, or too strange (and too political and too sexual) to risk it, and they had already—or were in the process of doing so— satisfying any need they saw for "politicized" women's writing by publishing the work of white feminists dealing with the politics of heterosexual love and romance (Erica Jong, Marilyn French, et al.) and the work of middle-class (at least) African-American women such as Toni Morrison, Ntozake Shange, and Alice Walker. The politics of the constant book buyer tend to be liberal.

The new gay, feminist, and lesbian-feminist writers, as a consequence—or because they preferred to be independent of a mainstream which they found classist, sexist, heterosexist, homophobic, racist—founded their own presses. Some presses actually had a press; others used Xerox equipment or hand-cranked mimeograph machines. Suddenly, in verse, fiction, and broadsides, the "love that dared not speak its name" became a motor-mouth. Much of what it had to say was memorable.

The presses eked out a hand-to-mouth existence. The costs of the publications often barely covered the production expenses. Nobody got paid; skills, including fundraising, were learned on the job. Decisions were usually made collectively. Hardship was the rule, burnout was the norm; but the staying power was in some cases enormous, and it was almost exclusively fueled by the adamantine convictions which had got the presses going in the first place: that well-wrought words on a page could, by speaking the unspeakable, create and organize radical political activism.

How well wrought the words were was not usually of primary importance; "good" writing was useful writing, the kind that made gays and lesbians feel strong, comfortable in their own skins, angry, tough, and highly motivated to enforce change, perhaps revolutionary change, in the surrounding heterosexual world. That it worked, to some extent, is history.

But there was considerable talent giving good literary

and journalistic value attached to some of the presses. In Washington, D.C., Diana Press published *Women Remembered* (important women "lost" by the patriarchy), edited by Charlotte Bunch and Nancy Myron (1975), and Rita Mae Brown's *A Plain Brown Rapper* (tough political analyses), and reprinted Jeannette H. Foster's invaluable scholarship, *Sex Variant Women in Literature: A Historical and Quantitative Survey* (1975). On the West Coast, Amazon Press brought out *The Lesbian Reader: An Amazon Quarterly Anthology*, edited by Laurel Galana and Gina Covina (1975); in Oakland, The Women's Press Collective, which devoted itself exclusively to work by lesbians disfranchised by race or class, published Judy Grahn's *Edward the Dyke* (n.d.) and *A Woman Is Talking to Death* (1974), both of which found immediate movement acclaim. In New York, Karla Jay edited, with Allen Young, *After You're Out: Personal Experiences of Gay Men and Lesbian Women* for Quick Fox in 1975; and Times Change Press published *Amazon Expedition: A Lesbian-Feminist Anthology*, edited by Phyllis Birkby, Jill Johnston, Esther Newton, Jane O'Wyatt, and myself (consciousness-raising, personal narratives, a noteworthy essay on manhating by science-fictionist, Joanna Russ). The best presses today are Barbara Smith's Kitchen Table: Women of Color Press, Faith Conlon's Seal Press, and Joan Pinkvoss's Aunt Lute.

Arno Press was located on Madison Avenue instead of in a damp basement or an illegal loft. Arno belongs in this context, however, because it had the vision to recognize the writing on the wall as early as 1975, when it began the Arno Special Collection, fifty-four reissues of lesbian and gay classics dating from 1811 to 1975. Jonathan Ned Katz was the editor.

· · ·

Parke Bowman wanted nothing to do with the presses. The radical politics, the nonprofit status of most of them, their collective organization—it all smelled strongly of the left wing to Parke. Parke got involved in publishing women writers because she was in love with June Arnold.

Daughters Publishing Company, Inc., was not a press. Both partners, June Davis Arnold and Parke Patricia Bowman, were rather touchy about the distinction. "Publishers of Fiction by Women" (eventually, they would reluctantly include some nonfiction), their writers got contracts, advances, royalties, royalty reports, etc., identical, according to Parke, to those issued to writers by the mainstream houses. Parke and June referred to all mainstream publishers as "Random House."

Parke's stated goal was to run Daughters as if it were Random House and thereby compete with Random House in the marketplace. To Parke, Daughters was strictly a business whose business was profit-making. She wanted to publish novels with both literary merit and commercial appeal, and if the works were perceived as feminist, so much the better. But from the start she made it clear that she would never agree to publish a novel for political content alone.

June idealized the back-breaking labor at the presses, and she was in complete agreement with their political sentiments. June claimed that Daughters' reason for being was to publish the novel-length fiction which the presses could not afford to publish. As soon as Daughters was founded, June began looking for manuscripts in keeping with the spirit of the poems, short stories and nonfiction of the presses: deep-thinking personal revelations about the nature of oppression.

In 1972, June believed wholeheartedly that a full-scale feminist revolution was at hand. With the patriarchy (and mainstream publishing) in ruins, Daughters would replace Random House, and the works published by Daughters would sell like hotcakes in the new world of empowered women.

Parke enjoyed the idea of Daughters' replacing Random House, but the last thing on earth she wanted was a feminist revolution, or any connection whatsoever with "prerevolutionary" women's presses, which she more or less privately referred to as "a bunch of damn dumb dykes." The way to beat Random House was through the tried-and-true methods of cutthroat capitalism.

Throughout the life of Daughters, Parke longed to have a quiet, deeply closeted life with June. What Parke had in mind was something closely resembling a standard upper-class heterosexual monogamous marriage. She would eventually get just that, but not until June's hopes for a women's world, and her own personal ambitions, had been severely disappointed.

From the start, therefore, the partners were at odds about the aims of the company. Throughout Daughters' brief life (less than a decade), June and Parke went through an ongoing struggle to dominate the company and realize their opposing views. Compromises were grudgingly made, or else one or the other of the partners would back down and wait for the next time. It's a miracle of a sort that the company lasted as long as it did. The miracle, of a sort, was money, lots of it.

At first, I was only another of the Daughters' novelists. Then I became their "senior" (their only) editor. Officially, my relationship with the company ended there. Unofficially, I was the third side of a triangle that rivaled the old Lesbian Gothicks in terms of booze, blood, tears, madness, violence, and operatic grand passions—so much so, I often wonder if Daughters wasn't something I wrote instead of lived.

For a while, I loved Daughters and Daughters loved me. I applied—I misapplied—three tenets of feminist doctrine to the way I loved Daughters: that trust, solidarity, and strength arise from making oneself totally vulnerable to women; that one may trust women totally, but never men; that male oppression is the sole cause of mental and emotional ill-health in women, and feminism the sole cure. It's difficult for me to confess to something so banal, but here goes: I needed a good mother.

Founded in 1972, Daughters published its first list in 1973. By 1979, Parke and June had dissolved Daughters in the manner of any publishing company going out of business. All titles abruptly went out of print; rights reverted to the authors; leftover copies of the books were distributed among the authors and to remainder houses. Parke sold the townhouse in Greenwich Village that had been company headquarters. June and Parke severed their connections with feminism and their authors (including me), and retired to an insulated haute-bourgeoise life in Houston, June's home town. At the time, June was fifty-three and Parke was forty-five or forty-six. I hoped never to see either of them again.

Late in 1975, I had rented, along with the feminist theoretician Charlotte Bunch, space in the Manhattan loft building June owned and where she and Parke lived on the top floor. After midnight, in late December of 1977, my phone rang. It was June, in one of her classic rages. She shouted into my ear that I had to be off her premises no later than the next day, my lease notwithstanding. The person I was in bed with, she announced, was an FBI agent who was sleeping with me for the sole purpose of gaining access to Daughters in order to destroy the company.

The person I was in bed with had about as much to do with the Federal Bureau of Investigation as I did with professional ice hockey. June's accusation was so very far off the wall that I wondered for an instant if the time had come, finally, to phone for the guys with the straitjackets. I got my breath back; I told June that it was my distinct impression that whoever went to bed with me—including that time back in 1910 (or was it 1902?) when it was J.Edgar Hoover himself, in full frontal nudity, lusting after me—did so to gain access not to Daughters but to my body, okay?

June told me to start packing. I was gone the next day, as ordered.

After June's death, Parke would confess that it was she, not June, who'd wanted me out of the building, no holds barred. That made plenty of sense to me, for two reasons: The FBI had had a strong grip on Parke's imagination for some time before the night I was caught in bed with J. Edgar Hoover. And Parke had been in love with me since the day we met. If she couldn't have me, nobody could. Rita Mae Brown, with admirable succinctness, once described Parke as a femme in butch clothing, and June, vice versa. She was right. June had to evict me on Parke's behalf because Parke didn't have the necessary machismo.

After the fiasco of my eviction from June's building, I never expected to hear from either Parke or June again. But in 1979, June telephoned from Houston and rather warmly told me that she and Parke would love to see me, would I come and visit? I said yes. My nearest and dearest suggested that I was out of my mind to go near Parke and

June again. I replied that I was certain that Parke and June must want to apologize, heal old wounds, effect a reconciliation: did that sound like I was out of my mind?

I was out of my mind. June met my plane; Parke waited in the car. June drove and pointed out the sights. Parke sat in stony silence. June told me that they lived in Houston's most fashionable suburb. It seemed like any fashionable suburb to me—spookily silent, absolutely white-skinned, so rife with self-protection the entire neighborhood seemed to be wedged inside an invisible condom. Their house was hidden behind a locked fence. It was long, low, enormous, and replete with many faux Tijuana-hacienda touches which I recognized because I'm chief of the aesthetics police. Outside, surrounded by a rose garden, there was a swimming pool that passed my inspection.

Parke disappeared in the house. June showed me a guest room approximately one city block's length from their bedroom, then she disappeared. I hung out in the guest room for a few hours. Then Parke showed up and told me to give her five dollars; she was going out for burgers, five bucks should cover my share. I gave her five dollars.

We sat at a table in a dining room suitable for Kiwanis Club banquets and unwrapped dinner in silence. For some reason I wasn't hungry, so I decided to make conversation. I introduced the subject of combat women in the military, a controversial topic in the news at the time, and asked whether they thought it was a feminist thing for women to turn themselves into cannon fodder—or did they think that turning women into cannon fodder was just another male plot to get rid of uppity women?

That broke the ice. Instantly, Parke and June flipped from restrained hostility into the active kind: unlike me, they weren't lily-livered pacifists. They believed in their country. They were one hundred percent behind any war their president cared to wage. Young women as well as young men should be prepared to die for their country, and any other point of view on the matter stank of communism.

Okay, I said. I figured they still thought they were dealing with J. Edgar Hoover's girlfriend, complete with wires. I considered congratulating them on being, as of that moment, completely in the clear with my superiors at the agency. I kept my mouth shut.

The next day June told me she'd asked me to visit because she needed help on her new novel, *Baby Houston*, hadn't I understood that? No, but. June handed me the manuscript. I sat down in the extraordinarily decorated living room, which was about one-third the size of the New York Public Library's main reading room, and got to work. Parke dropped in at regular intervals to collect for the next meal.

I stayed in Houston with Parke and June long enough to urge June repeatedly to replace the pretty writing in *Baby Houston* ("Baby" was her mother) with the rage she was so far keeping between the lines ("You're wrong," she told me), and to experience a representative slice of how they were living their new lives. June spent her days working on *Baby Houston*, swimming and gardening; Parke watched movies on TV, swam, gardened, worked the *Times* crossword, and read English novels. They visited with June's girlhood chums and played a regular bridge game with some of them in the evenings. They shopped a lot at Houston's glitziest mall; they were compiling new wardrobes of French designer clothing. From the neck down, June looked sleek and chic, but her face looked haggard— stressed and grim, as if, inside, she was grieving. Her face would have more appropriately accessorized sackcloth and ashes. Parke's threads were as upscale as June's, but were still in Parke's favorite understated color, *merde*. I was still in my basics—basically my only basics, except for the vintage evening dresses I reserved for dates with J. Edgar —which were, then as now, white shirts and black jeans. One night, when we were about to go out to dinner with one of Parke and June's new friends, June said, "I'm so glad to be here, where I can dress in nice clothes again. It's hard for me to even look at that New York movement drag any more." I quickly changed into my basic variation on my basics, white jeans and black shirt.

Houston had grown some lesbians since June's early life there (when, she once asserted, there weren't any), but except for one or two, all of June and Parke's close women friends were heterosexual; the one or two lesbians they hung out with were wealthy. They no longer felt comfortable among people too different from themselves. Too much difference, I surmised, was too little money. They had never felt comfortable among people different from themselves.

The last time Parke asked me to fork over, I made bold to ask if by any chance they needed a loan to tide them over. Parke fearlessly stepped on the irony. She told me that from now on they were keeping every penny strictly for themselves; they'd had enough of getting ripped off by the women's movement.

I wasn't the women's movement. Far from ripping off Daughters, or Parke or June personally, I had, minute by minute, inch by inch, paid my own way during my friendship with them and my time with the company. Parke had insisted on it, down to the last dime, even when I was traveling with the partners on Daughters' business exclusively. She justified this un-Random House-like exploitation of an employee by impressing on hand-to-mouth me that she had to save up for her old age.

I gave her money for the next meal. I don't keep score; I'd rather be ripped off. And I was, as ever, afraid of Parke's barely suppressed anger. Evidently, Parke had either demoted me into the "damn dumb dykes" category, or was possessed by the idea that I was so deeply in her debt (though for what?) that I had to make some recompense by paying for my own food while I was a guest in her house working on June's novel.

Parke was as uncommonly stingy with money as I am cavalier. Which may go some distance in explaining how she, with June's knowledge, could break the most fundamental rule of hospitality: but it doesn't begin to explain the rage that accompanied her demands for money. I've finally remembered how I actually felt each time I was faced with both her anger and her open palm: I had been invited to Houston to experience humiliation.

I did what I could with *Baby Houston*. June thanked me and drove me to the airport. I chalked the monetary and emotional costs of the trip up to being out of my mind.

Within two years after Parke and June returned to Houston, June was diagnosed as having cancer of the brain, the incurable kind. I thought, when I heard the bad news, of the trope—the human brain; cancer of the brain —I'd used in *Lover*. I had a nightmare about fiction's being able to assume an extraliterary life of its own to do things its author never intended.

Not long after June died, I acted like a Manhattanite and went to a psychiatrist. I felt disabled; I felt that I was disappearing, and neither love nor work nor sex was helping me. The psychiatrist was tall, fat, and mid-fortyish with a little-girl hairdo. She was so white she looked like an Easter bunny. Her clothing led me to believe that in her professional opinion dainty pinks-on-pinks was a good cure for what ailed her patients. She wore a lot of showgirl makeup—glitter on her eyelids, lashings of pancake, and fifties-red lipstick, and she had flat feet. She wanted me to hold rocks which she described as "crystals" while I talked; she encouraged me to attend events at which a woman entered a trance and then, in a voice belonging to an Egyptian from the Old Kingdom dynasty, answered questions from the audience: "Should I buy General Motors?" and Cheops would answer, "Go with the flow." I spent most of my energy during sessions with her trying not to show how thoroughly her mind and body revolted me. In no time, she had me driving her around New York, feeding her cats, and moving her from one apartment to another. I was paying her top dollar; we did not have a bartering arrangement. After a year of this, she urged me to give the little girl inside of me a great big hug. I suggested that she go fuck herself and, at last, departed.

I might have filed a complaint with the psychiatric police, but I couldn't imagine what nature of complaint I could file against my mother, or Parke and June. I spent the rest of the eighties virtually a recluse, one who cannot be had because she is not available to give herself. I avoided old, genuine friends; I felt contaminated, therefore unworthy of their friendship. It doesn't surprise me in the least that I've been unable to complete the four novels I've written since life with Daughters.

By 1975, the year before *Lover* was published, Parke had given up even the pretense of being a feminist, but June was still avidly talking lesbian-feminist politics. Neither of them had yet gone mad—or, if they had, I was so enchanted by being in service to Daughters, I ignored the symptoms. When others suggested to me that something might be seriously wrong with Parke and June, and therefore with the company, I became their apologist and defender. But after a while even I became aware of some serious contradictions between what June was publicly saying—the politics *du jour* (the personal is political, etc.) —and what she was privately doing: to me, in particular.

June and Parke were the first wealthy people I'd ever been close to. I thought it exotic, at the very least, that June swore by politics which, if they were successfully put into practice, would be the ruin of the sources of her money. But I didn't say so. I didn't want to spoil the loud party, I didn't want them to be disappointed in me. My mother got a lot of mileage out of telling me how disappointed in me she was. Nonetheless, I did wonder if June had found a solution to that tiresome riddle, the one about how much easier it is for a camel to pass through the eye of a needle than it is for a rich man [sic] to enter the kingdom of heaven.

Our closeness, which would end in my near-imprisonment, started when Parke went after *Lover,* insisting that I sell it to Daughters even though she hadn't read a word of the manuscript. Parke told me that she had read my first two novels and that she'd been impressed (Parke later brought *Confessions of Cherubino,* my second novel, back into print). This is how Random House operates, she said; they buy sight unseen too if a writer's earlier work suits them.

The partners took me to dinner. They were charming, amusing, and warm; every few minutes, Parke would say something hilarious. In the middle of this love feast, June explained that publishing with the "male" houses would brand me as "male-identified;" I would be just another one of those feminists, *so-called,* who did exactly that with their books. Parke said that Daughters was *not* a feminist house, that it had no political definition whatsoever be-yond "Publishers of Fiction by Women." June said Daughters *was* feminist. Then Parke threw her glass at the restaurant wall, and we were asked to leave.

I was delighted. I was finally in the cast of an opera; somebody definitely throws a glass against a wall during *La Traviata*. In the street, Parke told me to swear that when people asked me why I published with Daughters, I would not tell them it was because Daughters was femin-ist; I was to say, instead, that I published with Daughters because, like Random House, Daughters gave big ad-vances. I understood her point. Parke was equating femi-nism with impoverishment; I was ashamed of being poor. I swore to defend big advances to the death.

About ten days later, they took me to dinner again. They explained that what I would get by publishing with Daughters was a guarantee that *Lover* would never go out of print; none of their titles, they promised, would ever go out of print. No publishing company on earth could offer that guarantee but Daughters.

I more or less fell on my knees and cried, *I am thine!* Most writers will understand how I felt, though few are as naive as I was. I knew, of course, that *Lover* wasn't going to be a bestseller, or even come near bestsellerdom: effemi-nate aesthetes like me don't write bestsellers. But I hoped that given time, plenty of time—maybe twenty or thirty years—a first edition might be bought out. Daughters, according to the partners, guaranteed that time. When the euphoria wore off, questions occurred to me. How could Daughters make that promise? If, just for example, the partners died, then what guaranteed the future of the company promising in-print eternity?

Parke and June laughed my questions off. I was too

unworldly, they told me; I didn't understand how businesses operated. They were right. I was unworldly, possibly even other-worldly. Far from understanding how businesses worked, I did arithmetic by counting on my fingers. I was ordered to stop worrying. I decided to stop worrying and become a true believer. I felt safe with June and Parke, as if my time for being a beloved child had at last arrived. I was happy to let them have *Lover*; I feared that neither *Lover* nor I was good enough for them.

The only regret I had in publishing *Lover* with Daughters—and I suppressed it, it seemed audacious—was that *Lover* would not be reviewed by the *New York Times,* whose policy then, and for some time to come, was not to review original trade paperbacks. But the physical beauty of the Daughters' editions was well worth the loss of the *Times*. The elegantly designed covers and the dimensions (eight and a half by five and a half) of Daughters' paperbacks have now been adopted by nearly every good publisher—Virago, for example—both here and in Europe, but it was Daughters' designer, Loretta Li, who created the look.

When I finished *Lover,* Parke and I had dinner again. I handed over the A&P brown paper bag containing the manuscript and Parke gave me a company check for ten thousand dollars, the same advance, Parke assured me, that Random House gave its authors of third novels. Harcourt, Brace's Hiram Haydn, in 1969, had given me one thousand, six hundred dollars for my first novel *Catching Saradove,* and two thousand three years later for my second. I was giddy with the thrill of big bucks at last. Parke suggested we do some drinking and dancing over at Bonnie & Clyde's, a movement bar on West Third Street, to recover and celebrate. After a few hours, we realized that we didn't have *Lover*; one of us had left the only complete copy of the manuscript under the restaurant table. We found our waiter reading it. "Hot stuff," he said.

I thought Daughters was hot stuff. Parke and June thought Daughters was hot stuff, and with good reason. As far as I know, they were the only women around at that time who were putting so much money where feminism's mouth was.

I'm extravagant in my affections while they last. Compare me, if you will, to Tosca or to the family dog: I'm the very model of the cheap date. Parke and June led me to believe (that is, they lied to me) that they were gambling every cent they had on Daughters. Parke, for instance, had given up her law career to work full-time for the company's success. I imagined what June had given up; what I imagined her giving up was what I would have spent a fortune on if I'd had one: Europe, with special attention to Italy and France. My eyes glazed over with hero worship. When people started complaining to me that June tried to ram her politics down their throats and slapped them upside the head, in a manner of down-south speaking, when they failed to swallow her very hard line, I would try to explain away their indignation by urging them to *look,* June could be whiling away pleasant hours in Paris right now, or soaking her tootsies in the Bay of Naples, or lounging in a gondola—but *instead* . . . so the least we can do is be tolerant. Nobody swallowed my line either.

After I gave June and Parke *Lover,* I gradually handed over most of my life to them and to Daughters. I justified my self-abandon by maintaining that I was merging my personal with my political in an area (writing and publishing) for which I was most suited. I thought how lucky I was that they wanted me.

Since 1972, I'd had full-time employment at Richmond College of the City University of New York, where I taught in the Women's Studies program. I had other serious, time-consuming responsibilites, both professional and personal, as well. I had been, except emotionally, a self-sustaining adult since I was sixteen. But in 1976, shortly after *Lover* was published, June asked me to take on all her editorial work so that she could write full-time. Without pausing to consider when, with both a full- and a part-time job—and a life—I would find time to write myself, I accepted. My mother's chief contribution to my upbringing had been to beat my legs and back with a walking cane every time she thought that I was, in her words, "showing off" or giving the appearance of believing that I was "better than other people." By the time I met June and Parke, I had become so adept at self-effacement that I could make myself disappear at will. My mother told me that because of me, she'd been cheated of everything she ever wanted. I am, to this day, very careful never to compete with other women; I will go to any amount of trouble to help a woman get what she says she wants; if I must sacrifice something I want in the process, so much the better. Sometimes this behavior is mistaken for feminism; it is penance.

I understood immediately that it was more important for June to write than for me to write. June, I would eventually realize, also thought that it was more important for her to write, so much more so, in fact, she would have preferred that I stop writing altogether.

After a while, Parke and June began pressuring me to resign from my assistant professorship at Richmond College and work exclusively for Daughters. Neither offered me an ordinary reason to do so, such as a salary equal to what the City University paid me, health insurance, a pension—nor even an extraordinary reason. I was supposed to do it simply because they wanted me to do it. No mundane consideration prevented me from giving them what they wanted, it was rather a fear of being eaten alive combined with the twitchings of some half-paralyzed adult instinct for survival that kept me full-time at Richmond until 1976. But I wondered why they wanted me around full-time, and for what? Daughters simply didn't have enough work to justify my full-time employment unless I added most of Parke's work—bookkeeping, mailings, dealing with the printers, etc.—to my editorial duties, and this was clearly impossible. As we all knew, I was inept with money and the arithmetic that handling money demands; Parke, furthermore, would never have put the secrets of the company's account books into my hands.

But in 1974, when they were leaning heavily on me to say it out loud—*I am thine!*—I was, in any event, nearly always on duty at Daughters in one way or another when I wasn't teaching. Parke was running the ordinary day-to-day business of publishing with intelligence and keen competence; distribution, however, was an on-going problem for her, fraught with stress and anxiety. Except for gay and women's bookshops (and there were then relatively few), other, general-subject book dealers and their customers were still wary of taking a chance on such unfamiliar, sometimes openly lesbian, writing. The grand design for Daughters that June and Parke had conceived—beating Random House at its own game—was being continually frustrated in the marketplace.

Nor were women, movement women, living up to the partners' expectations as book buyers. I think now that it's possible that neither Parke nor June, sheltered as they were from the exigencies of ordinary women's lives, ever fully understood that, for most, buying books was an unconsidered luxury; although both June and Parke knew the facts of life—that women were (and still are) paid considerably less for work than men, and that most women who were single mothers led—and still do lead—lives devoted to acquiring the bare necessities—neither had directly experienced those disquieting conditions: so they resisted and ignored them. As well, it bewildered, and often downright aggravated them, to see women who had some discretionery money spending it on a night out, in company, instead of on Daughters' books. They also avoided looking at the bottom line: that most people, men as well as women, would rather do nearly anything than read unless the book is "useful" nonfiction or escapist fiction; and it's cookbooks and children's books that are the entirely dependable sellers. The war against Random House was being constantly lost.

Given their temperaments—Parke and June were highly competitive, ambitious, and proud; they were quick to take offense, they often perceived offense where none was intended; and they did not easily tolerate frustration or disappointment—it isn't surprising that the partners were frequently in a state of emotional turmoil which too often was directed at outsiders in the form of insults and hostile confrontations. Many of those outsiders were people who could have done Daughters and its authors considerable good.

Part-time editorial work, for which I was fairly paid, soon began to include unpaid labor: witnessing the often violent personal fights between June and Parke; monitoring their often combative meetings with writers; trying to con people whom the partners had insulted into believing that they hadn't really been insulted; and consulting with the partners over their growing enemies list. The "enemies" I knew of were those who had disappointed or frustrated the partners by not buying June's lesbian-feminist party line—and then, having been offended by the partners, offended them in return.

By the time the partners dissolved Daughters, the enemies list included all of mainstream and women's publishing, the entire membership of the women's movement, and last but not least, the only good Indian, me.

Almost from the beginning of our association, every move I made away from June and Parke, no matter how slight or temporary, met with their displeasure, then with suspicion (consorting with the enemies), and with charges of "disloyalty." My heros, friends, publishers, and employers were underneath it all a creature known as *folie à deux,* which consciously, and conscientiously, never stopped trying to turn itself into an *à trois.* It's hard to find good help: but Batman, perforce, needs his Robin, the Lone Ranger his Tonto, and even seething paranoids crave someone to lean on.

Soon I was seeing my friends on the sly; after a while, I woke up one morning and realized that I never saw my old friends any longer—and that I didn't know how to see them without Parke and June finding out. I couldn't understand why I was afraid of their finding out, nor did I yet understand why it was so crucial to them for me to know only the two of them. They once berated me for inviting the eminent scholar and critic Catharine R. Stimpson over for a drink without first asking for their approval, and for not asking them over as well. I waffled. By "berated," I mean the sort of loud, infuriated name-calling and sin-listing inquisitorial attack known as verbal abuse. I was afraid that Parke was going to hit me; more often than not, when words failed to score the point she wanted to make, Parke used her fists.

The truth was that I didn't want them to become acquainted with my friends any more than they wanted me to have any friends other than the two of them. I was afraid that one, or both, would lash out at people I cherished. I had learned my lesson early on when I invited June to meet my dearest friend, the painter Louise Fishman. I don't recall the preliminaries but in short order after the introductions, June was, unprovoked, raging at Louise, insulting her life, her work, her background, while reserving special (and mysterious) contempt for the fact that Louise had played basketball in high school. Louise's response was sensible. She put on her coat and quietly went out the door as if she were backing away from a barking, potentially dangerous, dog.

I put the scene out of my mind. Unless I wanted to walk out behind Louise—and to my eternal shame, I did not—I would have to, at all costs, avoid thinking about June's assault. I put it out of my mind—and kept it in that overcrowded "out there"—until now: that is to say, their tyranny over me, and my cooperation in being tyrannized, survived their deaths. June has been dead, at this writing, for ten years; Parke died in February 1992, less than a year ago.

Beneath the fragile gift-wrap of her professed politics, June Arnold regarded herself, by virtue of her socialite Houston upbringing, as a singular aristocrat; as such, she tended either to patronize or lavish disdain on any woman (or man) without class characteristics she could honor. It was as simple as this: Louise had played basketball; June had grown up riding her family's horses. Poverty irritated June; she understood that one might be born poor but to go on being poor into adulthood, she felt, demonstrated either an annoying weakness of intellect, or some pre-embryonic poor judgment in not getting oneself born an heiress, or some perverse refusal to grab hold of the legendary bootstraps and give them a good yank.

It was, however, the "common" woman who was being canonized by radical and lesbian feminism in those days: the more victimized by sexism or by patriarchal institutions, the more, so to speak, sainted. There was an unspoken taboo against personal ambition. "Using" the movement to achieve individual goals was tantamount to committing the mortal sin of "betraying the revolution," or betraying the women's movement, or all women. It was also a time in feminism, coincidentally, when mothers, as opposed to fathers, could do no wrong—a response to the Freud-inspired years of blaming mothers for everything.

Daughters, to some extent, practiced the politics June preached, by publishing literature by women overwhelmingly trapped in circumstances beyond their control—*Born to Struggle* by May Hobbs, for example, and *A True Story of a Drunken Mother* by Nancy Lee Hall, and *I Must Not Rock* by Linda Marie.

But in real life, June was dealing with her feminist embarrassment (not guilt: good feminists had nothing to feel guilty about) over hiring a maid and having the money to pay her well, by tying a big pink ribbon around the new mop she'd bought her, as if it were a gift.

Without money, class, or horses, I could only assume that what separated me, in June's view, from the common feminist herd was my small literary distinction. But it wasn't enough. June wanted me cut out of the herd absolutely. June decided, and Parke went along with it, that it would be better all around if I came from a more socially acceptable background, one rather more like hers or Parke's.

June's politics were by and large for public consump-

1

tion only. She swore, for example, by one of the most fundamental tenets of the women's movement, the one on which consciousness-raising, the first step towards liberation, was based: that one woman will unquestionably believe what another woman discloses about her life and the nature of her background. Privately, however, June persisted in reverting to type. In one of my most memorable encounters with the partners, I learned that after close and careful consideration, June had decided that I must be lying about the circumstances of my birth and upbringing in order to gain movement credentials. *Nobody,* said June, could be as bright, as educated, as good a writer, as well spoken and well mannered (and so forth) as I was—yet come from the deprived circumstances and cruel mother I had only very slightly, and very casually, filled her and Parke in on. It's impossible, said June, *we do not believe you.*

While I was profoundly moved and impressed by women such as Linda Marie, who could tell the story of her horrific childhood in clean, spare, glowing language (in *I Must Not Rock,* which I had the honor of editing), I was myself so ashamed of being my mother's victim, and of my helplessness in her power, I made every attempt to conceal the facts of my early life even from intimates, even from myself: I had, for example, spent most of the first four years of my life in a crib which was, in effect, a cage; my mother had ordered a sixth side carpentered for it, a hinged "lid" that locked me inside for most of the day and all the nights. One day my father was moved to take me out of the cage and destroy it. Within the hour, he began teaching me his dance routines. I did not think of myself as a victim; I thought of myself as incredibly lucky. I'd escaped, I'd survived; I was therefore undamaged: wasn't

I? If anything, I had embellished my childhood for June and Parke to make it seem reasonably "normal" to them —more eccentric than awful.

I began very gradually re-entering the world three years ago in my own circuitous, aberrant fashion, through extremes of physical exercise. After a while, I remembered that the one thing during my childhood that I'd loved (beside beauty) was dancing with my father. So I added a dance class to the extremes of physical exercise. My teacher is the dancer and choreographer, Beth Easterly. There are more ways than one to exit a cage. In my case, it has taken more than one dancer to unlock the lid and help me out. I'm out; I am, for instance, writing this introduction to *Lover* and one of my novels-in-progress, *You,* is nearly complete.

When June declared that they *did not believe* me she was within her rights, but for the wrong reasons. I did not fight back, although I might have used the opportunity to tell Parke and June the unvarnished truth; but within the topsy-turvy context of June's disbelief (that the earth's disinherited cannot acquire manners and education, or be gifted), the truth would have worsened my position because the truth was much worse than the "eccentric" half-truths I'd told her. And when June was convinced that she was right nothing could persuade her that she was wrong. And under certain kinds of attack, if the attacks come from women, I become paralyzed. I was paralyzed. I felt that June, and Parke with her, had unscrewed my head and filled my body with buckets of melancholy. I felt as helpless as a beaten child. I had no words. I don't recall how I replied to the charges. Apologetically, no doubt.

On the other hand, I couldn't bring myself to commit a version of suicide on June's behalf. I clung to the identity I had disclosed; it wasn't much, but it was all mine. June never stopped disbelieving it.

Aside from the stunningly classist (and positively un-American) attitude built into June's disbelief, there was the partners' ongoing conviction that if they battered long enough and hard enough at what I had indeed come from, and still was (despite the renovations I'd done on myself) they might eventually erase my difference from them—my origins, my memories, my history, and my people.

Doing away with my difference, the stuff of my human individuality and of my art, would also serve another vital purpose. Separate a writer from her typewriter and she'll find a pencil; separate her from her autobiography, through disbelief, and she will become silent: and June knew it. The patriarchy had been successfully employing the technique for a long time.

June and Parke had filled my days and nights with personal and professional crises; nonetheless, I was still writing. Furthermore, *Lover* was receiving the sort of critical attention June had craved for her second novel, *The Cook and the Carpenter* and for her third, *Sister Gin.* Worse, I was the second novelist published by Daughters who, June felt strongly, had gotten more attention than she deserved.

June and Parke became lovers in the late sixties. The first half of Daughters' life was located in Plainfield, Vermont, where June owned a farm. Later, June and Parke moved into the top floor of June's Manhattan loft building, but kept the farm. Parke bought the townhouse on Charles Street in Greenwich Village to serve as company headquarters; the Charles Street house also gave Parke a place absolutely hers to escape to when the fights with June, which were usually over June's involvement with lesbian-feminist politics and presses, began to escalate. Parke called sleeping at Charles Street "running away from home." June had her own escape hatches. She would retreat to the farm or rent small apartments in the Village, where she wrote and saw movement friends privately. June's politics had always made Parke nervous: that's how Parke put it, "They make me nervous."

Ironically, June's politics are what brought them together. June was one of a group of women who, in the late sixties, took over a long-abandoned city-owned building on East Third Street and made it, rather comfortably, a shelter for women and a day-care center. When the city ordered them out, they resisted; the cops dragged them out. Parke was one of the lawyers who went downtown to get the women out of jail. Parke told me how June's firebrand temperament initially thrilled her; how glamorous she seemed. But Parke's romance with June's temperament, and the politics which inspired it, was soon replaced by "nervousness," which in fact was a fear (which would graduate into paranoia) of June's drawing fire at the two of them from both the society at large and from parts of the movement June was at war with, which eventually included most of the women June had been with in the Third Street action.

June has been written about frequently, sometimes within the context of warm feminist praise for her fiction and her politics. Once in a while, a few details of June's life are woven in with discussions of June's books. It always interests me to find that the writers generally assume that June, with sterling altruism, deliberately turned her back on her Houstonian social rank and discontinued any immoderate personal use of her wealth once she became a feminist and a lesbian-feminist and a publisher of books by women: as if she had pulled herself *down* by the bootstraps.

In fact, June risked nothing, and lost nothing, when she left Houston for New York and the women's movement. She had absolute control over her fortune, and very sensibly she never neglected to foster it. She never felt the cost of Daughters, nor did her generous handouts to feminist enterprises ever make a noticeable dent in her wealth. She enjoyed the enviable position of being able to indulge in charity (and buy alliances) without feeling the pinch of self-sacrifice. She once told me that she was always very careful not to give to feminist causes any of the money she meant her children to have. Her mother, she said, would want her grandchildren raised as much as possible as she had been, and well taken care of after her death.

When the partners decided to terminate Daughters, and retreat from New York into Houston, they might have sold the company to other women. That they did not allow Daughters to continue, in new hands, publishing women's writing which might otherwise never see the light of day, was their revenge, their particular Tet offensive, against women in general and the women's movement in particular.

As well as money, June brought to a movement determined to create equality not only with men, but among women, a profoundly inbred sense of superiority and a bottomless need to be recognized as an exceptional woman.

Born in South Carolina, October 27, 1926, June was raised in Houston, where she was a debutante; she went to Vassar but after a year transferred to Rice University back home in Houston. According to June, the Vassar girls were "snobs;" they didn't regard Texans as their social peers. Attending Vassar was June's first attempt to gain status in the Northeast: where status counted. Leaving Vassar was her first flight back to established, albeit provincial, status. June had all the well-known vanities, and thin-skinned pride, of the Texas millionaires. She often spoke of how "cultured" (despite the fact that they were Texan?) her mother, and her mother's family, the Worthams, were. The family money was made in cotton and insurance. In Texas, cotton and insurance counted as "old" money. The parvenus were into oil.

After college and a tour of Europe, June married and bore five children, one of whom died in early childhood. She eventually divorced Mr. Arnold because, she told me, he was using up so much of her money in business failures. But not long afterward, according to what she told me, she went to New York and married a "Jewish psychiatrist" whose role as her New York husband, she said, was to give her an excuse to live in New York, away from her mother. June took her second husband down to Houston to meet the family. At the big barbecue thrown to fete the newlyweds, June's new husband fell in love with all things Texan and refused to return to New York. So she divorced him too. Otherwise, June told me, she'd had lots of male lovers before she met Parke: which is the way it was, she explained, for pretty and popular Houston socialites in her day; she would rather have been a lesbian, of course, but she couldn't find any lesbians to be a lesbian with.

One of the biggest and loudest fights the partners went through in my presence was about sex. It was bad enough, according to Parke, that June had had sex with men but she also suspected that a woman lover was lurking in June's past. Parke hated the fact that June had had any lovers, male or female, before her. Sometimes Parke could, in a self-satirizing way, joke about her jealousy. I remember some madcap murderous schemes she came up with to punish June's first husband for ever laying a hand on her.

I often felt that June, after the honeymoon wore off, was not at all happy with Parke sexually. Parke was a romantic and she had a romantic's need for June to be the romantic's ideal of womanhood, the chaste-and-malleable-maiden part of the ideal especially.

Ruinously at work in Parke and June's relationship was Parke's enormous need for the kind of security which demands an all-encompassing monogamy, historical as well as current. They joined forces to demand of me "monogamy" with them. Long before they caught me in bed with J. Edgar Hoover, they had more than once heavily hinted that I might be better off without lovers. As I write this, I realize that it wasn't Louise Fishman's high school basketball playing that made June attack her, it was because I'd had an affair with Louise, and had been in love with her, and continued to love her.

Parke Bowman was intrinsically shy, passive, and fearful of every kind of rejection. She showed every sign of being deeply inhibited sexually; her personality was the opposite of June's. Both, however, got a kick out being verbally abusive (they called it "honesty;" what I heard was sadism), and Parke also enjoyed becoming physically violent. I find it probable that Parke felt that beating up a woman was somehow more "decent" than having sex with a woman. She smiled while she was doing it; she seemed orgasmically blissed afterward.

In one blistering scene I was privy to, June argued that any woman—Parke, for instance—of her generation who had not gone to bed with men back in the days when there weren't enough lesbians to go around wasn't sexual enough to be a real lesbian. There was a lot of more-lesbian-than-thou one-upmanship going on in the movement then: the fewer the men you'd gone to bed with, the more lesbian you were. But June was not so much regretting Parke's lack of heterosexual experience as she was marshaling a defense against possible movement charges that she wasn't lesbian enough to understand and write well about lesbian experience. As far as I know, those charges were never made against June or her writing. But New York feminism was electric with charges and countercharges during the seventies. June couldn't exactly pretend to be a poor woman, not with her real estate and her publishing company, but she wasn't about to have her extensive heterosexual past, which included four children, used against her.

With a few well-chosen words (including, "The reason you screwed guys so much is because you're a slut") Parke responded to June's charges that she wasn't lesbian enough by redefining insanity and sanity: Insanity, Parke said, was a woman with the morals of a slut who thinks that the way to become a lesbian is to go to bed with a lot a men; sanity, however, was a lesbian who controls her animal urges until she finds "true love": as *she* had.

I always had a hankering to get into some serious legal trouble so that Parke could win my case in court.

Parke had enjoyed consummated "true love" in only one relationship with a woman before she met June. She was by nature deeply conservative and conventional; she voted a straight Democratic ticket mainly because she hated Richard Nixon's guts. "True love" meant marriage for life.

But "animal urges" sometimes overwhelmed Parke's high moral tone. On many occasions, Parke decided that I was her true love. I am reasonably certain that each was preceded by a quarrel with June. Compared to June, I was easy to control and manipulate; and Parke was a control freak of the first water. But I was not so much controllable during my life with Daughters, Inc., as very agreeable, evasive, and diplomatic. I was the unreconstructed feminine (or the unreconstructed daughter of my mother); I was vulnerable to bullying, I would do nearly anything to please. One night, I was at home alone writing *Lover*. Parke rang my bell, marched upstairs, smashed a vermouth bottle against my kitchen stove, and got down on her knees and declared that she was in love with me, would I run away with her? I replied, evasively, diplomatically, that sex and running away together would destroy our friendship. This answer seemed to mollify her. Another time (we were closeted in the Vermont farmhouse pantry whose shelves displayed a survivalist's supply of canned petit pois), she insisted that I promise her that when I turned fifty—not before, not after—I would "marry" her. She was serious. She said that June would probably be dead by the time I was fifty—a miserable prediction that miserably came true. I was in my mid-thirties at the time; June was eleven years older than I was. I don't recall what I answered; possibly I lied, and said *Why not?* I loved Parke's charm and humor; it was her body I was rejecting, but I couldn't bring myself to insult her body. Parke feared rejection, I feared rejecting.

I was not as diplomatic as I thought I was; Parke knew why, in the first instance, I'd said no, and in the second, the reason for my evasiveness. She never forgave me, yet she never stopped, behind June's back, trying to seduce me. With every rejection, her hostility grew and expressed itself in ways that ranged from the mean (such as refusing to let me get some laundry done in the washer and dryer at company headquarters), to attacks on my friends, then straight on to eviction.

One of Parke's favorite forms of revenge was turning me, when she could, into the company's scapegoat. Midway during the company's lifetime, June commissioned a novel from a woman in San Franciso, and, I suppose, gave her an advance. When the completed novel arrived, neither partner thought it was any good. I wasn't allowed to read it. The writer had published some fine short stories, so I suggested that they send the manuscript back and let the writer turn it into a collection of stories or replace the novel with original stories; I reminded June that mastery of short fiction did not necessarily mean ease with novel-length fiction.

But June was embarrassed by the impulse that had made her commission the work; she had committed, in her mind only, a shaming lapse of judgment. She wanted the whole matter to disappear, as if it had never happened. Parke told me that in order to protect June's reputation, I had to return the manuscript and write a rejection letter to the author which she herself would dictate to me. Parke stood over me, I typed. The letter was scathing and insulting; it was designed to demolish the author's ego and make her resist any rash inspiration to show it around to her friends and associates. Then Parke told me to sign the letter I'd typed; my name alone would be at the bottom of Daughters' stationery: whereupon the worm turned and suggested that we write another kind of letter, the sort that points out to a writer that many novels commissioned by many publishers sometimes—very often, in fact—don't pan out. If we send your letter, said the turned worm, this woman is going to hate us for the rest of her life. Parke replied that I, not "us," was going to take the rap; I owed it to the company—for example, *Lover* had not earned back on sales the ten-thousand-dollar advance she'd paid me and probably never would. June added that the writer deserved the letter for pretending, during June's visit to her home, to be too poor to afford a television set when everybody (and everybody knew it) could afford TV.

The letter Parke had dictated was sent, with my signature only. Amnesia has mercifully erased all memories of the responses I got for that letter.

Another book June commissioned that Daughters never published was *Not by Degrees,* essays in feminist education collected and edited by Charlotte Bunch. *Not by Degrees* would have appeared on Daughters' last list. Charlotte did her work, the book was ready; but it transpired that June and Parke had expected each essay to be a diatribe against Sagaris, a feminist educational institute created by Joan Peters and Blanche Boyd, who was one of Daughters' authors. Sagaris had enjoyed a groundbreaking life span of one summer during the early seventies in Vermont. I taught writing at Sagaris. One of my students, Dorothy Allison, would later publish her award-winning novel *Bastard from Carolina* as a consequence of her own courage and talent. Charlotte Bunch had taught feminist theory at Sagaris. Charlotte refused to negate the Sagaris experience by complying with June and Parke's wishes. *Not by Degrees* was later published by Crossing Press.

In the early seventies, Susan Sontag was diagnosed as having drastically advanced cancer. The literary community, worldwide, was frightened for her. One of her friends, and mine, spoke of her fears in front of Parke. It was not long after Parke had decided that I would "marry" her once June was dead; Parke suspected (as if I were June) that my friend and I were sleeping together. On the basis of that suspicion, she hated my friend.

When my friend said that she was afraid that Susan Sontag might die, Parke promptly replied that she hoped that Susan Sontag *would* die. June agreed with Parke.

No matter what I said to June and Parke about this assault on my friend's feelings, their answer was always the same, endlessly repeated: Susan Sontag wasn't a feminist, so she didn't deserve any pity; if Susan Sontag were the literary genius she thought she was, she would have long ago said a few good words about Daughters; Susan Sontag, being "male-identified," occupied the place in the literary firmament which rightfully belonged to June and if the women's movement had done its work, instead of screwing around so much, the male literary establishment would by now have been replaced by Daughters, starring June instead of Susan Sontag.

Parke was secretive and close-mouthed about her personal life, her background, and her political beliefs. She behaved as if a sort of House on Un-American Activities, manned by a sort of Joseph McCarthy and Roy Cohn, had its ears to her ground waiting to use anything she might reveal about herself against her. It's possible that her extreme reserve happened in reaction to the political demands radical and lesbian feminists were making at the time: that class, racial, ethnic, and sexual bounderies separating women could be abolished only by a detailed public disclosure along these lines about one's own life. Knowledge, in effect, would invariably bring about understanding of the "other," and understanding would accomplish a united front. It was acknowledged that lesbians, especially poor and/or black and/or disabled (and so forth) lesbians, were the most "other."

But Parke loathed being identified as a lesbian, and she was deeply suspicious of the "most other," who, she was certain, would be breaking down the doors to garner for themselves her money and her privileges of skin and class if they were given half a chance.

Meanwhile, June was out there competing for movement prestige by proclaiming herself a lesbian and enthusiastically letting it be known that Daughters was offering the great unwashed half a chance. June made it impossible for Parke to stay absolutely nailed in the closet. When

June was addressing women's groups, or giving readings, Parke kept herself in the deep background: she didn't want to seem to agree with June's lesbian-feminist stance but at the same time she wanted to be around to defend June in case the "most other" went for June's highly privileged throat. No wonder Parke was a nervous wreck.

Parke was born on February 7 in either 1933 or 1934. She told me that she had been raised, for a while, by her parents in New Jersey, where she would eventually go to college and law school. But while she and her brother, she said, were still children, her grandparents decided that they didn't want Parke and her brother to be raised by "flappers," so they went to court and got custody of the two children. Parke gave me the impression that her parents were a sort of *jeunesse dorée*, New Jersey style. Parke also once told me that her father was someone very important with the Atomic Energy Commission. Which is how, Parke told me, she'd learned how to keep her mouth shut; loose lips sink ships, the government had warned the nation during World War II.

Parke told me that the grandmother who'd raised her finally lived in reclusive splendor in a big isolated house in upstate New York and ordered all her food (mostly cans of petit pois) from S. S. Pierce. The conclusion of Parke's life was not unlike her grandmother's.

According to Parke, she had severed every connection with all members of her family very early on. She never told me why. She was neutral and cautious when she talked about her beginnings; if she had any feelings for her family, she did not betray them to me. Given the more difficult aspects of her personality—intolerant, hostile, judgmental, unforgiving—I imagine that she was raised harshly. When June spoke of her own upbringing, and she did, frequently and nostalgically, it sounded to me as if she enjoyed endless love and spoiling, especially from her mother.

The first writer Daughters published who got more attention than June felt she deserved was, of course, Rita Mae Brown.

Daughters Publishing Company, Inc., "Publishers of Fiction by Women," was created in 1972 to disguise, and legitimize, the fact that June was forced to resort to vanity publishing. Her first novel, *Applesauce,* written while she was still living in Houston, was published in 1966 by McGraw-Hill and was reprinted by Daughters ten years later.

She wrote her second novel, *The Cook and the Carpenter,* during her first two or three years with Parke in Vermont. Her first version of the work was an explicit tale of lesbian grand passion, a *roman à clef* of her relationship with the "cook." That version, had Parke not interfered with it, might have gotten the mainstream publication June wanted for it, although probably not until June had excised the gender-neutral "na" she used and replaced it with the usual pronouns. But Parke, as she would tell me in detail, was appalled to find herself destined to be in print so openly a lesbian. She demanded from June, and got, cuts, rewrites, equivocation, and dense disguises in the novel's final version. *The Cook and the Carpenter* was rejected by all the mainstream publishers.

Hence, Daughters, at a time when June still loved the women's movement, which would, June was certain, recognize her feminist literary masterpiece in return. And so it did—the educated, habitual book-reading part of the women's movement, in time, did show a proper appreciation for *The Cook and the Carpenter*—but not fast enough and never, in June's view, sufficiently. Nor did the "right" women (the poet Adrienne Rich, for example, and Susan Sontag) ever respond appropriately, or, perhaps, at all. What the movement did respond to, immediately, and with love, was another novel on Daughters' first list, *Rubyfruit Jungle* by Rita Mae Brown.

Rita Mae Brown's first novel is as far removed from the woeful tradition of the Lesbian Gothick as it is from *The Cook and the Carpenter*'s stylistic mannerisms and equivocation. *Rubyfruit* is a funny, straightforward tale of the picaresque adventures of Molly Bolt, and Molly Bolt is lesbian *mens sana in corpore sano* entire. In no time, Molly Bolt became a conquering heroine. To a greater or lesser extent, every woman, gay or straight, who read *Rubyfruit* wished she could be more like Molly Bolt.

Parke rejoiced in *Rubyfruit*'s financial success. She had joined in creating Daughters to become a businesswoman. But Rita Mae Brown's success humiliated June. The popular acclaim June had counted on from the women's movement had gone to someone else; nor was there any praise forthcoming from New York's literary community. June's covert purpose in founding Daughters was annulled in little more than a year. Nearly as demeaning, the same mainstream houses that had rejected *The Cook and the Carpenter* soon began trying to buy the rights to *Rubyfruit Jungle* from Daughters. Parke wisely held on to the rights until she got what she considered top dollar in the deal.

Even worse, Rita Mae had unwittingly scored another sort of triumph over June. Like Molly Bolt, Rita Mae Brown was still in her twenties; she was attractive, sexually desirable, and sexually active. Rita Mae's outrageous *mots*, and singular fearlessness, coupled as they were with warmth and charm, endeared her to most women. June was old enough to be Rita Mae's mother. June had, in middle age, the body of a teenage athlete (but so did Rita

Mae) but only Parke got to see it. At last a lesbian, June was confined (it was as bad as being a wife) in a relationship with a woman who wasn't all that crazy about sex but was certainly crazy when it came to sexual jealousy. When June tried to be charming, like Rita Mae, she often came off like a deep-fried version of Scarlett. When she tried to be outrageous, she sounded either pompous or scary. June had a scanty sense of humor; Rita Mae was able to make people laugh. Up from poverty, Rita Mae was a self-made woman. If anything, June's wealth mitigated against her in the women's movement, which tended, in that era, to equate poverty with political virtue.

Officially, the women's movement didn't have stars, but it was composed of human beings so of course it did; and Rita Mae, who had great native charisma as well as political wit, was one of the movement's first stars. Rita Mae had, in fact, along with Charlotte Bunch, and other members of what was to become the *Furies* collective in Washington, D.C., been among the first (during the sixties) to posit, and see into print, the politics of lesbian-feminism which June espoused. June had hoped, since the time of the Third Street Building takeover, to be that too: a movement star.

Daughters' degeneration began with its first list, a year after its founding in 1973, with—as June saw it—the unjust victory of an inferior woman over a superior one. The rest of that first list was, to June, simply high-quality filler.

Parke was proud of Rita Mae's success. But a united front was crucial to both of the partners. Parke finally, reluctantly, agreed with June that *it wasn't fair*.

June and Parke had approved of all my manuscript choices until I presented them with M. F. Beal's *Angel Dance*. It was late in the life of Daughters, which was, by

1977, becoming more of a armed camp than a publishing company. The screws were tightening on Parke's paranoia, which she had lately begun to express as a fear that "something might happen" to June if June didn't withdraw from public view.

By then, however, June was up to little more than talking old-fashioned lesbian-feminist cant at nothing more dangerous to her health than Modern Language Association Conventions. I once listened to June say at an MLA seminar—which was perhaps entitled *Whither Clit Lit?*— "We've [Daughters and the feminist presses] gotten rid of harsh expressions like screw and spread your legs . . . and reclaimed fat and wrinkled as adjectives of beauty." Parke was fat, June was wrinkled, and leg-spreading in their bed was on the wane. Parke sat beside me during June's presentation checking out the audience, some of whom, she'd warned me, would be FBI agents masquerading as academics and writers. Anyone who couldn't look her in the eye was an FBI agent.

I hadn't taken Parke's fixation on FBI infiltration seriously because more often than not she made a joke or a game out of it. I was therefore surprised when the partners initially resisted my desire to publish M. F. Beal's *Angel Dance:* in which a strong-minded feminist revolutionary, who's survived the male left of the sixties, fights her way through sinister attacks from both the left and the right, and ultimately enjoys sex with a women's movement star in a snowbound cabin. There was nothing wrong with the politics of *Angel Dance* that I could see, and it was also a heady novel of suspense written with confidence, ease, and sophistication.

When I (wrongly) persuaded Parke and June that *Angel Dance* was going to be a bestseller just because I loved it, they let me go ahead and write M. F. Beal a letter of acceptance. Working with M. F. Beal was an interesting change from the usual. As soon as M. F. Beal returned her signed contract, Parke told me that she'd had word from Beal that while I was working with her on the book, I must under no circumstances send anything in writing to her through the mails; all editorial work had to go on over the phone, but it had to be over a public pay phone, never a private one.

What?

Parke hinted darkly that the plot of *Angel Dance* might be based on the author's real-life experiences, which (Parke suspected) were replete with dangerous emissaries from the right, and desperadoes from the left, and roughnecks from the Federal Bureau of Investigation.

True to form, I did as I was told by the boss. Parke liked me to call her the boss. I enjoyed getting out of the office, even when the local street nuts tried to horn in on my pay-phone conferences, but nothing in my conversations with M. F. Beal gave me reason to believe that she was anything but a good novelist who wanted the best for her book.

It took me a while, but eventually I understood why Parke was buying surveillance equipment, adding locks to the company doors, and regularly inspecting its telephones for taps: government taps. I got it; Parke wasn't playing cloak-and-dagger games, she was dead serious.

With considerable braggadocio and swagger, Parke had gone up against "Random House" when she'd entered into the Daughters' partnership. She had, for years, precisely followed the rules of capitalism to achieve success for Daughters, and had openly showed her contempt for the feminist presses for not being intelligent enough (or rich enough) to do the same. But, in her view, she had failed; "Random House" had won. Daughters, Parke felt, had earned little more than a small *succès d'estime*—and that, only when she was talking to the right people: who were never the "right" people, who were the New York literary establishment.

Inspired by *Angel Dance,* Parke looked in another direction for grandeur of another kind. If the FBI was seeking to find incriminating evidence against Daughters, or to plant some, then Daughters was important. Thereore the FBI was after Daughters because Daughters had to be important. It was true, of course, that the FBI had routinely monitored feminist meetings and individuals since the sixties; and certain of the sisterhood who entered the women's movement after working for left-wing causes were loathe to give up their dangerous-character identities.

But we were, as I pointed out to Parke, entering the late seventies; I suggested to Parke that it must be common knowledge, even to the feds, that feminism as a fomenting revolutionary force was now a back number if it had ever been a number at all. Guilt by association, Parke answered, now that we're publishing *Angel Dance.* They're going to try to nail us.

Angel Dance was published in 1977. That same year, the Women in Print Conference that June had organized among women's presses, large and small, nationwide, took place during a heat wave and a plague of grasshoppers in a deeply rustic Girl Scout camp surrounded by cornfields outside of Omaha, Nebraska. June was responsible for that choice of location. It was central to all the presses; fairness was the issue, not comfort. Neither Parke nor I wanted to summer in a hot cornfield; I had wasted three days of my extreme youth with the Girl Scouts trying to get a close look at some eighteenth-century "chewed paper" chairs, so I hated the thought of a Girl Scout camp.

But the Women in Print Conference was June's most ambitious stab at achieving movement esteem. A Nebraska cornfield, a Girl Scout camp—Nebraska itself—would serve to demonstrate that she could be a common woman with the best of them.

I told June that speaking as a common woman, I myself preferred hotel rooms in San Francisco or New Orleans to cornfields in Nebraska. Parke told me to shut up, we'd get a kick out of slumming—besides, if we didn't go along with June "something might happen to her" out there in the alien corn all by herself.

At least a hundred women in print showed up. We all had to take turns going into Omaha to shop for food, then cook it in the unrelieved heat. Some of the hundreds were vegetarians; some, macrobiotic; some spat out anything with sugar in it. The politics of food was under constant discussion. I don't cook. I was finally coerced into representing three-personed Daughters at the stove, so one night I fried fish and wrote on the chalkboard menu that it was fried grasshoppers—free food, therefore the most feminist food.

There was a major cornfield abutting the cabin where Parke, June, and I slept. The first night of the conference, while June was out working the camp, Parke had a look at the cornfield, then tiptoed over to me and whispered this: The cornfield is full of FBI agents. I laughed. Then I looked at her. She was trembling with fear, tears were in her eyes. It got worse: The FBI, she was certain, had been monitoring feminist presses, and the single feminist publisher, for a long time. Now that everybody was corralled in one place, they'd have an easy bust; any minute, the feds would be slapping the handcuffs on every "pinko" woman in the Girl Scout camp, but they'd take June and her first because they were the most important—and because June was a well-known "ringleader." She and June were going to the slammer, they'd be locked in separate cells, she was never going to see June again. Parke began weeping.

I was afraid of all that high-as-an-elephant's-eye corn myself, but then I'd always been an indoor type. I made light of the corny agents; I tried to reel Parke back in by reminding her that what Daughters did—*all* Daughters did—was publish fiction by women: therefore nobody, but especially the FBI, took us seriously. Fiction wasn't taken seriously, I said, women were taken less than seriously; fiction by women? Just a big joke.

Wrong. Women were *dangerous,* lesbians were even more dangerous, books about dangerous women . . . and so forth.

If June, and Daughters, could get famous no other way they were going to get it as Most Wanted. Parke refused to sleep or eat. She crouched under a window and aimed her binoculars at the corn. I went to find June. I told her that Parke thought that the FBI was hiding in the cornfields and that I thought Parke was having a nervous breakdown. June seemed indifferent; her expression was blank. She said that if I thought Parke was having a nervous breakdown, then I must feel free to take her back to New York; then she returned to the business of Women in Print. I returned to Parke. On my way, it struck me that June's response to my announcement was eerily calm; my news, I saw, was old news to her. By the time I regained Parke, I was convinced that June had traveled to Nebraska hoping for agents in the cornfield. More than one woman whose ideals and personal ambition had been disappointed by the women's movement half-hoped to achieve immortality in those days by becoming a martyr to the cause—and June wasn't the first.

I went and scored some speed (I didn't inhale) from a San Francisco sister, then told Parke that if she would lie down and grab some sleep, I'd keep watch. I kept watch until it was time to go home.

Once we were back in New York, June asked me never to bring up the matter of the FBI in the cornfield again.

Not all of the FBI hysteria bounced off *Angel Dance* or snaked its way out of the partners' delusions of grandeur. Shortly, in the fall of 1977, one of June's favorite "sister" presses, Diana, in Baltimore, would suffer a devastating break-in and subsequently get the fervent attention of every woman in the feminist press movement. The grapevine was hot with rumors: did Casey Czarnik and Coletta Reid, the founders of Diana, do it to themselves? Was it *men?* A rival press? *The FBI?*

Parke and June certainly favored the FBI as the villains. Along with *Angel Dance* it made for an airtight conspiracy theory. June's frustration and anger grew more intense. She envied the attention Diana Press was getting. Eventually, Parke would arrange for Daughters to be threatened by my lover, J. Edgar Hoover. Throwing me out of the building was also a good way to get even with me for sleeping with somebody besides her.

With Women in Print under control, June, who thought of herself, and Texas, as southern, announced that it was time to take the South. She had by then published her third novel, *Sister Gin*, whose story was designed to persuade younger women that in spite of the author's privileged upbringing and wealth, she was not only as politically correct as they were, she was more so: now she was menopausal, she was old. The older the woman (according to *Sister Gin*), the less the older woman had to lose; therefore the older the woman, the more the older woman was inclined to embrace lesbianism, which is what the older woman had wanted to do all along but when she was young, men had stopped her.

The novel is set in the South. June arranged readings in Atlanta and in North Carolina for her and me. As usual, when on company business, I paid all my own expenses. There was an unacknowledged understanding between me and the partners that because of June's very generous handouts to feminist presses and other enterprises, I was responsible for picking up the slack. It was only right: they had paid me ten grand for *Lover* and *Lover* wasn't earning back the advance.

The southern sisterhood (the few of them who showed up for the readings) fell hard for June. One extremely attractive sister fell hard for me and the fall was mutual. Parke efficiently blocked every move we made to get an hour in bed together.

In Atlanta, while she was reading to an audience of twelve in somebody's front parlor, June (rather like Luciano Pavarotti) became suddenly overwhelmed by the sound of her own words in her own voice and began crying. Pavarotti weeps, but goes on singing. June wasn't so professional. By then, I too craved success for June; my motives were base: anything to shut her up. Without a break in the reading, I put one arm around her shoulder, swept up *Sister Gin,* and replaced her voice with my own.

Our small audience was deeply moved by what they saw. What they thought they saw was sisterhood in action, a feminist bonding and twinning, one woman taking up where another woman must leave off, an emotional correlative of the political. What they saw in fact—on my part—was a purely theatrical gesture, a professional move deeply instilled in me by my interesting childhood.

One Christmas at the state asylum for the insane, my father and I were only two beats away from entering the stage tapping his flamboyant grapevine step for a captive audience of two hundred or so medicated schizophrenics: but suddenly my father folded. His knees were trembling, his skin was dead white, and damp; he had to sit down. His bad cold was in fact pneumonia. But: *Go!* he croaked, and I did, instantly, holding the right hand of an invisible ten-year-old girl and tapping as my father would have. So I tap-danced for June that night in Atlanta just as I'd been tap-dancing for June, Parke, and Daughters all along—and most of the time, in spite of everything, I enjoyed it. The emotional tone was familiar, as in of or relating to a family, mine in particular. And I loved tap-dancing for the sheer hell of it.

June told our little audience later that she'd started crying during the reading because she was so moved to be back "home" in the South again, where women truly understood her. But I knew that her tears came instead from the depths of her disappointment in these same women. They loved her, and they showed it; but once again there were too few of them to love her the way she needed to be loved.

The southern tour was in any case designed to disguise a personal agenda of June's, just as Daughters had disguised June's vanity publishing. June's son, although intelligent, sweet-tempered, and athletic, was not academically inclined. June, however, wanted him to have a degree from a distinguished university; the family honor was at stake. The readings, and Daughters' promotion tour, went first to Chapel Hill, North Carolina, so that June could remind the university that one of her ancestors had been the state's attorney general, and then to Atlanta, where, June told me, she was going to offer Emory University some sort of deal. After Atlanta, we came back home.

June's trouble with *Rubyfruit Jungle* returned in another form when *Lover* was published. When Diane Johnson wrote a friendly review of *Lover* for the *New York Review of Books,* where no Daughters' book had been mentioned before, June's response was that she'd known all along that *Lover* was "reactionary establishment" writing.

When some feminist *salonistes* phoned the company to ask for my number so that they could invite me to give a reading from *Lover,* June replied that I did not give readings unless she too was invited to give a reading. A month later she told me about the invitation, adding only that she hadn't bothered to tell me about it till then because she'd known that I would agree with her.

Sometimes I believe in a spooky kind of destiny. I happened to be in Houston, for once minding only my own business, when June was diagnosed as having incurable brain cancer. Furthermore, I'd randomly landed in a small hotel less than a block away from where Parke and June lived. They had traded up out of the suburb into Houston's museum district.

Predictably, I dropped everything and ran. Predictably, what June wanted me for was to help her hurry up and complete *Baby Houston*. Parke and June, this time, were under the gun. They put up a show of geniality and graciousness. None of us referred to the past or to the discourse in *Lover* on brain cancer. I set to work. *Baby Houston* was long, wildly disorganized, and packed with extraneous material. June was evidently trying to get every novel into it that she half-suspected she might not live to write; *Baby Houston* had to be her unqualified masterpiece. I did my best; June argued against every change and cut I urged.

After June's death, *Baby Houston* went through serious editing in other hands than mine and was severely cut. The Texas Monthly Press published it in 1987, five years after June died.

June did not believe that her cancer was incurable. She went through two or three fruitless operations and endured lengthy radiation treatments. Parke spent her days and nights tending to her, often with the help of local friends and June's daughters. It took June a long time to die. Neither she nor Parke had medical insurance. June had once told me that insurance was a scam, good for nothing except making insurance companies rich: she knew because much of her family money had come from insurance. The wise, she'd explained, make good investments, then cash in when an emergency arises. June's system worked. The expenses for her care and entirely futile operations and radiation treatments ran into the hundreds of thousands.

When June was dead, Parke sold their house and bought a summer cottage to live in year-round on a straight Fire Island beach. Her neighbor was her oldest friend, Loretta Li, and at least once Parke traveled with her to Hawaii, Loretta's birthplace. Parke spent most of her last years, however, as a virtual recluse: although there was one bright period when she fell wildly in love (albeit only electronically) with Diana Ross, and then later with an amusing and attractive young woman with whom she wintered for a while in Key West. I advised her, regarding this young woman, to *try*, to go for the elan vital for a change. Parke couldn't; she told me that she was too afraid that her friend might say no, and then despise her for being a lesbian. About a year before Parke died, she returned to Key West alone, and I visited her there. She seemed lifeless and physically frail. She spent most of the time that I was with her silently watching reruns of *Operation Desert Storm* in her darkened living room, but one day decided that we should invite a mutual friend to dinner. At the grocery store, she told me I had to pay for the food. I paid for the food.

A few months before Parke died, riddled with untreated cancer, she bought her own place in Key West. She died in her new home, cared for by Loretta Li. June's heirs were her children; Parke's were Loretta Li and Loretta's son.

Parke told me that about a year before June died, she finally accepted what she had been told all along by her physicians, that her case was hopeless—and so took charge of the matter of her death. She told Parke to go get the gun, kill her, and then kill herself. Parke told me that she got the gun and tried to pull the trigger, but couldn't: which infuriated June. I asked: Was it like this? If June couldn't live, neither could you? Parke answered, Yes, of course. And if you, Bertha, had stuck with us the way you should have, she would've tried to get me to shoot you first.

It no longer matters who they were; it's what they did, in spite of it, that continues to matter. They published twenty-two good books by eighteen women, many of whom would not have been published had it not been for June and Parke.

What matters, in no particular order, is: *Kittatinny: A Tale of Magic,* a children's story by Joanna Russ; *Shedding* by Verena Stefan; *Nerves* by Blanche Boyd; *X: A Fabulous Child's Story* by Lois Gould; *Applesauce, Sister Gin,* and *The Cook and the Carpenter* by June Arnold; *Angel Dance* by M. F. Beal; *Rubyfruit Jungle* and *In Her Day* by Rita Mae Brown; *Early Losses* by Pat Burch; *A*

True Story of a Drunken Mother by Nancy Lee Hall; *Born to Struggle* by May Hobbs; *The Treasure* by Selma Lagerlof; *You Can Have It When I'm Through with It* by Betty Webb Mace; *I Must Not Rock* by Linda Marie; *The Pumpkin Eater* by Penelope Mortimer; *Riverfinger Women* by Elana Nachman; *Daughters in High School,* Frieda Singer, ed.; *The Opoponax* by Monique Wittig; and my two, *Confessions of Cherubino* and *Lover.*

Parke and June, as far as I'm concerned, have therefore been assumed, along with *Lover*'s sexual subversives, into the "heaven" of *Lover,* where I want them to have a good time, at last.

Lover's *Beloved: 8*

I wrote *Lover* for Louise Fishman. The bowerbird (family *Paradisaeidae*) falls in love. Immediately, he sets about building a bower of love, a chamber or a passage made of choice twigs and grasses so elegantly made it appears architected. The bowerbird adorns the bower with *objets trouvé,* bright and shiny bits of paper and glass. When his bower is completed, the bowerbird dances in front of it. I am told that his dance is complicated, that it's so sophisticated it seems consciously choreographed. It works.

I became a bowerbird. I wrote *Lover* to seduce Louise Fishman. It worked.

LOVER

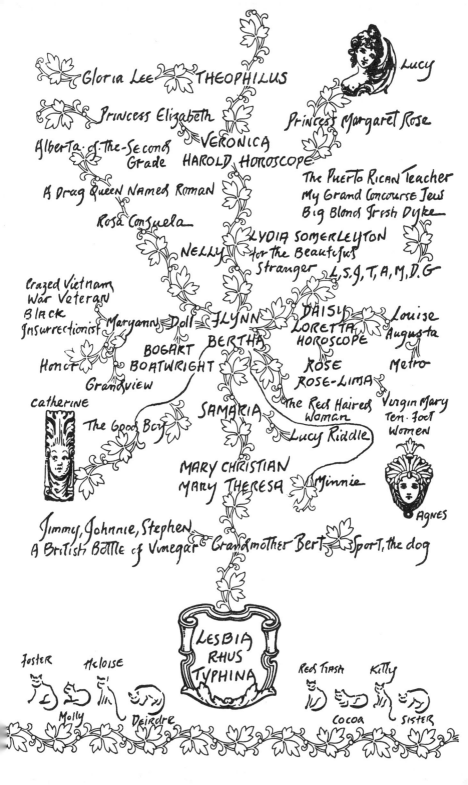

Gloria Lee THEOPHILUS Lucy

Princess Elizabeth Princess Margaret Rose

Alberta-of-The-Second Grade VERONICA HAROLD HOROSCOPE

The Puerto Rican Teacher My Grand Concourse Jews Big Blond Irish Dyke

A Drag Queen Named Roman

Rosa Consuela

NELLY LYDIA SOMERLEYTON for the Beautiful Stranger L, S, G, T, A, M, D, G

Crazed Vietnam War Veteran BLACK Insurrectionist Maryann Doll FLYNN DAISY Louise LORETTA HOROSCOPE Augusta

Homer BOGART BOATWRIGHT BERTHA Metro

Grandview ROSE ROSE-LIMA

Catherine The Good Boy SAMARIA The Red Haired Woman Virgin Mary Ten-Foot Women

Lucy Riddle Agnes

MARY CHRISTIAN MARY THERESA Minnie

Jimmy, Johnnie, Stephen A British Bottle of Vinegar Grandmother Bert Sport, the dog

LESBIA RHUS TYPHINA

Foster Heloise Red Trash Kitty

Molly Deirdre Cocoa Sister

The lights go down, the curtain opens: the first thing we see is the Marschallin von Werdenberg (played by a middle-aged woman) in bed with Octavian (played by a very young woman). Their passionate declarations of love are disturbed by sounds of footsteps which the lovers fear belong to the Marschallin's husband. Octavian hides and dresses up like a girl, a lady's maid. But it wasn't the husband. It was a dirty old man, Baron Ochs, who, without bothering to knock, enters the bedroom to demand help in his courtship of lovely young Sophia Faninal (a young woman played by a young woman). But the Baron no sooner sees Octavian, disguised as a girl, than he lunges for her. Some clumsy acrobatics—in sharp contrast to the opening scene of love—ensue. Meanwhile, the Marschallin—as was the practice of aristocratic ladies in those days—has her morning interview with her attorney, head cook, milliner, hairdresser, literary adviser, animal dealer, Italian tenor. The Baron leaves. The Princess asks Octavian if she will, according to the custom, be the bearer of a silver rose to Sophia, act as the Baron's representative. The first act ends with the Princess wondering rather sadly when she will cease attracting her young lover.

Octavian, in a suit of silver, the silver rose in her hand, arrives at the Faninal house. Upon the presentation of the rose, Sophia and Octavian fall in love. The Baron enters, with the marriage contract. Sophia is disgusted by him; Octavian draws her sword and wounds him in the hand. Sophia declares she will never marry the Baron. Her fath-

er, of course, rages: Sophia will either marry the Baron or become a nun. Sophia's father wants to link his wealth with an aristocratic name.

In the third act, Octavian—again disguised as the Princess's maid—makes and keeps an appointment with the lecherous Baron at an inn. There, Octavian has arranged a magic show so full of trickery, disappearing acts, and sleights-of-hand that the Baron thinks he has gone mad. To clinch the Baron's downfall, Octavian has a woman arrive to claim the Baron as her husband; and surrounds the Baron with many little children who hail him as "Papa." Octavian's timing is perfect—Sophia and her father come to the inn at the height of the brawl and see the Baron disgraced.

Octavian, again in her suit of lights, sings with Sophia and the Marschallin a final trio: love, and the loss of love. Octavian and Sophia are alone together.

> —a synopsis of the plot of the opera,
> *Der Rosenkavalier*, a comedy in three acts.
> Music by Richard Strauss,
> words by Hugo von Hofmannsthal

To save herself from marriage, Lucy gouged out her own eyes; but Agatha appeared to her and declared, "Thou art light."

This one was lying strapped to a table. Covered in her juices, Samaria was being pulled through the lips of her vulva. That is how Samaria met her.

She was being pulled, yelling already, through the lips of Daisy's vulva. That is how Flynn met Daisy.

Veronica, however, came out of nowhere, and so she used to go exclusively with Veronica. They were childhood sweethearts. On February 14, 1947, Veronica gave Veronica a red heart-shaped box of candy and then they sat together in the porch swing that warmish February afternoon. Arms entwined. Sucking on candy hearts with messages for the tongues: *Be Mine Valentine. I Love You. Thine Alone.* Like eating the camellia blooms that bounced against their hair when they swung backwards.

Next, a series of snapshots, brownish with unnatural lights, of Veronica from the early forties, beginning with her head: her dark hair seems stuffed into packages of curls, one big parcel above her brow, two more above the ears, a hint of snarl at the back, tickling the neck. On the face, smears for the eyes and mouth; and the nose, even beneath a microscope, invisible.

Even then, Veronica gives the impression of being all heart; and, like candy, hard on the teeth. This is not true. Really, she is pretending to be St. Sebastian offering his body to the arrows of the assasins.

5

In December, near the date of her thirty-sixth birthday, she buys herself a little white china monkey with painted features and red fingernails. The monkey is hollow, and a cigarette lighter fits inside the hole in the top of its head. Veronica uses cigarettes like a murder weapon against herself. She once heard Jenny make that remark about her own mother. Then at Christmas time, Veronica's lover gives her an old silver cigarette case, with the initials *BH* engraved in one corner of the lid. Her lover gives her a second present, and this is an ivory and tortoise-shell cigarette holder. Both gifts are made to hold only non-filters. These presents are truly ancient of days, Veronica declares; and lights up. She stuffs the case with Balkan Sobranies, then flips it open again and holds it open in her left hand like a little book. She stretches her arm toward Jenny, offering the open case. *See-garette, my dair?* she leers. The waiter passes the hot hor d'oeuvres. Though she is hungry, it would be inappropriate to eat in such circumstances. In the lobby of the Algonquin Hotel, Veronica is a man in a 1939 Twentieth Century Fox movie. She is David Niven in a pin-striped suit and a pencil-line moustache. She leans across the table and leers, "*See-garette, my dair?* Don't be nervous. Trust me. Soon I shall reveal all!"

In the photographs, Veronica seems about three or four. Beneath the head, the torso is long and flat. The arms and legs seem unnaturally short and the fingers and toes, when visible, oddly attenuated. The same as now, but pretty women still let her kiss them in dark corners at the ragged edges of parties.

Picture number one: wearing white shoes that lace up above the ankles. Her pinafore is too long in front. Her back is to us. We can see nothing of her face but a blur of cheek. She is facing a bush, an empty street, and an empty sidewalk. To her left, there is a toy piano the photographer

6

has borrowed to add interest to the scene. It is unbearably hot, and everything in the picture is as tight and sealed as a drum. Veronica looks as tight and sealed, as soundless, as a drum.

Pictures number two and three are all bright light and sepia. In these, Veronica is a water baby standing in the shallows on the cluttered shores of a place named White Lake. She is wearing a scratchy wool bathing suit appliqued above the heart with a single duck. Her fingers curl inward, brushing her thighs. Her thighs are without edges; they flow into the water. She could be alone in space or only an extension of the space in which she stands. If there is ground beneath her feet, it is the same color and substance as her skin, of the water behind her, of the light around her. Veronica is partial to snowstorms, but at the time of the photograph she has never seen any snow at all.

When someone touches Veronica, or whispers to her, while she is sleeping, she screams. Like the author of a novel, she has the ability to appear and disappear—like the ghost on the ramparts, like the rabbit out of the hat. Like the author of a novel, her hair and eyes will change color; she will wear thick spectacles one moment and have 20/20 vision the next; she will grow down, then up. But there is no mystery, and she no body at the bottom of the swimming pool. There is simply always a moment in your life when she is either there or not there.

Veronica began life as a religious poet composing ecstatic meters about drowned nuns. She began life as a bigamist, as a twin, as a married woman, as a lover. And still, at any moment, she can render herself again into an exact replica of all the creatures she started as. At the drop of a hat, she could become, for instance, Veronica the wife of Theophilus—which, indeed, she has already been. The wife of Theophilus was the wife of a railroad engineer. Theophilus

7

engineered the trains of the Southern Railroad back and forth over short distances. Although Theophilus and short distances can never return, Veronica, the wife of the engineer, can.

There was once a Theophilus who had a son named Johnny who had a daughter. Occasionally, the daughter will try to remember which man knew all the sinister, tosspot verses to "The Rising of the Moon." But any Mick prick (she recalls, as *envoi*) is bel canto in his cups. Flynn, the granddaughter, did not sing. On those occasions, Flynn danced. She danced in starched ruffles, done up for Sunday by the lady dripping tears into her frying pan. She tap-danced with bamboo cane and top hat holding Johnny by the finger *a la* Shirley T. Like Bojangles, like Fred.

That was stolen chicken in the frying pan, therefore sweeter. Neither the business in pistachio nut machines ("Give Me Five Salted Peanuts with Your Heart in Beside 'Em") nor illegal (but still mismanaged) juke box enterprises was lucrative enough for store-bought. What drives a wild Irish rose to transplant, to suck up whiskey like the morning dew, to fall in love in horrible detail (like from the roof of a ten-storied building), to join circuses, commit murder, act Hamlet, balance herself high above the ground? What urges her secret contemplation of old age spent as the Staten Island Ferry's number one shopping-bag lady speaking in strange tongues around her mouthful of jelly doughnut? Women, Flynn will answer—all of them, aged unborn to very old. What she really wants (she will insist) is not women at all; what she really wants is Harris tweeds and sensible shoes and a room of her own and a life of thoughtful solitude.

And then she points to what she's got: exertions of the flesh, one clitoris in the hand worth one in the mouth; a pistol to point at the horizon of the Atlantic Ocean one

8

autumn afternoon; a lover as fantastic as a loony bin; a cat, two turtles, old baby pictures of Veronica. A daughter named Nelly, enough eggs for breakfast, and herself as lover.

But none of these things are Flynn. They are a lie about Flynn, or they are pictures of herself her fantasies have contrived, or they are her overworked imagination forcing memories of things that have never really happened to her. They could be an elaborate drag or a system of disguise devised by an outside agent, a masterful forgery of the authentic Flynn, whose only accomplishment in life, so far, has been an invention of a brain machine which can (at last) irrevocably separate spirit from matter, thought from action, mind from flesh. That the real Flynn has become interchangeable with her fake is not her fault. Still, no one, not even Flynn, can tell them apart.

She has a grandmother named Samaria, who was also, like Veronica, married to Theophilus; but Samaria could be any grandmother—for instance, that one who, in her nineties, kept a bottle of whiskey in every room of her house in order to avoid unnecessary travel. Or, perhaps Old Mother Hubbard in black net stockings and whipcord trousers—avoiding lightning-quick backstage changes. Flynn imagines her as a kind of boring, but necessary, adjunct to three meals a day, like mom's deep-dish apple pie. Really, Samaria is the kind of woman it is impossible to love until she is gone; and then loved and remembered with a yawn. A yawn (we have been taught) is as inescapable as orgasm once it begins. For Veronica to meet Samaria, Theophilus could not die before Daisy lived: Theophilus' daughter, Daisy, living to be every daughter's dream of mother.

And every daughter's dream of a mother is our dancing daughter. She was born to do it til dawn—rhumba superbly, fox-trot unflinchingly; every possibility of love it is possible to arrive at (on public transportation) stretched out in white latex beside the diving board. When Flynn considers settling down, it is Daisy who sits on her lap while she repents. But Flynn is half princess, half gorilla—her mother's very own, especially when the mornings are cold.

It is as if her other girls, Rose and Rose-lima—her little girls—don't exist. Hardly anyone, including these twins, recognizes that they *must* have had a mother, and that the mother must be Daisy. Everyone believes (Rose and Rose-lima believe) their origin was in the lusts of late Victorian literature—pink-bottomed sexual chimeras with highly-developed killer instincts. The twins fancy themselves the children of the garden. They tilt their hips and dance—*Wild Thing, I think I love yeeew!* For good reasons, their names are Rose and Rose-lima. But it doesn't yet matter, for they are still little girls and still don't need a mother as, for instance, Flynn does, who is older and has been very ill.

St. Dorothea is often depicted in art with roses in her hand or on her head. Before her martyrdom, two apostate women were sent to pervert her, but Dorothea reconverted them. Dorothea, therefore, was beheaded.

Flynn, coming up from fever: I know it's a dream, but knowing doesn't save me from it. It sucks on me like a baby on her orange. When all the juice is gone, I'm split open and my flesh chewed out; that's real to me. My mother Daisy in her wedding dress again—elbows out, chin up, upper lip gnawing lower lip. Icy fingers up and down her spine to snap the little hooks and eyes together.

The fire behind Daisy, my mother, snaps and clicks, eating through another coal. It wants to get outside the grate and eat her up. It isn't the season for a fire, but tell that to the Marines. I am tall off the floor in her tall bed, sick and hot in her bed. They think I am my mother in her bed, so they are coming to burn me to death or smother my head. I am her case of mistaken identity. The fire sheds like mica from the mirror. One reflects the other; both fire and mirror collapse and lay hidden in the tufts of the red rug to catch bare feet if they should pass.

Two fires, then, are climbing my mother's skirt. They make her twirl, they make her swirl, and coal thunders down the grate and the sift of ash is even louder than fire burning.

I am sick and too hot. The fire is what is coming apart in her hands. The fire is the breeze down the chimney that lifts her skirt as though it were a hurricane wind and makes the skirt spin off its flat embroidery into a dimensional juicy harvest. The grapes, apples, pomegranates once off satin and into space and air turn to real fruit; and they all hit me and I feel smothered once more. My mother spins until the skirt rises into a cone above her head. All of her above the waist is hidden. Below the waist, she is all naked hips and green stockings. She is whirled until she's blown through the roof. Then the fire goes out, and I'm left in the dark.

My grandmother Samaria keeps eight cats, one for every room in the house; a gray Manx, Foster; two black Persians, Molly and Heloise; a black-and-white short hair, Deirdre; an orange calico, Red Trash; a Burmese, Cocoa; two tortoise-shells, Kitty and Sister. They eat, then go outside. They are hardly ever around to see. Occasionally, one or all or some of them hunt and bring home a dead squirrel to lay across someone's pillow. Someone will see the squirrel, but not the cat who caught it. Nobody loves them; there is no question of loving them. But a sense of their presence is available. They stink of the woods and their encounters there. They vomit and shit in secret corners where it is hard to find. Turning a corner, opening a door, running down stairs, there is often a sudden splash into smell; then one step more, and it is gone. Then it is the jolt of walking dry land after riding a boat on water. Some day, Veronica tells Samaria, she intends to skin them all alive and make herself a fur shirt. Her intention is to tease my grandmother.

Somewhere a dog is barking now. Daisy my mother married a man again. An insect with a green body and multi-colored wings is flying, like the story of the Holy Ghost, through my window. I am rubbing my heel, good back and forth, against the bottom sheet; and way off, from outside, I hear the sound of Samaria releasing the bow; and then of her arrow hitting the target.

Because she resisted the attentions of one Quintian, a man of consular rank, Agatha was persecuted and tortured in various fashions. For instance, they cut her breasts off. In art, she is often depicted carrying her breasts on a plate. After her death, the volcano of Mt. Aetna erupted over Catania.

Unborn, to very old, Veronica broods. She props herself up against cushions, on Grand Street, remembering women:

I met this one as middle age came creeping up behind

her for a last embrace, for a final struggle: up all day, all night for long-legged advancing and retreating, for mysterious scuffles in dim corners. I await the news of her heart-attacked on West Third Street, two a.m.; rushed *sans* Blue Cross to Bellevue. Which would, nevertheless, resolve the dilemma of how hard she means to fight for the best room with the best view (of Katz's Delicatessen? The White Cliffs of Dover? The parvenu trees of East 61st Street?) at the Old Lesbians' Home.

The obituary (mimeographed and handed out at subway entrances) will compound every cliche: last words; with her boots on. But all else a record of shifts and quakes. The plot shifts, the geography earthquakes. When the queen dies, the idylls are blue-pencilled and rewritten with greater economy. Who knows what tomorrow will bring? is the burden of their song—the princess snorting forward on her noble steed, an hour too late for a death-bed reconciliation; a thousand-acre inheritance of Australian kangaroos; the crown of the Romanovs: proof she was Anastasia entire. Because she cannot stay still, nothing will arrive at its proper time and place. Inconstant—unlike, for instance, Harry S Truman, who could be counted on to stop, look, and listen, with the faithful regularity of a Big Ben alarm clock—and give the condition of near-death classical symmetry. No surprises, no sudden dips and curves in the routine. No abrupt deviation in the morning walk from Elm to Oak.

Wasting your time on enchantment with death's surprises—I am surprised at you, Veronica, at how you've turned out—if you know what I mean. It's a little terrifying—if you know what I mean. And remember, once we were all each other had. Where's your pilot's license? I got mine. But you'd rather be a sky-diver, if you weren't so scared of heights. Long tumbles through space; the parachute gone (unopened) with the wind is what the dream is really saying. Waking, believes that what she really wants is the wraparound hug of castellated Gothic. Blood, and hoot-owls and midnight bells. Were I in fact the knife-edged street dyke of my fantasies, I would say, "fucka-you" and pass it all right on by. But am only how I find myself; but could, if necessary, live without baroque, could become as tightly sealed and plain as that stone Assyrian tomb at the Brooklyn Museum. Sealed and soundless as a drum.

But there she is; and despite the creaks and halts of one more year over the hill, still full of health and vigor, still cashing in on those early years of physical education in summer camps and Episcopal boarding schools; and that industrious era of sweat when she labored as hard as a draught horse to become a dancer.

The Red Shoes, final reel: Moira Shearer bloody on the train tracks, in the white light of the Riviera: "Adrian . . . take off the *red shoes*!" Cut to Grisha sobbing in front of the impatient audience, his tears drenching the ballet slip-pers (red) he clutches to his breast. Is it blood or just the same old Capezio shoe dye? "Mizz Page will not daunce *Zee Red Shoes* tonight . . . or, indeed, ANY OTHER NIGHT!"

But it served her right. She could now be chewing choc-olate bon-bons with her feet up, on Grand Street, like me, and visiting her work that hangs under other names at the Metropolitan Museum (like me) had she not been so stub-bornly faithful to what she thought of as her calling. She's trying now to keep on a slimming vegetarian diet (she saw a film documenting the horrors of the *abbatoir*) and wor-rying about decaying teeth and, in secret, is tracing her an-cestry via William the Conqueror back to Nefertiti. Her facts are only what she deserves; and they serve her right.

14

Her first lover was big, fat, gloomy, hairy; is presently married (to her male first cousin) and raising goats in West Virginia. No rumors of either happiness or discord. The plaintive smell of goat on a green hill faraway. Her second, on the verge of early retirement (when they met) from water sports and field hockey, tortured Maryann into a platonic (but urgent) contemplation on the nature of things; then departed for Provincetown with one who was more her own kind. She could be, by this time, dead, rich, or transfigured. Her third was an English real-aristocrat with the sexual moves of a monkey.

Goats, water, green fields, monkeys; then she was born.

Ursula promised to marry Prince Conan of England but only if she could bring her eleven thousand handmaidens with her. She and the eleven thousand were slaughtered by the Huns while passing through Cologne. She died a virgin and a great beauty.

I am standing hunched up against the glass door of our golden-floored living room where Maryann is working at her desk and where Maryann also sleeps at night with Honor; and where the rest of us, daily, gather to smoke, drink, quarrel. I am looking at the outside where my daughter Nelly and her friend go for a walk up the road. It is April, but still wintry cold (Honor's only words to me all weekend: "The robins are back."). The children are barefoot. Nelly holds a green shawl around her shoulders. The other wears a denim jacket with "Lesbians Unite" embroidered, like a merit badge, in a red circle on the left arm. I know they are doing sex together and that presently they will turn off into the trees, out of my sight, and spread the shawl on the river bank.

In their twenty-four hours together here, they have connived to take two naps and two baths together. I am furious with jealousy, and Maryann knows it and laughs at me. Nelly's friend is black and her mother is a street-whore who lives apart from her several children. The child disgusts me. Her salacious tittering about underwear, her songs about sailors and bow-legged women, her sly whispers about what is done in bathrooms disgust me. I am furious with class hatred. I want my daughter to be nothing but a brain kept living in a tank full of marvelous liquids. I want to call a halt to her happening breasts and pubic hair. A brain in a pure white skull, all safe. Nelly is nine, the other ten.

Thecla, the perfect disciple, cut her hair short and put on male attire. In the process of her martyrdom, she was subjected to such tortures as fire and wild beasts. Late in life, she became a famous healer, but had to flee the jealousy of the doctors and conceal herself inside a rock which had miraculously split open to receive her.

It had been Daisy in her wedding-dress again, involved once more in her own normal course of events. Flynn, however, eventually wakes from dream and fever. Her upper lids break free of the crust on her lashes. It seemed the nightmare had taken a hundred years. The light washes over her, and she lets herself float in it until her eyes remember vision; like an empty boat, a stick, a bleached-out piece of bone.

She feels herself with her hands. All the flesh burned away, a bag of bones. She is either eighteen or one hundred and eighteen. She is only eighteen. It is only the second great sickness of her life, not the sickness that lasts forever: forever, a hundred years: the sickness whose cure is a kiss. Daisy gets married, and then she is gone. This is now the third time.

But Flynn's mouth is parched and she doesn't any longer give a damn what her mother does. Daisy can marry anything she wants. Daisy can marry the stud cat, she can marry the farmer's mule or a goddamn movie star. Daisy could marry the mother of god, and Flynn wouldn't give a damn. Daisy can marry and bear litters of kittens or three-eyed beasts or Siamese-twinned starlets or baby Jesuses: but Flynn will never let it make her sick again. All she wants is for someone to stuff scoops of cracked ice into her mouth and lead her to a Panama Canal that runs with gallons of coca-cola. Or help her to the lake where her giant mouth can suck it all up—scum, minnows, frogs, mallards, all. Or someone could hold an orange to her lips.

She opened her eyes wide. She saw the room recovered from its nausea of distortions: bedposts steady, upright; the ceiling that had buckled and bulged, flat once again. She spoke out loud: "I have been very sick. Nobody is here taking care of me." But she said this because she sensed someone had recently been there and standing beside the bed and looking down on her. But if it had been Daisy, rambunctiousness would still be filling the space she had stood in. It had not been Daisy.

On the wall opposite the bed, the windows shone and dust filtered through the sunlight. Thirty framed photographs on the wall to her right now hung dead quiet from their nails. They were pictures of children Daisy would tell lies about when she was at home, unmarried; while she was undressing for bed. She would tell the stories to Flynn, who would be in her own bed, around the room's corner, who would lie there listening until she could sleep. They are all my own children, Daisy would say, I am their natural mother. When I go away, it is to visit them—*not* to do what you think I do. I have a mother's natural affections. You must not be bitter and jealous and deny a mother's natural affections for her other children. But the children behind the glass all looked as if they had been clipped from magazines, from "Save the Children" advertising campaigns. They were black, brown, yellow, white; and ragged and huge-eyed. Some had distended bellies. All were barefoot. All were female. Neither Flynn's face nor those of Rose and Rose-lima were among the photographs. It had crossed Flynn's mind that her own photograph might be hanging on a stuccoed wall in Mexico or tilted against peeling wall paper in Appalachia.

Nothing ached any more but her bladder. The fire was dead. She was well. But time was gone, and it was impossible to tell how much of it remained. Maybe so much time the number of children on the wall had increased; but Flynn hadn't time to count them. She felt too weak to walk. But how to piss without first walking?

It was simpler than she thought: she began wetting the bed. The big bedroom was L-shaped, two rooms knocked together to make something big enough for big Daisy when she was at home, and big enough to share, at Daisy's request, with skinny Flynn. In between Daisy's absences, Flynn shared with Daisy: hooks, chests, bathroom, the rug, the fire, the sight of the photographs. *But not this.* The sound Flynn heard, she had heard before only in her imagination: the sound of Daisy being married to her husband. It was a vast and freezing sound: and if it had words to it, they were foreign, and were always shouted, never spoken. Flynn heard a huge rubber hammer beating up and down on the other bed. It was Daisy's body up and down astride another husband. Did sick make her invisible so that they didn't care if Flynn were there? Flynn screamed, No. Then the noise stopped.

Then quiet. Then footsteps lumbering around the corner *coming to get me.* But Flynn could not scream again. It was too late for help. The big mouths would open and swallow her up, and there would be no trace left.

It was two gold faces, tall as people. Rattling gold-skinned faces, five feet high, with big red mouths painted open and grinning, and each nose twin caves. Then they were upon her, but Flynn did not faint.

Rose and Rose-lima threw the masks beneath the bed and then talked to Flynn.

"Look at her. Look at our big sister. Her hair stinks of vomit. She's puked in her hair."

"She smells like shit to me. That's worse than vomit. The cats could have been here."

"Her bones stick out. I don't believe she's got breasts anymore."

"She doesn't deserve breasts because she's a big baby."

"Babies get sick when their mamas leave them for a man. You'd never believe she's a big girl and not a baby. Not us. We are darling girls. We will grow up to be darling big fat ladies like our mama and not get cancer of the brain because we don't have husbands. Flynn will never get a husband. She might get cancer of the brain."

"We are going to have big fat breasts. Flynn wet the bed, Rose-lima!"

"We will get her big breasts away from her because she doesn't deserve them anyway. You must take your hand off her, Rose. You might catch the disease that makes you bleed and then you get sick when your mother gets married, and you vomit in your own hair."

"We're getting away from you, Flynn, because you yelled at us for pretending to be mama and the new husband in bed. That makes us mad. The husband might come here and find out you wet the bed, then he will be mad. He will beat you up with his wangwong."

Their own faces were tiny, pointed, pink. And their bodies, naked except for ragged underpants with holes the size of silver dollars back and front, were tiny, pointed, pink. They had long-legged, lean, freckled, identical bodies. They had been born together, face-to-face, joined at the abdomen; then separated by surgery two months later. Their scars were white and crinkled and vaguely the shape of Manhattan. Daisy had looked at them, after they were separated and said, "They should have been left Siamese. They could have gone to the circus. They could have grown up to be successful gospel singers in Carnegie Hall. The money for the surgery could have bought Carnegie Hall for them."

Their hair was wiry, red-gold encircling their skulls like brush fires, then dying out in darkening snarls and knots below their waists. In full sunlight, their hair seemed to disappear, and then their heads seemed haloed. Until husband number two, Daisy's hair had been exactly the same. Then that husband, a hairdresser, had taught her how wrong it was and had bought her lotions and taught her how to sleek and roll the hair into exactly twenty-one fat curls which were then arranged, by him, into a nosegay on top of her head. When someone admired the new arrangement, she would tell how she kept it that way: "I fuck on top," she would say. "That's how I keep my hair so neat." The twins' eyes seemed brown, were really yellowish. Their chests moved more quickly than seemed normal, even

20

when they were still.

Now, they linked arms and strolled in a procession step to the door, arousing from nowhere Deirdre and Foster, who flashed past them, snarling and tangling to leap through the window to go rolling and fighting down the sloping roof.

Then Flynn was able to speak. "Please don't go. Please stay with me and help me." Flynn was crying, with piss all up and down her body, just like a big baby. She turned her head into her pillow. "I want my mother," she said, but no one could hear her.

The twins were humming a tune, a sound like insects in grass. They were humming "The Merry Widow Waltz." "One-two-three," Rose-lima whispered, and they waltzed together back to the bed. They got into the bed and lay down in the cold wet beside their sister. They held her tight and kissed her, and helped her cry for their mother. But then Rose stopped crying and said, "Big sister, don't cry. We won't let the cancer of the brain get you." Then they moved their sweet little hands down her body.

Goats, water, monkeys: then she was born.

Irene, with her sisters Agape and Chiona, was martyred at Salonika. After her sisters had been burned alive, Irene fled to the mountains, but was recaptured by the governor who then sent her naked into a brothel. She was, however, unmolested. After she was executed, her books were publicly burned.

Third, fourth, and fifth lovers attained in rapid succession, exploded into tiny pieces just as quickly. The situations were without romantic detail, so now the lovers are nameless, but they were lovers nonetheless.

Maryann, age forty; Honor, age twenty-seven; and Grandview, age thirty-nine, on this day almost exactly a year ago, are climbing into the Ford Microbus. It is just past St. Valentine's Day—more winter to come, but the house cats are restless. The ice is cracking in the rivers. All of them are in a state of cold-fingered nervousness. Getting ready to go, early in the morning, they begin to gell their various fears into the single issue of what shoes to wear. How closely does a bank, which must give you a mortgage on a house, look at your feet? Do they have trained cloven-hoof detectors that can see through even the most respectable leather?

They get there too late. The bank guard is locking the door and adjusting his holster. The Holiday Inn is both a reprieve and a reward. They can go barefoot and stuff themselves full of hot showers, bloody marys, clean sheets, color television. All this makes them feel so prosperous that by morning, greatly relaxed, they lace themselves up into their accustomed stompers.

This house, near a lake and with a golden-floored living room, has been on the market for over three years. On Grandview's credit, on Maryann's cash (earned modeling with a foam-rubber doll on television commercials) they take the bank.

The house is big and white and clapboard and cold; and surrounded by ten plain and wooded acres. The bank's information about a river is inaccurate. The river is in fact a small lake, and it is on their property. In the town records, it is named White Lake. They consider changing the name to something symbolic, but never get around to doing it.

Maryann is terrified out there alone at night when the rest of us, beginning Mondays, go back to the city to work. No one who has a share in the house is on welfare this year.

Maryann is terrified of: the dark. Crazed Vietnam war veterans looking for something to shoot at. Black insurrectionists who believe white women are after their black women. The supernatural. When she hasn't enough money to speed, around midnight, to a hotel, she leaves all the lights on, all her clothes on, and sticks a bread knife in her belt. Near sunrise, about the time of the false dawn, she collapses wide-eyed on the bed, then sleeps. Bad things happen every day. Why shouldn't they happen, at night, to her?

Flynn goes to teach school and quickly becomes entranced by such stories as the one about the Puerto Rican teacher who has been educated into an adoration of ethnicity and trained to speak with the same sharp-edged speed his Marxist professors had formerly kept to themselves. When he was twelve, he was selling himself on Times Square along with all the other little chickens. Now he teaches a course entitled "Urban Third World" and displays his knife-wound scars to his favorite students. His textbooks all have the word "man" in their titles, and their cover designs are stark black and white, to seem dangerous. He likes to fuck young Jewish girls up the ass. He commits sodomy on young Jewish girls, so that they may repent of the sins of their slumlord daddies. Their fathers, he tells them, owned the rat-filled tenements of his youth. Parting their buttocks, the young girls remind themselves that this is going to hurt him more than it hurts them. It is only to revenge himself. On Times Square, it was only for money.

One day, a big, blonde Irish dyke falls in love with one

of his little women—the one he refers to as "my Grand Concourse Jew." And she with her, apparently. The two women disappear into the sunsets of Brooklyn. He finds another. He discovers that this one, during the long afternoons of his seminars, makes love with her roommate. It is not a coincidence, he realizes: it is a conspiracy. He beats hell out of the roommate. "Dirty cuntsucker!" he screams. Above West 83rd Street, his cries ring out and synchronize with the bells of noon.

Once, a much longer time ago, she tried to go straight. She married a man and then had a little baby named Nelly. After a year of this, visions of women were jumping in her head like balls of bubble gum in penny machines. She had learned all the rules, however, and intended to follow them to the letter. She served oxtail stew exactly at the dinner hour. She could sweep a floor. She became engrossed in the surgery, the widowhoods, the sounding brass of puberty on daytime television. Women still swarmed (although she clenched her teeth) like roses past her nostrils. But one afternoon, within a little dream, she took her hands out of the soapy dishwater, dried them off, and handed the little baby girl to Rosa Consuela in the basement, and walked through another door and then made love to the woman who lived there, beyond the door. Her husband had told her that this woman belonged to his best friend. Ho-hum ho-hum. She and the red-haired woman make love all the afternoon.

Years later, she is in bed with Grandview, and they are talking about the best friend. Grandview laughs and laughs. She pokes Grandview: "Watcha laughin' for, huh?" Grandview explains that she's laughing because she herself used to make love to the best friend's first wife; and then, later, her lover started making love with the best friend's second wife—and then *you* took your hands out of the dishwater

24

and made love to the best friend's girl friend. "I hear," she whispers to Grandview, "that he's married for a third time! There's a new one!" She and Grandview laugh and laugh.

They decided to raise money for the Old Lesbians' Home by having weekly dances to be called "The Alice B. Toklas Memorial Cotillion." These would be an alternative to the expensive bars. They would be held in neighborhoods safe as churches so that those with imperfect karate techniques would feel secure on the way home. They sat in church parlors to make arrangements. The lady reverends opposite them in the church parlors agreed that everyone has the right to dance, cha-cha-cha. One lady minister describes a phenomenon called human liberation which boils down to dancing in her church on weeknights as long as there is no smoking, no drinking, no kissing, no dope, and no rubbing up together as it is done in the expensive alternatives.

On the living room floor, they dance. When the music stops, they wait a moment and then begin again. She likes heroic noise that is bloodied but unbowed: Scottish bagpipes, St. Patrick's Day parades. The sword of Nefertiti hung up to rest. It is late autumn. The man who lives two fields away—whose father originally owned this house—daily delivers another load of firewood. He stops at the door; he stays and stays, telling Daisy the awful details of how his wife lies dying of cancer of the brain. Daisy shakes her head in inexpressible sorrow. Her head moves in perfect cadence with the rise and fall of the story. The next day, however, his wife feels better, and Daisy smiles.

"I don't know what name I was born with. I was baptized Samaria in the orphanage. The Woman of Samaria was a person of Hellenistic background whom a prominent young Hebrew of her day used as an example to show that it is the spirit of worship that counts rather than inheritance or culture. A puzzler, that one. A paradox, some would say.

"My life, as plain and tasteless as white bread in its beginning, has become richer than fruitcake. Already, I've had everything—love, passion, loss, grief, mutilation of the spirit, and sex. These things taste like the candied fruit inside dark cake. I live in the boathouse now, writing my memoirs and getting strange. Everyone who happened to me was extraordinary—but I didn't realize they were until I had left them and was gone. *Je ne regrette rien,* as the song goes. Actually, I'm afraid of being arrested for murder if I show my face.

"At the beginning, I opened my eyes in the orphanage. I was ten years old. Before that, of course, my eyes were also open; but then nothing stayed still so that I could take a look at it. At the orphanage, nothing ever moved an inch. My mother was a whore, and my father, many sailors. My mother and her sister did twenty a day between them, working the docks in Wilmington, North Carolina. They told me they did them through their mouths. They said it was easier to clean your mouth than your insides. They said that's what the sailors really wanted anyway—though they pretended otherwise. A woman's mouth seems safer to men than a woman's inside.

"I opened my eyes the first time between my mother and my aunt, and it was warm and bright. I *know* a woman doesn't get babies through her mouth, but nevertheless I was conceived and grew to birth on the back of my mother's tongue. Our house was beautiful. You think Grand Street is beautiful, where you're dedicated to fretting about a hundred *objets* worth nearly nothing. The Tarot deck in its gilt box, the china monkey that's really a cigarette lighter, the eighteenth century inkwell your first beloved pressed into your hands—she took it off her own table and put it in your hands. The bunches of books and pictures and papers, and the brass candlesticks and the orange cat. You should have seen our house.

"The house we live in now—long and low, white clapboard and cold. Our house then was long and tall, white clapboard and hot. Its porch wrapped nearly all the way around. Out in the yard were hollyhock, larkspur, and azalea, and anything that could grow wild without tending. And seedlings in coffee cans everywhere you put your foot.

"My mother's name was Mary Bridget and her sister's name was Mary Theresa; and their house came to them from their mother, whose breast was amputated and then she died. There was biscuits and fried chicken and mashed potatoes and gravy. The ocean was not far away.

"We would wake up afternoons in a bed full of quilts. But I woke up first and spent the time seeing the pictures on the quilts. There were stars and flowers and velvet and moons and threads and knots. I would go to sleep wrapped around my mother's back, and my arm grew longer every year until it could go almost the entire way around her waist. But three in a bed is not the right number. I was a little girl; my mother and Mary Theresa were grown women. But we would wake up together in the bed anyway, and there would be bright light through all the windows—I'm recalling it like it's just a play I've seen up on a stage with the curtain rising and falling. I was in the play, but when I remember it, I'm sitting in the dark, in the audience, watching." (Samaria begins to tell the plot of the opera *Der Rosenkavalier*, as though it were the story of her childhood:)

"First, there is music like solid silver; then two women in bed together begin to sing. Then one of them gets up—the younger one, Mary Theresa—who is still young enough to jump and leap with fright: they think there is somebody coming. But it isn't the man—they shouldn't be afraid. I'm the one who knows for sure that von Werdenberg's gone forever. He never once comes back. He's gone for good. But *they* don't know.

"The younger woman in the bed is a girl pretending to be a boy who has to pretend to be a girl. She bangs around in leather boots. She hides behind a painted screen. She sees a fat old man come to ask my mother, who is the older woman, to get him a pretty girl. Mary Theresa, the younger woman, changes to ribbons and skirts, and then the fat old man wants her. I see that the fat old man wants a boy dressed up like a girl. The last I see of Mary Theresa she's wearing a silver suit of lights and she's carrying a silver rose in her hand, leaving my mother behind; and that is how I lost my mother for good.

"But at the orphanage I met Lucy Riddle. Lucy Riddle taught me in secret, at night in the bathroom, how to tap dance. She had black frizzy curls and big gray eyes and could tap dance in silver shoes like a little star. Before the orphanage got her, Lucy Riddle had taken years of tap dance and toe. Then we were seventeen, and could leave and get a job.

"We served behind the cafe counter at the bus station.

28

When Mary Theresa got off the bus one night, it had been nine years since I'd seen her. She still had her good suit—the blue and gray tweed, and a dark red necktie—not silver the way I sometimes remember it. It felt like my brains had moved to my stomach. It felt like she had come to take me back home to my mother, and then the whole show would begin again. It would be early afternoon, and all the light would be pouring through the windows to show the secret. It would be a second chance for me.

"But she didn't know me. My hair was dyed red and all swollen into curls Lucy had fixed with rags. I had the yellow uniform on, with the green triangle apron. I smelled like grease and sugar doughnuts. I don't blame her. It was the middle of the night, and she was tired and she smelled like the long distance bus.

"She put her left hand flat down on the counter. I put a cup of coffee and a doughnut in front of her. Lucy Riddle came up then, and Mary Theresa lifted her left hand and held it out to her. Mary Theresa touched Lucy at her waist. I told the boss I was sick. I went home to where Lucy and I roomed and boarded, the Ivy Inn; and I stayed there, losing my job until Lucy Riddle finally came home two weeks later.

" 'I never intended to marry an old man and a widower,' Lucy says to me. 'But he's in love with me, and I've already done wrong with him, and he's got a good steady job at the shipyards in Wilmington. Will you stand up for me?'

"I behaved like a crazy woman. I yelled and screamed. Then the florist's boy comes with a dozen white roses with a note from Mary Theresa that reads, *'With my heart in beside them, I send them to the one I love.'* Poor Lucy is torn in half with the excitement of the roses on the one hand and scared to death on the other, of how I'm carrying on. I couldn't explain to her. I know now that my heart was broken—but I didn't know that then to tell it to her. She held her face in the roses and kept asking, 'Why, Samaria, why?' with smiles she couldn't help across her face.

"The only words I managed were, But what about your big tap-dancing career in New York City? What about the Rockettes at Radio City? Which made absolutely no sense to her. I might as well have said nothing at all. The subject of tap dancing had been dropped the minute we left the orphanage. She had grown out of the silver shoes. I was the only one of us who even knew what the Rockettes were, and I was the only one of us who remembered her tap dancing like a little star.

"She sat there flabbergasted. She twisted her hair in her fingers and didn't know what to say. She finally got up and put her roses in our water jug, then got a cold rag for my face. She went off to tell the landlady it was all right.

"When she came back, I pretended I would be maid of honor, and then we both went to sleep. In the middle of the night, I took my suitcase and left."

Samaria waited at the bus stop for the rest of the night, and in the morning took the first bus that went out through the country and past the orphanage. The driver let her off at the gates. She told herself that she would get the facts, and then she would know what to do next. She was wearing her good blue dress with the red sash, and she had hidden her dyed red hair beneath a green Hawaii scarf. Her suitcase was cardboard.

"You found me in the house by myself," she said. "You were afraid I'd burn the place down. Or you took me because of child neglect, that kind of thing. That's why you took me here, wasn't it?"

"No, that's not why. People have the right to leave an eight-year-old in charge of the house. A big girl eight years old can be all right. No complaints."

"Then tell me why."

"Just because."

"Because, just because."

The head of the orphanage had breath that smelled of the orphanage—cold potatoes and yesterday's breakfast grits fried into today's lunch. But a strong smell of beer in the middle of the other smells. "You really don't remember, do you?" the big man grinned.

The room became quieter than it should have been. It grew too hot. Samaria had the feeling that flies were about to buzz. A year behind the counter at the bus station had taught her the smell of beer. She had never tasted it. It crossed her mind that she would like to taste beer.

"I'm going to tell you." The man lurched a little forward in his swivel chair. He picked up a fly-swatter from the desk and began to slap it against the window sill, though there were no flies in the room. It was like a dream in the room. The room did not make good sense.

"Your father," the man said, "might be an English sailor, but then again he might not be. I myself believe you've got Cherokee in you. But the father in this case is irrelevant. It was your mother. She'd been working the docks—as far as we knew—for as long as she could get up on her feet and walk. *She* said that she was just a decent 'workingman' going to work down there. *She* said that she put on her overalls every morning and went to work at the shipyards like a decent 'workingman.' Have you ever heard such shit in your life? What we knew was a woman, a bad woman in a red dress. The Bible says . . . the word is *whore.* You tell me—what woman can be a decent workingman and at the same time be a scarlet woman? Answer me that. But as long as we let her go on talking, that's what she said."

"That was not my mother. That was her sister in the overalls. You didn't listen closely. There were two of them and then there was me." Samaria felt a fly crawl up her wrist, and she felt quite cold. When she looked, the fly was gone.

"What sister? No sister we knew of. No other family we could find anywhere. No orphanage wants extra children for no good reason."

"There was our home. There was a big white house where you could have gone and found the truth."

"It was just her, I said. No home. No big white house. In this town, there is no *house* of any kind for women like that. They go to rooming houses that should be burned to the ground. They hide out in the colored section. She must have hid out in the colored section and had you there with her. But she was slippery as an eel, and she could disappear in daylight. It took us two years finally to track her down. We had other problems on our mind. You weren't our sole concern. We wiped her out and we got you. You could say thank you. You could thank your maker."

"Thank you," Samaria said.

"It was in a cornfield, five miles outside of town in the middle of the night. She was with a man, but he got away. They were both drunken and naked. She was trying to put the man's private member inside your mouth. You were eight years old. They were laughing their heads off. You were lying on the ground, still as stone. Don't you remember anything?"

Samaria remembered a song she had forgotten. It went: *Eff U Cee Kay, Tell Her I Love Her.* There had been a man who sold newspapers at the bus station. He had no legs, but he wore pants anyway. The pants legs were folded up behind him and pinned at the waist. The man was strapped to a little wooden platform, and he pushed himself along

32

with little paddles. Why would her mother want to put a man's leg into her mouth?

Samaria gets a new job at the Railway Luncheonette, which served excellent breakfasts. For forty-nine cents, you could have a glass of juice, two ham biscuits, and all the coffee you could drink. For a dollar, you could have eggs and bacon (or ham or sausage) with grits and gravy and toast and jelly, and all the coffee you could drink. Samaria waits on, and keeps the place clean.

Almost simultaneously, Veronica is employed by the British Royal Family. She is to be nursemaid for Prinesss Elizabeth and Princess Margaret Rose.

In order to save Bethulia, her city, Judith beheads Holofernes, who is a general sent to invade Palestine.

The little princesses dance along on either side of Veronica's heavy-footed stride. They are dressed in their precious cream-colored coats, and both have new permanent waves. Veronica is taking the little princesses to view the seals at the zoo. The seals have been brushed and combed for the occasion.

To entertain them on the way, Veronica tells the princesses what is going to happen, just as if the future were a story:

"Shortly before the winter of 1920 closed down hard and fast on the little farming town of Lepetty, North Carolina, U.S.A., and the simple country folk began to settle down indoors for a season of fornication and conning the *Farmer's Almanac,* Flynn Burns's grandfather was killed in

33

a railroad accident—crushed inside the engine he had so expertly fired his whole career. Because death was instantaneous, Theophilus Burns hadn't an instant—before the angels bore him to a heaven paved with shamrocks—to reflect on the agents of his death *which were . . . ?"*

"Sex, booze, jealousy, lust, violence," chimed the little princesses. This story was one of their favorites.

"And even had Theophilus lived," Veronica continued, "it would have taken literally herds of great professors to make him perceive the appropriateness of such a death to the life he had lived. And the professors would have failed, even using words of one syllable, even using such familiar plain talk as . . . ?"

"Eff U Cee Kay," Margaret Rose piped up.

"Exactly! You are a very bright little girl. Theophilus was a man almost entirely devoid of brain. A great sweet space filled his skull, where, among the normal, evil thoughts and rich designs on nature lurk. Brain cancer is the last thing he would ever have caught. He had almost no place to store them; and he had forgotten the reason for March 15th . . . "

"Margaret Rose and I are bloody British imperialist swine," Elizabeth said.

" . . . and he never once concerned himself with anything not directly at hand. He thought he knew what he liked to eat, for example, but he would eat anything set before him. He never complained for what he did not have. When desire beset him, he did not rave (like spoiled little girls sometimes do) but waited patiently for desire's object to appear and be taken. He could read only a little, but there was nothing he needed to read. He could write his own name and the names of his two wives *which were . . . ?"*

"Samaria and Veronica!"

" . . . and he had memorized the names of the ten station stops it took to get from one to the other of them.

"There also lived in Lepetty a gorgeous creature named Gloria Lee. She was the grocer's wife who—until her sexually ravenous thirties invaded her—lived to enjoy two things in life: her reputation as the county's best barbeque cook and her gift for glossolalia. And *what is glossolalia?*"

"The gift of speaking with tongues!" cried the bright little girls.

"Especially on hot Sunday afternoons, when Gloria Lee could combine her talents into one helluva double-header: leaving the pigs basting on the spits, she would lure the sinfully expectant crowd into the tent. And there, while tossing her long yellow hair and shredding her lace-covered bosom . . . "

" . . . and massaging her pure white bosom, white as the driven snow . . . " chorused the princesses.

"She would give tongue to the forgotten languages of the Holy Ghost . . . "

"Yenkettenkettunketblahblahjesus," Elizabeth intoned.

" "Almost, but not quite. There are many imitations, but there are no substitutes for the real thing. Gloria Lee was the real thing. And, as it is to be expected with reality, one thing led inevitably to another. The proof of the pudding occurred early one spring. Gloria Lee cast fame, reputation, her mystical and her marital duties aside—and washed and untangled that lengthy yellow hair—and began an *affaire* of such heated proportions the whole town seemed to liquefy in its presence. Pig and prayer were gone forever. They were not regretted: Gloria Lee, newly transformed, was better than ever.

"The lover was unknown. She did it behind the schoolhouse privy, hardly waiting for the last child to run home. She did it in the fields, the woods, beneath parked pickup trucks. She did it in the choirloft. Once, with her skirts hiked up, she did it against the wall of her husband's store. By August, she had stopped putting up her hair at all. As a matter of fact, by this time, she had hardly any hair left—she had had the barber cut it short because it got in the way of what she enjoyed doing most. She scarcely kept her front buttoned. By October, she wasn't going home at all . . ."

"And on November 22nd, she was getting her throat strangled in the middle of the railroad tracks . . ." said Margaret Rose.

" . . . where her husband had finally caught up with her after a circus chase down Main Street."

"Frightening the horses," said Elizabeth.

" . . . and right on schedule, here comes Theophilus. And promptly, out of nowhere, also comes the unknown lover. Both of them, just in time to be in for the kill. Lover, wife, and husband—triple-locked into . . ."

". . . their death-struggle . . ."

". . . their struggle unto the death. No one of the three would be the first to roll away, although each must have heard the train coming, and felt its heat."

"*Crash!*" screamed Margaret Rose.

"Their heads were cut off, their bodies dismembered," Elizabeth uttered. She nodded graciously to one of the seals; and graciously the seal (whose tag named it Veronica) returned the salute.

Because she refused marriage, Agnes was placed naked in a brothel by the father of her suitor. But hair grew until it

covered her entire body. Next, she was tied to a stake. But the fire went out. She died by a sword through her throat, at the age of thirteen, and is the patron of chastity.

In the dream, she is sitting yoga-legged in a pale room: peaceful, dim, Oriental. The room is the shape of an oval, and a few feet within its perimeter has a low fence made of white wooden slats. Her back is leaning slightly against the fence.

Although she feels no fear, she experiences a certain nervous sense of being in public, of being watched. But she knows she is alone. But then she knows she is not alone. There is a person she knows is a surgeon crouching behind her on the other side of the fence. He is opening the base of her skull, slicing with his scalpel ear to ear. He is a jolly doctor, he expects nothing but cooperation from her. She realizes he is removing her brain. He accomplishes this quickly, silently, without giving her pain. She sees his hand slide her brain into an enamel pan waiting beside her knee. She believes he is going to leave it at that and go away. She is certain of this, and immediately becomes ingratiating, charming, cute. She will perform any trick to bring her brain back home; she would even suck his cock. It lies there beside her, silver, silent, quivering.

The doctor then does something else—also painless—inside her skull. She will never be sure if he has put her brain back.

Then she is in the foyer of an Oriental palace made of dark wood—not too distant, she understands, from the site of the brain removal. The atmosphere is hectic and panicky. There she glimpses, just before they disappear, little brown men in yellow loincloths. They are slipping around corners hunting for children to execute. The order to kill comes from a war lord who resides on high. But if any

37

children are killed, it will be her fault.

There is a faint rapping on the door behind her. She surreptitiously cracks it open and sees a raggedy little boy waiting there. She snatches him up and hides him against her body.

The woman in bed with Maryann tries to wake her. Maryann curses and rolls over. The woman presses her hand between Maryann's legs, but Maryann's dream is relentless and keeps her asleep.

Then she is outside the wooden palace, standing in a dark garden near the place of the surgery. She feels herself exposed inside a deep erotic flow, and the women are all her own size, the same height, the same weight. Everything else disappears.

Maryann is making love to Honor. At the same moment, just across the street, ten women (whose husbands are baby-sitting) are opening up their own cervixes with plastic speculums and staring up into themselves through pocket mirrors.

The Marshallin—the Princess von Werdenberg—at the end of the first act is alone again. She is looking into her mirror, watching charm fade. She has dismissed her hairdresser, her attorney, her literary advisor, milliner, animal dealer, chef, flautist, Italian tenor. And the Rosenkavalier is gone, too, bearing the silver rose to Sophie—sixteen, slim, pretty. This will be their first meeting.

"For seven years, she let me sleep in bed beside her. But then one morning the footsteps in the corridor *were his*. He was back from World War II, and I had to run and hide.

Teresa of Avila, of a noble family, underwent, in 1555, a "second conversion." After that, she experienced inner visions to which, with great brilliance and charm, she gave practical and delightful application. She left behind her writing of sound literary value and frequently prays for souls still in purgatory.

Samaria said, "He courted me out of the Railway Luncheonette. He would eat first, then court me. He would eat hotcakes and syrup, ham and eggs, and drink a whole pot of coffee with cream. First he would eat, then he would court me. He had a head like a turnip and hands like hamhocks. I married him after a while and gave up working at the Railway Luncheonette. Then I had a little girl, Daisy.

"Then I found out about his other wife. He carried pictures in his wallet of little boys I knew must be his—they had heads like turnips and hands like hamhocks, just like his. So of course I knew he must have another wife and these boys must be hers. The other wife turned out to be Veronica, but I'm never certain those boys are hers. Only *they* think they are.

"Between finding out about Veronica, and Theophilus getting killed, was a year's time. All that year I thought about almost nothing but Veronica. I would feel my heart get so big there would be no room in my chest for breath. When Daisy was five years old, I began telling her my thoughts about Veronica. Sometimes we would do things like shell peas or pare apples while I told her, but other times we would just sit while I talked, with our hands uselessly in our laps. She drank the words in. She has never forgotten a word. I could never see Veronica's face in my mind, but I imagined her exactly my size—the same height, the same weight. There would be light around my picture of her. I told Daisy that someday we would get on the train and sit on red velvet seats going to visit Veronica that each of us would carry a big bouquet of roses in honor of. Daisy wanted her bouquet tied with silver ribbon. I went to the five-and-dime and bought three yards of silver ribbon, to be ready. When we got off the train, she would be waiting. Sometimes she would look like Daisy—the way Daisy was then; with wild red hair. Sometimes she would look like me—like a Cherokee. She would be short, or she would be tall. She would look like either of us.

"When Daisy was fifteen, she began telling the stories instead of me. One of hers was of Veronica as a ship's captain. The ship's captain would be wearing a silver silk dress and diamond earrings and buckled shoes. She would take the ship to France, and return with a princess costume and toe shoes for Daisy.

"Then Theophilus died, and we buried him. Then the truth, because of the death, came out, including her address. The address of Veronica. I said to Daisy, I am scared to death. Daisy answered, You are going, nevertheless. But she was, by this time, really disinterested. She was spending all her time in front of the mirror or sewing new dresses. She sang, all day long, like a movie star, "Some Day My Prince Will Come." How did she know I would hate that?

"She sewed a new dress for me to wear and bought me a hat. She dressed me up and sent me off. Daisy had become a Roman Catholic, and the hat she gave me to wear looked like the wreath of flowers the smartest girl put on the head of their Virgin statue every first of May. And when I was gone—and I was gone for a long time—Daisy took a lover. She carried on in broad daylight it was so bad with her. It was the kind of thing that could end in death. But with Daisy it ended in Flynn. Flynn, now, wishes she could chop off all our heads from our bodies and keep us just as brains, but I could be wrong, and if I am I'd admit it.

"I had never worn a hat. For clothes, I wore the color blue. I had never worn that same color of blue before. I got off the train in the town where she lived and began to walk. It was a town that was one pretty neighborhood after another, as if people never cooked or worked, but had nothing more to do than tend their gardens. It was nearly dark, but there was still light enough to see that. It was the sort of light that's the color of milk being poured— it doesn't seem to shine, but does—you know it's light because you can see. I began to think I smelled the same as that hot planted earth that began just beyond the people's fences. Sometimes they would have a grape arbor, still vine, not yet grapes. If the flowers from their bushes leaned over their fences, I would break one or two off and take them with me. Pretty soon, I had a large bouquet. If Flynn had been my little girl instead of Daisy's, it would have been that night I conceived her. Counting back, later, I knew it was that night Flynn was conceived.

"Shortly, they began turning the lights on inside their houses. It was supper time, and I could see inside. I recall white hallways, golden lamps, dark wood staircases leading up to their bedrooms. In one upstairs, there was a woman fastening a necklace around her neck and wearing nothing more than that necklace on her body; but I kept moving on. When it became entirely dark, dogs started barking at me, so I threw the flowers away.

"It was that time of night, I think, Flynn was conceived, but in Daisy, not in me. Daisy put me on the train wearing

41

her navy-blue school uniform and her Girl Scout shoes. When I got back to her, her belly was swollen beneath a red smock and she wore dangerous high-heeled slippers with pointed toes. So we have Flynn. Before long, the sidewalks ended, the houses grew farther apart, and the tended grass began to go. At the last house, I turned a corner and had nothing left to walk on but the dirt road, and no flowers left to see—even if it had been light—but that flowering mimosa tree which will take root anywhere. There was dust up my nose and a band of sweat beneath my hat, and I was afraid I would soon have to be beholden to a colored lady for a glass of water. But then I saw where I was going.

"A plain house, a dirt-farmer's house, its paint flaking and leaning to one side. It was all by itself, alone in a great field of nothing but closing-up lilies and Queen Anne's lace. There was no path to the door. There was no way either in or out of the place I could see. So I just stood there for awhile, beside the ditch running past the flowered field, and thought, does she expect me to *fly*? No other answer to my problem came to me, no matter how far down I thought on it. So at last I just went on. I went on past the house, straight up the road, getting scared of the dark until finally I happened on the way that was there all the time. It was like trying to find something you want to see in a dark room. If you look directly at it, you can't see it. You have to look to one side of it, pretend not to be looking for it, then it will leap up against your eyes and you'll have it to put your hand on if that's what you want. That's how I found the way. It was a path that was a tunnel. Big water oaks grew on both sides, met overhead, and made a tunnel. As soon as I was inside, I felt safe and hidden from danger. I could have been a cat out hunting for the night and getting ready to tease a mouse to death. The tunnel curved, then I caught sight of the house again.

I stood in the dark, the house stood in light. It was like the time I went to a theatre.

"I imagined, then, Theophilus coming to it from his work at night and catching sight of it like this. But he might have had his kerosene lantern to get him through the dark. The whippoorwills started up, then it was dark for good. I imagined Theophilus going past the light, putting himself inside the house, and finding her home and trying to put his tongue inside her mouth like he did me.

"At the last minute, I lost my nerve and could go neither forward nor backward. I spent the night sleeping in the weeds underneath the trees. I slept deep and thoroughly.

Margaret of Antioch, having refused the attentions of the governor, found herself cast down deep in a dungeon with a dragon. The dragon swallowed her alive, but Margaret swelled inside him to such proportions that the dragon split open and she emerged from its belly unharmed. Frustrated by the miracle, the governor had her executed. Her help is summoned by women in the pangs of childbirth.

It is July 13, 1973. In New York, L. massages the pain in her right eyeball, continues to paint with her left. I cannot find S. because she is gone from Staten Island into a disappearing act on the upper West side. If I go there to track her down, I'll be wading up to my ass through memory solid as sewage: Nelly and me living on eggs and pasteurized cheese at the top of the 82nd Street walkup, gnawing my way through five mysteries a night, abandon-

43

ing my cat because it's either him or me. Up there, I will stumble over a dog squatting to shit; and the dog will not have been there a single instant before, and some cat—not that one—will be watching me through a window. Sidewalks too wide, trees too young. I will have to cross Amsterdam Avenue and will therefore be thrown in the air by a bus. L. has new paint, more kinds of yellow than she's ever had before. J. is marrying, in church, T. She describes her wedding suit as French satin, white-on-white, cuffs in the trousers, with a blue ruffled shirt. T.'s dress is a secret, but the clue is "Jean Harlow" and naked as the law allows. I have exactly ten minutes left to buy a wedding present. If I'm late, I'll miss "Oh Promise Me." When I was a child, my mother took me to a great assortment of weddings, where women married men. At each of them, I prayed earnestly that the pretty bride would answer: NO, I will not, and trample the lilies beneath her feet. A. goes to dinner with me, and I want to lean over the table and slide her hair through my mouth. In ten minutes, for three hours, I am in love with her; but instead I eat veal parmesan. Tonight, to keep my strength up, I will eat boloney, eggs, milk, carrots. Instead of one pack of cigarettes, I will smoke two. With the cigarettes I will drink an unpronounceable vodka, because there is a long night ahead. She won't talk to me on the telephone because I have interrupted something—a lot, I hope: a woman's anatomy can cool in the twinkling of an eye. They will have to drink a cup of tea and feed the dog instead. M. has burnt me, like another bridge, behind her: I am a liar, without consciousness, and a dirty fighter. She has burnt me—not like a bridge, but like a witch. Her mind is a star chamber; condemned there, I burn in the process of missionary's faith, but like a light bulb, General Electric, hundred-watt, much illumination and little heat. There are no troublesome ashes to dispose of. In North Carolina, mother still works as a telephone operator and lives, for the most part, on pimiento cheese sandwiches; and, a hundred miles away, M. has apprenticed herself to a plumber who gets her wrapped around the pipes and then asks, just one more time: What is it, exactly, you do with your girl friend? I don't remember from one day to the next, M. replies; and makes good money. On one of my rare days off, I lean back into the pool players and justify the wasted time by contemplating the universe: In all of us, I conclude, lurks essential bar dyke and her release. Shoulders move before the legs do. Large D. spreads like cumulus above that brown earth. It would have been the easiest thing I'd ever done in my life, last week (like rolling off a log) to pick up the steak knife and put it through that old bastard's gullet while he first picked at his salad, then picked at his nose: that was last week in the restaurant, when I wanted A.'s hair in my mouth. I drink with G., because she's a real cook-book of a mother but I must suddenly hurry home (I am easily embarassed) when she tells me that the logical solution to her personal despair would be to stick her tongue up a friendly cunt; only, she adds, as I stuff my mitten in my mouth, I'm not attracted to women.

Sometimes, on Canal Street, I become a serpent. Reflected by industrial plastics storefronts, I slither inside, then outside, my Appalachian pool, all poison drained; defanged—as near death, as vulnerable, as the Godzilla that science will conquer on late-night tv. I spoke to I: I am without substance, a liar, a dirty fighter: it takes only one of you, however, to kill me. The nice doctor gives her lithium to eat. Having no alternatives to offer—none but the same old helping hand—I give her the hand to hold. I understand more than I think I do. But this whole place seems full of women shivering with anxiety as they tick off

the number of years they have remained together in pairs—
the next Ark will have to multiply into a fleet—and they
concern themselves with why I drink (instead of, for instance, jog) but never think why I stay, uncured, Irish,
out of that grandmother off that boat. That grandmother
called (short for me) Bert, who, upon hearing the news of
her husband's death in a train engine, simply slapped her
hands together and announced: *That's that.* The genuine
class difference among women exists between those who
had paradise and lost it and those who never did but think
they do. Street games with a stick and anything hard
enough to hit: sweat fanning past from the body just
ahead; street lights coming on ahead sudden and disastrous
as thunderstorms. I beat the shit out of the boy next door:
although bigger and stronger, his arm snapped like raw spa-
ghetti in my fists. And, like a good boy, he died, grieving
those who loved him, although, now, I cannot remember
why I needed him to die. If she came to my door this
minute, I swear I would turn her away. And she would die,
grieving those who love her; and then the alphabet would
end. I want my mother, she told the woman who had made
her scream and cry for hours. You may want, but not have,
the woman answered. Your mother is a married woman.

*Winifred, a seventh-century Welsh maiden, refused to mar-
ry the chieftain Caradoc; whereupon he beheaded her. But
on the ground where her head fell, a new spring opened up
and its waters were healing.*

The arrangement with the bank seems to work; the mortgage gets paid. We took possession in the spring, and now it is winter. We have been here, we are still here. The lake is now frozen over with a thin layer of ice. We have had time to fan through the house and find natural hiding places. The man's wife came over last week for her first visit, arms folded beneath her breasts, head bent to watch her feet crossing the field: in the manner of all country women who cross fields to visit the neighbors. Once inside, her visit had only one purpose: *Where are mother's curtains?* she said. Honor's first act had been to pull down all the starched dimity at the windows and hide them in a cardboard box. "Would you like to have them?" Honor asked her. The wife looked bewildered. She shook her head, no. Before she left, she made one more effort to make Honor understand: See, I meant *mother's* curtains, she said.

After a hard, lugubrious talk about the future, they are drinking, variously, martinis, bloody marys, black coffee. Then, a sudden charge of energy through Maryann manifests itself in a blast of heroic noise from the machine, in the appearance of a derby hat on her head and a plastic machine gun in her hand. She disappears; then as suddenly reappears in the doorway to drop two brown eggs on the floor; which is hilarious. She promptly wipes up the mess, after everyone has put down her drink to clap her hands and laugh. Then she begins to dance, like this: arms stretched stiff some little distance from her trunk, then one foot, then the other, inching across the floor; her head bent, watching the floor she's crossing. L. and I wait for half the music to be finished before we do what we have been counting on doing.

Our dance, it appears, turns out to be what we imagine Swan Lake could be: Zeus, disguised to catch Leda unawares. But some say it was Nemesis—a thoughtful maiden, occasionally represented with measuring rod, bridle and yoke—he caught unawares. To the sound of Scottish bagpipes. First I am the Prince, but then she wants to be the Prince. Because of greater agility, she gets her way. I am more interested in the comic: the notion that Helen pecked her way out of an egg that rolled from a maiden's body! It is awkward for me to dance with a woman I want. At any moment, she might notice I want her—and so might this lover or that lover already established in the nature of things—and the establishment is always the first to get the message and convey it broadside back to the revolutionaries. Some like it scrambled, some like it fried, but if you're all out of butter, I'll have it crucified.

Samaria did not starve or go thirsty all that night she spent in the open. A little while after she slept, Veronica crept out and dropped an orange, a cake, and a bottle of water into her lap; then was gone before the sudden weight of the food could wake Samaria.

Olympias, widowed at twenty, determined to remain single thereafter and devote herself and her considerable wealth to good deeds. She was charged, however, with conspiring to burn down a cathedral, and from that time until her death suffered constant harrassment from the authorities.

Waking up again, this time absolutely cured, Flynn recalls all that has happened to her but not the proper chronology. It might have been three hours ago—or ten minutes ago—that the twins left her at last, revolving out of the room, snapping out their last bits of dialogue: "We will go—get help—for Flynn—from a grownup—Flynn is—so sweet—but mean and ugly—sweet but mean—but we are the little princesses!" The twins could translate everything into three-quarter time and then do it. They waltzed.

Flynn thinks, those children should be in the hands of the state asylum for the insane. It could have been hours ago, or ten minutes ago. I don't know. Now it is summer, and in summertime, as in any other season, light changes—but doesn't show the change in summer until all at once it is dark, and then you know it is a summer night. Summer light, summertime—*sneaks*. It is not like winter. It is not matter-of-fact.

She is not too weak any longer to get to the window. Out there, it is like a lighted tent, with the skin stretched tight as it will go to hold inside the luminosity, and the flavors, and the colors. In summer, that which is most dependable about Flynn—her harshness, her furies, her grimness—slacks out of her control. It is always a shock to her to find herself all of a sudden like some pulpy fruit, like peach or plum. She remembers herself as stone, but the stone gets fattened, by heat, into something edible and she hates that. She could be compared to a rich orange dropped out of the night into the lap of an unconscious woman. A toothsome delight.

She hates that. She despises herself when she gets this way: leaning on the sill, twitching her nose, simpering at the green and the gold. It doesn't take just weddings, she understands, to drag her down. She can be as healthy as a horse, her mind as poised as a fresh mousetrap, her mother, husbandless and reunited with her maidenhood—but the first of summer will shoot Flynn down; and she is never prepared when it happens. Forewarned-is-forearmed is not for people like Flynn.

For instance, now, stretched out beneath her are two green acres of oak, elm, water oak, judas, dogwood, cedar; and all stitched up by sun and shade and shot through with flying birds to keep it all in motion; moving, so that she will understand it lives, that it is not a painted marvel. Even the fabled Bluebird lives in this place and on schedule, merrily reproduces itself. And just beyond the land, there is the lake, a little of which Flynn can see now, through the trees. She interprets what she sees as shine. Dragonflies skim the water, turtles colonize its shores, fish and snakes trouble the surface. Its other side is swamp and wild wood and a boathouse where no one bothers to go. To her left, the bamboo grove rattles, without benefit of wind; to her right, the swish and slam of Bogart and Boatwright choosing either to enter or leave their home in the old garage. Bogart and Boatwright live alone together; they gave their goats away some time ago, but Flynn was delirious at the time.

Flynn understands that men and women do it like Nature: monkey see, monkey do. Mother and men do it like nature because nature is so pretty. If nature were funny-looking, like me, drawn like a comic book, like me, they would stop doing it because they would no longer imagine themselves Art imitating Nature. They would be mother and a man aping something funny-looking, and they would stop out of embarrassment. Be like me, in winter, mother, Flynn wants to tell her mother: black-and-white; no birds' nests, no leaves. Something ugly would bring the whole thing to a standstill and be then like Flynn in winter. (Flynn does not yet realize that among women with men Daisy does it *only* when she wants another child, another daughter. It is in this way that her mother is like nature, and that is why her husbands leave her.)

Question: How did Greensleeves get green? *Answer:*

From rolling on the grass. Flynn was sick to death, but even the twins were doing it, and it made a noise. But she leaned on the sill, getting better; but bemused, as caught as anyone. She put her hand between her legs, touched herself. Then she knew there was no hope. Fuck it, she said. Why should I care, if no one else does? The world had once promised her everything—had presented her with nothing but its round, shiny behind. *The anals of human history*, Flynn adds. Old pictures stuck ineradicably into the fissures of her brain now sloped forward to be looked at. *All nature rejoiceth to show us the Way, to Innocent Pleasure, to Innocent Pleasure.* Wet colts nuzzling: that kind of thing, too. Old ladies withering into porch swings, their feet dangling unseen behind buckets of wet ferns; safe in their daughters' houses, passing the time waving at the traffic. And hollyhocks, purple and blue, planted beside the corn; and a little rose garden inside a circle of staked-up tomato plants: all these kinds of things.

Flynn is the only person she knows who never once forgets that the mind is a big gray muscle called a brain. When she was twelve—just when her body was heartily popping forth those tits the twins so coveted—Flynn (instead of eating her supper) listened to a radio story about two scientists and a brain. Neither the story nor its meaning have ever abandoned her. One scientist is good; one scientist is evil and crazy. The good scientist does not recognize the symptoms of evil and madness in his colleague—a blindness common among the good; and his ignorance, of course, leads him into a situation which, in his opinion, is personal disaster. The evil scientist, after drugging him, severs his head from his body in order to test their theory that not only can the brain survive without the body, it can also continue to dream and intellectualize. Although the bodiless scientist would not agree with her, Flynn regards his

51

fate as wonderful and begins, from that time on, to want it for herself. The evil scientist, according to plan, arranges his colleague's head in a container of a miraculous pickling solution and attaches the necessary wires, tubes, microphones. He toasts himself with a glass of Amontillado and sits back to wait for the voice of truth: a head without a body, according to their theory, will speak only the truth. At last the truth!

Flynn cannot remember the nature of truth (although midway in the program, the head spoke.) She recalls only a mess of grieving utterances concerning the vileness of the separation, the damage to one's immortal soul, unethical medical practices. On and on. Looking a Gift Horse in the Mouth, spitting in the Face of Fortune. At last, the head's daughter bungles her way into the basement laboratory (for a mason jar of pickled pears?), recognizes her vanished father (she had been told he had gone suddenly to Chicago, or Vienna) and they have a conversation about rejoining each other someday in Heaven—if she will only *now* do her part. She pours her father down the sink—she pours his fluids down the drain, and unplugs the apparatus. Instantly, she is attacked from behind by the evil scientist (whom, since infancy, she has called "Uncle Al") and her head is about to be substituted for her daddy's in a fresh tank. But she is rescued at the last minute by her boyfriend Jack, who breaks the door down, shoots Uncle Al and takes the sobbing Lillian in his arms ("My darling!"). Jack's name, in real life, is Albert.

Flynn figures it must be noon. The bee-loud glade is louder than ever. She is sweating. It is hotter than hell. But she can still concentrate on how to do it: first, some complicated—possibly troublesome—arrangements with a surgeon. Then, a haircut—all black curls that have posed for Veronica's cherubs-made-blond shorn, shaved away, until the skull is as clean of hair as the shiny behind. Then off with her head. Ready the tubes—input, output, drainage; ready the microphone to broadcast the truth. Herself inside a roomy plexiglass box, hunky-dory; the lid closed forever. I will be horrible. I will be placed on the round table in the front parlor, where I will be horrible. Horrible will control. Horrible absolute controls absolutely, so I will control. Wonderful for me, horrible for them: for *them*, without the body, without all the little entrances and exits of the flesh, it is horrible.

Flynn depicts, on the glaze of nature before her, little scenes of religious ritual: Veronica, Samaria, Rose-lima, Rose trucking in baskets of the first fruits and sacrificial lambs. Jugs of wine, glass balloons of olive oil. They are wearing striped loin cloths. Were they not humbled by awe, they would be dangerous. They wear false (but long and thick) beards. They are attended by dancing girls who look like Yvonne de Carlo, who click castanets and wrench their naked bosoms to and fro. But how can she imagine now, unfreed, what her brain will imagine appropriate once her brain is let loose of herself?

But, after all, she can't stop. Her knees are knocking. She has been hungry for a long time, and must still add and subtract like everybody else. For instance, once deployed through the mouth of the brain, what will happen to the platter of Chinese fried chicken, the bowl of lobster Cantonese, the hot fudge sundae? Will the brain know to shit?

It is clear that she must shuffle off the mortal coil, but first she must piss. She must get off the window sill and on to the toilet. The dream of food is a diversionary tactic sent forth by the enemy agent. The enemy agent, seated, pisses; and is relieved not to find menstrual blood coloring the water below. Somebody said, Writers write for three reasons: fame, fortune, and the love of beautiful women—

which, Flynn agrees, is indeed the case. But if the glove wears, fight it. She wipes herself, she tells herself to ship out or shape up; but on the other hand, she is not bleeding. "Rough winds do shake the darling buds of May . . . " she recites. She recites. Then she free-associates: liplicking, leering, kneepatting, lap-dogs: eighteenth century lap-dogs, a temporary genre of Veronica's quickly abandoned. Little Pekingese smothered beneath billowing pink silk (crinoline too) going lap-lap, a busy, snorting little Pekingese. Alberta-of-the-second-grade who could touch her nose with the tip of her tongue. And those who fuck in the back seats of fish-tailed convertible automobiles. And the minnow-sized monstrosities of Hieronymous Bosch up the ass.

Defeated absolutely, Flynn comes. Then Flynn washes, dresses, brushes; enters the sane continuity of grown-up days. Faintly, from below, the voice of Galli-Curci warbling "Lo, The Gentle Lark." Therefore, it is lunchtime. Therefore, the lunch will be Samaria's version of that which is Olde English: rare roast beef and Yorkshire pudding; or else, shepherd's pie. "Lo, the Gentle Lark" means that her grandmother is once again Jane Austen and will describe herself by the food she serves. At this very moment, up Samaria's lane, the vicar comes wandering to be fed. He slashes with his stick at the hedgerows of blooming clytemnestras, both pink and orange, because he is bothered by sin. So there is no question of showing up barefoot, with her shame covered in girl scout shorts. Sickness is cause for alarm, but no excuse. She is the son (the Etonian necktie is found, finally, beneath the bed) home for the Long Vac. (or some such slaphappy shit.) And the son wears, also, white flannels, straw boater, high collar. He is, perhaps, an Edwardian son; but this will not trouble Miss Jane Austen. The twins will be wearing posy-sprigged Empire gowns, chintz, with (stuffed) low fronts. The vicar will create an opportunity to take a peek.

So Flynn goes downstairs, the legs atremble like a god-mother's wand, so she must take a rest on the landing and also an absent-minded look through the white-purple-green stained-glass Lamb of God. And therefore, she gets her first (and only) look at the stranger on the other (northern) side of the lake, who she sees wandering tiny as a pinpoint through the trees. The way he walks, he looks like he owns the place; but then he disappears behind the leaded line separating purple and green. Flynn straightens her tie (she will do anything for love) and goes down to eat.

"On Easter morning, 1951, my father for the first time had the florist deliver boxes of orchids for my mother, my sister, and me. We found the boxes on the kitchen table. My father was in the back yard cutting a bush back. My mother said to my brother, 'Go out there and tell your father to stop cutting back my bush. He will kill it. It's the wrong time of year.' My brother went outside and then came back: 'Daddy says he's only trimming it a little.' 'It will die,' my mother said. 'Go tell him to stop.' My brother came back again. 'He won't stop,' my brother said. 'He says he's only trimming it a little.' I looked outside. The back door was open, and I could see it all. My mother's big hydrangea bush was already just a stump, and my father was gathering up the leaves and blue flowers into a sack, leaving the place neat. I said to my mother, Why do you let him get away with that? Why don't you do something

55

to make him stop? My mother sat down, with her back to the open door. 'What can I do? He cuts my bush and then I go cut all the buttons off his shirt? Then he cuts all my dresses and then I cut all the legs off his pants? And then he will cut through all the pages of the book I'm reading and then I will cut through the tires of his car and then he will bide his time until I'm sleeping and then cut off all the hair on my head, so where will it end? My bush is dead now and there's nothing I can do.' "

Barbara, a maiden of great beauty, was born in Heliopolis, Egypt. Her father shut her up in a tower to prevent her associating with men other than himself. Later, he tried to cut off her head, but straightaway a bolt of lightning laid him dead at her feet.

I am older than you think. I am also older than I look. I am old enough to know what's what—that is, the truth of the matter. And I will testify to it. I will sit up all night, if necessary, to persuade any who say me nay (quibbler, lawyer, moralist, psychiatric bill collectors). I act within the full circumference of what I know to be true: that the real action is the action of the lover; and all else is that action disguised. All else, such as sleeping, eating, forging works of art.

I have known Flynn since birth. I have raised her to be what she is. I know, therefore, her fantasy of the independent brain for what it is. And I know what it feels like—I was once abandoned myself and spent the darkening hours stiffening into stone on the steps of the British Museum.

When she finally came to get me and take me home, it was too late. I did, however, achieve a poem from the experience. It begins, "Rough winds do shake the darling buds of May . . . " Any schoolgirl knows it.

But Samaria is the poet of this menage. I myself work as a forger of both great and minor works of art. Several dissertations have of late been published on some Tanagra I both made and buried—off the coast of Yugoslavia, causing the scholars to make radical and disturbing revisions of their theories of Boetian migrations of the sixth century. The Yugoslavian government, their cultural ambassador, paid me more money than I ever made before for that little performance in terracotta.

But Samaria is the poet, though she neither reads nor writes poetry. She reads nothing but fiction, a taste she acquired after the age of twenty-one; and she hates poetry. Like me, she would rather *act* what is there to be done; and do it three-dimensionally when possible—but I also paint. Samaria will not have her name writ in water.

The next morning, Veronica got up before the sun—before the sun could reach through the trees and wake Samaria before she could herself wake Samaria. She slipped through the false dawn, looking for Samaria sleeping—but, at the last minute, changed her mind and returned to her house without allowing herself even a glimpse of Samaria sleeping. She would let Samaria do it.

Three hours later, she saw Bogart and Boatwright roll away on the county school bus, off to make straight A's for one more day. She took her coffee to the front steps of her house, sat, and drank it. She had waited a long time; she waited a longer time. The coffee was long gone. But she did not stiffen into stone. She found the body of a horse-fly and occupied herself poking at its jewel-blue shell.

Samaria seemed so small from a distance, and was so fast-moving, that had Veronica not looked up from the fly to rest her eyes Samaria would have been upon her without notice. As it was, there was just time enough to discover that Samaria wore blue, that the garment was more some cunningly devised mold to cause reproduction of her torso than it was dress; that a heavy gold locket hung between her breasts and caused Veronica to blink her eyes. She also saw that Samaria wore adornment as though she were ashamed of it. She did not have time to see the hat that dangled from Samaria's fingers like a wreath of flowers.

"My name is Samaria, Ma'am.

"The Woman of Samaria was asked to draw water from the well. And she said, 'How is that, being a Jew, you ask me, a woman of Samaria, to draw you water?' And was answered, 'If you had asked it of me, I would have given you living water and you would never thirst again.'"

"I don't understand."
"I don't either. But I was named Samaria and told the story."
"My name is Veronica."
"Like the veil. Veronica's veil took the face on itself and afterwards no one could tell which was the real face and which was the face on the veil."
"Certainly not."
"Will you mind if I sit down?"
"I never mind."

"It's been a long walk from the station." (Sitting, folding herself against me).

"And a longer night sleeping?"

"It is you I have to thank for my refreshment?"

"Yes, me."

"And do you mind if I slip my feet out of my shoes? I am hot and tired, like I didn't sleep a wink."

"But you did sleep. I don't mind." (Little black slippers, buckled above the instep. Like a child's.)

"You know, I feel better." (Her feet, without her hands' help, shed the shoes. One fell into a patch of clover by the step. It was, I imagined, happy as a shiny black pig in clover now.)

"Now, those tight hot stockings," I told her. (She peels her legs bare, revealing about five fresh-clotted razor cuts. Mistakenly, she shaved for me.)

"Your dress unbuttons down the back. I'll do it for you."

"Daisy sewed it."

"Who is Daisy?"

"She is mine. My little girl, fifteen years old."

"Like you?"

"Not like me. Nor Theophilus either."

"That's wonderful."

"You want me to lift up a little? Then you can slip it over my head."

"That's what I want you to do. I'll take the petticoat at the same time." (Draping both across the boxwood, as though she were going swimming.)

"To save the awkwardness, I'll lift you and carry you into my house. Let me ask you, if you were still a little girl, like Daisy, what would you want to be when you grew up?"

"You, I guess. Like you."

"Why is that, when the right answer is Samaria?"
"It seems to me, then, that there're no right answers."
"Wrong!" said Veronica and lifted her up.

Reparata, a twelve-year old Palestinian, was first tortured, then executed with a sword. As she expired, a dove flew out of her open mouth.

But one is very much like the other, anyway. And if you can't discern difference between the original and the reproduction, then difference does not exist: they are the same, although they take up separate blocks of time and space and may change one's ideas about the course of history. "She reminds me of a character in the early fiction of a minor American novelist. Indeed, as far as I'm concerned, there is no difference between the two—between the living and the written—between the idea, the fantasy, and she who walks up and down on the wooden floor, shaking it with her heavy step, above me. No matter where I turn, I find a total disregard for the truth.

"Glamor. I mean, *magic*, whatever . . . . *Unreasonable*—that's the word I'm looking for! Some Princess Uncharming who does not trouble to slash through the hedge of thorns and awaken her with a kiss. She prefers the easy way out—seduction and abandonment; and home for breakfast. On the other hand, she will do anything at all for any woman at all. Especially if, in the doing, she becomes the woman's lover. She is a lover—that's what she adds up to.

"Her movements, for example. A chronology of her

movements from the beginning to the end of an evening. The sequence of events she executes to just get her own body next to another's.

"Her fingers bump across the other's knuckles until her fingers are caught in the other's palm. It is an irresistible takeover; and then she has three loose fingers and a thumb with which to cup the other's fist. That is the way she frequently begins—and it could end with only that. But not this time—because, almost immediately, her free hand starts. It takes the other's waist, it slides around to the other's back, the small of her back; then enters the clothing, insinuating beneath the waistband and shirt. At this point, the tips of her fingers are resting against the initial curve of the buttock. In this manner, she draws her toward her: until the shoulders, the breasts, bellies, *pubi*, the knees indent, one against the other.

"Then she moves, but only from the hips, and a little to the left. The lover's right thigh is then between the legs of the beloved. It is a tight fit, and the entire length of the thigh. The lover's first kiss is on that curve where the neck becomes shoulder. She kisses; then she licks there, then she sucks there. Sometimes she tastes perfume; sometimes she tastes sweat, or soap."

The beloved, too, becomes necessary. Some point is eventually reached at which one can not tell lover from beloved. A conglomerate of picture, sound, smell, noise charges past her on the red carpet pavement. There are cloudbursts, dingdong bells, shoo-fly pie, yumyum and the lover's indrawn breath (taken, now, from within the beloved's ear). But if she is smart she will neither grab, gesticulate, nor roar. She will take deep breaths. She will close her eyes, and hold on; but not too tightly.

The wizard tongue collects the eyelid, then the mouth's first corner, then its second, then all its insides—teeth, tongue, gums, palate; while the hands go up and hold tight underneath the arms and the two thumbs press, once, against the nipples. Once more, then, they touch the hips then leave the body entirely. The lover and the beloved are separate now, so the lover says, "I love you."

Later, it will all begin again; and go on. The beloved draws breath: "What can we eat? What do you have for supper?" She holds her breath until she gets an answer.

"I have a quart of gin, an ounce of vermouth. I have five pounds of kosher salt, a head of old lettuce, half a jar of harvard beets . . . " She shuts the icebox door and looks on the shelf. " . . . and a can of tuna fish and a can of Hawaiian punch. There is a loaf of bread, mayonnaise, and ice cubes. Can I make love to you now? Do I have to wait til later?"

"I am so fucking hungry! I am a big empty space with no food in it!"

The beloved's personal city map is of a great wasteland greened in secret places with restaurants, all miles apart. There is the Nathan's concession in the basement of the Brooklyn Museum, for example. There used to be the French Roumanian, but it vanished overnight four years ago. If it still existed, they could reach it on the E train. If they take the Sixth Avenue bus, they can ride for thirty blocks and then eat raw fish. They can go, by foot, to the St. Anthony Feast and have sausage-onion-pepper heroes and raw clams in lemon juice. There could be steak and baked potatoes if only they had ten dollars a piece. There is no longer any good guacamole to be had in Manhattan.

The lover puts her foot down. Under no circumstances will she go to Chinatown. She knows, for a fact, that they are substituting roast rib of alley cat for chicken on Bayard Street. Nor will she go all the way uptown for Cuban. She straggles back and forth through her three rooms, dressing with one hand, drinking her martini with the other. It is hard to dress because she doesn't know who she will be tonight. She could be Queen Elizabeth the Second if she had time to do her hair in pin curls, if she owned something simple and fuschia-colored, with a bolero jacket, if she had a pearl necklace. She thinks of T. S. Eliot; but her jock strap is at the laundry and her lips are too full. She wants to wear a stained trench coat and be a detective. She wants to squire this broad to a blue-plate special, then back to her place or her place.

But the beloved is pounding the mattress and yelling, "Empty! Empty!" so the lover makes the simplest choice. She becomes a drag queen named Roman. She laces white shoe skates with red pompoms to her feet and circles her recumbent beauty, flashing her brawny black-haired legs. She spins like a top.

"Oh, you are terrific."

The lover lifts her tiny pink tutu and curtseys to the princess. She puts on her yellow t-shirt imprinted with the faded legend, *Get Your Shit Together*. She hooks her pepper-and-salt beard behind her ears. She is ready. She takes the lady's arm. Then they go out. But they will return. Since her acquaintance with the beloved became a matter of intimacy, the lover has gained ten pounds. But skating is good exercise; and, because the lady overate, Roman the drag queen had to carry her home: weight-lifting is also good exercise.

Cecilia, a wealthy Roman, was married to Valerian; but persuaded him to join her in a vow of chastity. It was not

long before the governor tried to force her to perform an act of idolatry. Because she refused, attempts were made to stifle her in her bath. That failing, an executioner was sent to behead her. Her neck was struck three ineffective blows, and she lingered for three days. During that time, she distributed her wealth among the poor. At one point in her career, an angel fell in love with her because she made such beautiful music.

When I wake, I am starved to death. Samaria is like a white snake coiled over my breasts and belly. She is sleeping still, in the place where she at last collapsed. She is my long white snake for my religion—its ecstacy is snake-handling.

I am starved to death, although my mouth is still full of her. There is a distant noise of Bogart and Boatwright quarreling and nailing something together out in the shed where they also sleep and eat. They are building a hutch for their rabbits; and the rabbits were a gift from Theophilus. I dream of enrolling them instantly—miraculously grown-up overnight—in the Communist party so that I can see them eventually electrocuted by the United States government. They are Theophilus' twin sons. I have no idea who the mother is.

Samaria's hips, like a moon, rise before my face. I see through the window that it's already night-purple outside and the hedges are already without leaves and branches, have melted into hunks of green. I imagine, starved to death, that I am making love to her in my first memory. I am in some summer house, in some country with a season of heat no other place in the world can match. It could be Alabama; it could be the Isle of Capri and I a wealthy, pre-war lesbian. The place is very small. I think it belongs to my grandmother. It has a dirt floor. Its walls are nothing

64

but vine and leaf grown up invisible stilts. To do it there to her. There is nothing inside the summerhouse but the two of us and that broken shard of teacup where a sleeping garter snake lies curled. The summerhouse eventually collapsed, broken by the weight of the green.

I take my finger up and down the canals of stretch marks left on her hips by Daisy. I rub the craters my teeth have made. I will start again if she doesn't move and I will faint midstream and drown from starvation. Lust is this moment going to unfurl. So I move her beside me and get up, away. I return with steak, eggs, toast, jam, orange juice, and a bottle of gin. We eat in bed. Samaria eats like a boa constrictor swallowing a horse who eats like a horse.

Bogart and Boatwright going away. The telephone not ringing. No music playing; the ears of the angel bored by silence. We eat, then sleep some more. Off in the distance, there is the conception of Flynn; here, not a sound. The rugs are flat on the floor; nothing walks. I ate like a horse. I sleep like a lamb.

But not me. I am all aching back and nerves like pizzicato violins. My mouth is a cigarette machine. My mouth is like that giant Caucasian face of metal above Times Square which every five seconds, blows a ring of smoke. A thousand Japanese infants pluck the "Pizzicato Polka" from a thousand made-to-measure Japanese violins. The tune is sacred to the memory of Lady Plum Blossom, of Ko-ko San, Lieutenant Pinkerton, and Hirohito. Another summer, another trip to the country, where cigarettes are cheaper. This one, also northeast. We stay with friends inside their authentic Early American clapboard, and everything is antique and lemon-waxed. I fall backwards in a little rocking chair and break the rocking chair and apologize. It was not my fault. The rocking chair was one hundred years old and had never once been outside New Hampshire. Outside, I lie flat on my back stoking up enough oxygen to carry me through the long Canal Street summertime ahead and keep an eye on her. She is sitting beneath the gumyum tree silently weeping, as if her heart were broken. Samaria and Veronica sleep soundly through most of the night. In the middle of the night, they wake up refreshed.

She said, "We wanted each other like a hatchet in the stomach." She was a psychiatrist married to a man psychiatrist. Her work was—and she told me about it, seriously, a thousand times—*touching* therapy, where they scream. She made a great deal of money. She needed a babysitter to live in her house all the time and leave her free for the work. She moved me in; I was the babysitter. She wanted me to attend her therapy sessions. They were in her living room, so I went, for the last two years I lived there. But sometimes I wouldn't go. Those times she would make an excuse to run out and leave the crazy people and find me. When she did, she would hold her head and pull at her ears and whisper how much she wanted me. She would say she'd go crazy if she didn't have me. I never touched anybody in that living room, and I didn't let anybody touch me. We were never lovers. I could have died from it. She conducts group sex these days, I understand. I imagine her in an orchestra pit waving an illuminated baton, making them go fast, then go slow. The kid, the little boy I minded, used to sit in his room and make phone calls to the kitchen. "Bring me a hamburger, *now*, rare!" he'd yell over the phone. The cook would cook it and I'd serve it. That was eight years ago and now I am thirty-one.

66

Faith's sisters were named Hope and Charity, and their mother's name was Sophia. All three girls, however, were executed in A. D. second century during the reign of the Emperor Hadrian.

Just like nearly everybody else (even Siamese twins) Flynn grew for nine months inside the body of her mother, whose name was Daisy, a red-headed teenager. It occurred to Flynn sometimes that she, too, could have been a Siamese twin but that her sister had somehow been carelessly lost. The one thing she was sure of was her birthdate: February 14. Her middle name was Valentine. Those two items constituted all facts of the matter.

But the facts of the matter—solid as Gibraltar, she thought (although the moment she pictured Gibraltar, it exploded above a ton of dynamite, and dismembered apes clinging to bits of famous rock were whirled out to sea)— the "facts" were so encrusted with what she had learned to recognize as fictional topsoil that she increasingly felt the truth of herself to be some rotting Sutton Hoo or buried flint arrowhead or ruin of Troy—but a treasure—which every decade sank deeper down. This neither frightened nor depressed her. Her brain was the answer. Unleashed, her brain would be the whole truth. Flynn would dig up Flynn.

By the end of the lunch, Flynn was full and refreshed. She felt reborn—the word flashed past before she could stop it: reborn, washed in the blood of the lambchop presently turning the trick in her stomach, effortlessly besting the brain's resistance to turning turgid as a sleepy old cow. Roast leg of lamb rare; new potatoes, pickle-and-onion preserve, snow peas, trifle, cheese and biscuits. But the event was not a success.

Samaria, dressed after an engraving of Jonathan Swift, had spoken perfect sense to the subject of Flynn's illness: she had been near death; she must be careful. Others might die, but not Flynn. And Flynn had responded with sensibility: "I believe I did die. Is it possible that I, too, was Siamese and am the survivor?"

"If that is the case, I wasn't told."

In spite of the heat, Flynn did not loosen her necktie. "But," she added, "there is something wrong somewhere."

Entering the dining room, Veronica had said, "I can tell that something is going wrong" and had refused to join the table and eat. And had refused to change out of her red Japanese robe and into suitable riding attire. She sat in the corner, behind the potted palm, and watched out the window.

Samaria was angry; Samaria, at the head of the table, could not keep her little hips still in their chair. "What is it that's wrong?" she asked three times, and never got an answer. And the twins had refused dessert; had, instead, torn off their unbearable dresses and rushed, inevitably naked, outside. Rose had not wanted to be the charming daughter of the house. She had wanted to be a child murderer attempting to poison (arsenic in the sugar bowl) her family of twelve. And Rose-lima had wished to appear as an infant prostitute who had turned up at the Bath assemblies in red satin and feathers, who had seduced all the ladies, one by one, in the cloakroom between waltzes.

Shortly, Samaria was left alone with the dirty dishes. As she washed the plates, she began to assign motives of envy to Veronica. Veronica in her sleazy Jap robe was envious of Samaria's grip on literature. Veronica, she understood, wanted art all to herself. She wanted each of them only as she imagined them, as though behind glass, or on canvas, or wood. There is one Samaria in Veronica's mind, and there is another Samaria washing the plates—Veronica will bode no trespass of one upon the other. Samaria grabbed the spray hose and shot ice cold needles through the open window above the sink, and the bumble bee attempting entry instead fell out of sight. But nothing could be settled until Daisy came home. No one, not even Veronica, could tell one thing from another, then act, until Daisy returned. Her absence made everything inconclusive, formless. Always, Samaria concluded, some mother, some daughter kept disappearing and making things stop before they were meant to stop. Her tongue tunneling a vagina: everything felt, everything for sure. She wished she could apprehend Daisy as exactly. She wished everything could happen as exactly as *that* did: her tongue tunneling a vagina.

Flynn joined Veronica behind the palm. "If I were the Chevalier D'Eon," she said, "then I would play the part of Ophelia and would not care. But it is otherwise. I am not the best swordsman in Europe. I am not French. I could continue—I could tell you the reasons why there are no other roles available to me."

"Have a drink," Veronica replied. "Hold your glass steady. This same martini shaker has been by me most of my life. It is interesting to see you take an interest in our livelihood. That is interesting to me. I do have plans for you. I do have your interests at heart. But you are right. As the famous Baron Grimm once remarked, 'It is difficult to imagine anything more extraordinary, and, it must be admitted, more indecent, than Mademoiselle D'Eon in skirts.' "

"I understand. The . . . *chevaliere*. Forced to become

69

royalty's freak in skirts. Both Royalist and revolutionary and a career eventually injured beyond repair when, fencing, he tripped on his petticoat and got the immobilizing wound; thereby forced into retirement from the double-edged sword. Dead, in poverty, at the age of eighty-three.

When I mention D'Eon I *should* say *she*—obviously she was a woman disguised as a man forced by circumstances to dress as a woman . . . "

"It is too bad, Flynn, you were never forced to go to school. Your knowledge of the universe is a jumble of Raree Shows. If you could, you would make us all into dwarfs, giantesses, living skeletons, pig-faced women fit for nothing but the entertainment of gentry."

"*Strange Eeka!* The woman who tears living flesh limb from limb and devours it raw before your very eyes! I have sufficient learning to know that anyone can make anything she wants out of *Hamlet.* All I ask is not to be Ophelia again—nor any of the others. I want you to change my part. I want you to have me stage-center curled inside a large glass sphere throughout the entire play. I will speak whatever lines are appropriate through a microphone. I could even, at the interval, reenact the death of Theophilus and the lovers. Listen to my choo-choo imitation. The audience will stay to watch me instead of going out to trample cigarette butts in the flower gardens."

"You force me to rethink the design of the entire production—Hamlet as a hump-backed dwarf; Ophelia, an Irish giantess who can trace her ancestry back to defeated kings; Polonius, a conniver born without legs—I am raising the price of admission to five dollars a head. We will perform it *al fresco*, with only the stars and kerosene lanterns for illumination. We are going to enjoy a well-heeled winter. I may even be able to avoid laboring over Vermeer forgeries for the homes of Texans. I could spend the cold months with my feet up. There is enough left for us both to have another drink. The marvel of the martini, Flynn is *less* vermouth, even in such hot, hot weather as this."

"And myself curled stage-center inside a great glass sphere, like a brain without a body. My mother once told me she was raped because her mother left her alone to take a long trip away from home."

"Not true. Hold your glass steady."

"Another time she said I was born on the Lusitania during a stormy crossing. The boat was pointed towards America. She had been presented at the Court of St. James and the Prince of Wales had promised marriage, the lying young scamp!"

"Or perhaps she found you floating in a basket among the bulrushes out on the lake and became enchanted by the sweetness of your smile. You will be Gertrude at this evening's performance. There are no glassblowers available. All glassblowers were killed in the last war."

"I hate being fucking Gertrude."

"Remember, I said beneath the stars and illumined by lanterns. And except for your crown and bunches of diamonds, you will play Gertrude naked."

"Certainly, then, I will. And I will wear a long false beard."

"To cover your shame. I agree."

Petronilla, who did not wish to marry Flacco, obtained the grace to die; and was buried before his eyes.

On Nelly's tenth birthday, it is so hot I am being fried; in deep fat turned to crackling. It is, however, a little cooler than that original birth day. I measure the heat of every June against that day's weather report when it was not a question of living or dying but a matter of how death would come—from suffocation or from pain. The delivery room was air conditioned, for the babies' sakes.

The enema hurt me as much in the brain as in the bowels. Once, I read some pornography in which enemas, being given and received, were the climax of sexual pleasure between the man and the woman. All her little friends are here with her. But only Nelly has grown the first strands of pubic hair and has nipples so round and pointed I grow sick with fear.

I deliver Macdonald's hamburgers, french fries; and lemonade and chocolate cake. The new bicycle is the color of egg yolk. Soon she will leave me (as my mother used to sing) "stone cold dead in the market." My mother would sing that song on her way to bed with her husband. Nelly's new body is as frightening as the loss of love.

When it's all over, we sprawl on the floor where it's cooler and watch the evening news. A man has raped a nine-year-old girl and thrown her off the roof of a building. She was lifted over the parapet, and dropped. A woman's face (she is a neighbor) is on the screen. Her face is lined, plucked, avid. The invisible reporter thrusts his microphone to her mouth. "Did you see, *see* the little girl as she hit the street? I'm asking you, did you get a look?"

"No," the woman answers, "not that. I missed that part. Crowds were in my way."

In the middle of the night, we wake up again, rested and ready for talk, that second round of love-nesting. She is on one elbow. She says, "You are so beautiful." But they all

72

say that. What else can they say?

Am I? What do I look like? I expect eyes like stars, lips like cherries, skin like milk.

"An actress. A star of stage, screen, and radio."

Then what am I doing buried in the country seducing dream girls? Why am I not forty feet tall above Times Square and my story a scandal? How did she know?

"Your face is a thousand times bigger than a real face. You are made of gold, like real gold."

Samaria, I say, that is only my disguise. Sometimes my disguise is love, sometimes this pleasure—here.

But she took my hand away and knelt astride me. She pinned me down at the shoulders.

"I know all that. I know about costumes. Daisy has a princess costume. And kings and queens and spies and angels, and God more than anyone, go in disguise. You all wear costumes so that we won't know you. There are many old stories about you, and you can't fool me because I know all the stories."

Her hair is so long it brushes my mouth with every word she speaks. Samaria talks, and every part of her moves with her mouth. I am what she says I am. Now she sees me as round, as if pink: It's as though, through her eyes, my hair were gold and my eyes wide and blue, the colors of a savage. When she looks again I will be flat as a blade, dark as night, damp from Elsinore fog. And the murdered corpse at the bottom of the swimming pool. And the Slavic Anastasia; and Baby Snooks. It is wonderful that she is a woman and, unaided, creates the world.

She doesn't take my hand away. I collect her with both hands, pull her center to my mouth, reenact chaos. Theophilus thought I was a man, and that is what he loved—and that's where he went wrong. It is possible that she could learn all my secrets, especially in this fashion; and when

73

she does, every word out of her mouth will be the truth: angels, kings, queens, spies, gods, a woman at the stake earning sainthood. I am a pageant, like reality. Not very far away, inside her daughter, Flynn begins.

And eighteen years later, is Queen Gertrude in our rose garden theatre. The kerosene light sheds through her saffron veil through which our genteel audience can perceive the face of a virgin. Naked—but for the black beard so long it hangs beyond that deep place between her breasts. She also wears a crown of gold and ivy. She has grown to be nearly six feet tall. I approach her, as Hamlet, in a white wedding dress. The audience, understanding, applauds. It is a lovely night for my very lucrative production of "Scenes from *Hamlet*." The sky is sharp with stars.

Claudia Procla besought her husband, "Have nothing to do with that righteous man, for I have suffered many things this day in a dream because of him."

She owned houses and a dog named Sport. On hot pale evenings she would take Sport and me for long walks across cracked pavements. Her purpose was to steal flowers. She would pause, look right and left, then reach through the fence and snip them off, with long stems, with the scissors she wore on a black ribbon at her waist. I carried the basket for the flowers. She smelled, not like flowers, but like bouquets of candy; but I was a child with a sweet tooth. The rose would fall into the basket I carried, then we would walk on.

We would stop, too, to look at what happened behind

unshaded windows. Once, we watched a woman pull a dress over her head, then stand there, above our heads, quite still. We sighed, speechless, then went home.

In my mother's house, there is a photographer's portrait of her, taken when she was young. The picture is propped up on top of the old waist-high radio. Her shoulders are naked, her arms are draped in some white stuff which is pinned between her breasts with a worthless cameo. Her face is in partial profile. Her eyelids are lowered, to conceal herself. Her hair is a dark coil from crown to nape. The photographer left his spiky golden signature in the right-hand corner.

She held me on her lap, rooting me to her ground, kissing the top of my head as if it were a priceless work of art—one tanagra, for example, washed up on the seashore of her shoulder—and screamed contempt at the rest of them: Johnnie! You were the boy who traded his bicycle for a billy-goat! Jimmy! You married a British bottle of vinegar who'll murder us in our beds one night! Stephen! You drink on St. Patrick's Day but not another day of the year! What kind of man are you? She kisses the top of my head and rocks me.

I get drunk more days of the year than not. I turn vinegary women into wine. I never trade; I give everything away.

Now, this woman and I are walking, thirty years later, deep at night on the dead streets of Thomaston, Maine. We are out to look at the dimmed architecture and to let the dog, who is another woman's, shit. I tell her some of this about my grandmother.

Eugenia spent much of her life in male attire serving as abbot of a monastery in Egypt. Upon her return to Rome, however, she was beheaded. While in Egypt, she was accused of highly inventive misconduct.

Bogart and Boatwright live in the garage, and when they dress up they put on matching zoot suits. Their jackets are pink and tan plaid, with pads doubling the normal width and length of their shoulders; and nipped in at the waist. Their trousers are baby blue, and pegged. They have blue string ties, and blue suede shoes, and keyless key chains half a yard long.

They have a fast red car with lengthy tailfins, with white sidewall tires, with a coon tail on the radio aerial, with a special installment on the steering wheel which emits loud wolf whistles when punched. On Saturday nights, Bogart and Boatwright, omitting underwear, dress with elaborate excitement in their zoot suits, after first having examined them inch by inch for wrinkles, for stains and rips. The suits are always in perfect condition. No harm ever comes to the suits. They brush the week's worth of tartar from their teeth, they grease their hair into pompadours. They layer their cheeks with Burma-shave, and shave.

They drive their unmuffled car to a town. They whirl their car around and around the parking lot of a place named EAT and imagine their wolf-whistling is annoying bored young women. They pretend that they are crazy, hopped-up kids; they pretend they are going to run over the pink-nyloned car hops, who scream at them. They eventually park and eat. No girls will get into the car with them. But they are only pretending to ask the girls to get into the car anyway. They dare each other to ask a girl; neither does. Then they drive their car up and down the streets and through the shady neighborhoods, driving slowly, on the lookout for women to whom they can say (as they glide past): How would you like my great big cock up your cunt? On some Saturday nights, they are able to ask this question as many as fifteen times; the town is rather large. As they go along, they drink a six-pack of beer apiece and listen to the all-night disc jockey. They talk back to the disc jockey, suggesting what he should do to the high school girls who phone him for song dedications. They never speak to each other. They have already said, long ago, everything they ever had to say to one another.

After midnight, they begin to speed through the dark country roads and throw their empty beer cans at roadside signs. On the average, they hit one out of every ten. At least once, they stop to piss against trees. They also stop to reshape the 35 m.p.h. signs into 85's with their can of black paint. They have taken turns driving.

Back home inside their garage, they put on a record—the Ink Spots, or Elvis, and dance the dirty shag until they are too tired to dance any more. Then they take a long time folding and hanging up their clothes. Before sleep, they sit together, side by side, and masturbate in front of Betty Grable pin-ups glued to the wall. They are both virgin. Neither, except in important fantasies, has ever touched a woman. Women, through the cloud of their identical imaginings, seem to them to be either bearded or bald headed—the potent hair in some terrifyingly wrong place; and possessed with hidden woven nooses to snatch them up like rabbits and dangle them in thin air.

They more or less spend their lives waiting for a solution to this problem; and avoid the company living next door as much as possible.

Early on a Sunday morning, however, Veronica pays them a call. She knows how they feel—nevertheless, they must bite on the bullet. Bogart and Boatwright are still in bed, huddled together on the round queen-sized waterbed they have acquired through sharp trading. The single sheet is gray with summer sweat; and, in several places, the bed is quietly dampening the cement floor.

Veronica, slamming the door behind her, imagines the pair hurtling Niagara together in twin barrels. Bogart sucks his thumb; Boatwright, dozing, picks his nose.

"Gentlemen, good morning!"

They leap upright, horrified. Their bed sloshes, threatening to spill. The light inside their home is dim and dank. There is an immense unrecognizable shape spreading its arms against the light blazing through the doorway behind. It is black; or else they've gone blind. It is going to get them.

"It's only her! It's only her!"

"No, no, yes, it's only her!"

"Buggering your noses and sleeping your lives away like little babies."

Even with a name, she is no less horrible. The water rocks. They can't keep still—they must be ready to run at any moment. A new pinprick hole opens, squirts: Huckleberry Finn and Nigger Jim poling down the Mississippi, Veronica decides.

They slosh off the bed; they fumble their legs into their jeans. But it's too late—the bitch has seen.

Veronica sits, on a pile of foam rubber pieces cut into crude but familiar shapes, but most of them inaccurately formed. The foam makes itself into a chair, with arm rests, around her. She lights up a Lucky. Her form and colors settle: she is still too tall, but her shirt is blue; her shorts, brown. Her long, long legs are covered with scrolls of black hair.

"I am taking some time off this morning to talk to you. I want you to leave. I want you to go away from here. It is time you made your way in the world—I believe that's the expression."

They seem to understand. They sit together on a stack of three rubber tires. There is little room for both of them; they wobble, they are fat. Bogart must wrap an arm around Boatwright to steady himself.

"Do we understand you want us to go away from here? Leave home?"

"Do *you* understand that?"

"Fuck you, you crazy bitch," Bogart replies. But his voice shakes: she had given her head a shake—and her hair, sometimes dark, sometimes light, had cast a shadow over her eyes so that he could no longer see to guess what might happen next. Bogart was twenty minutes older than his brother and more reckless in his speech; but less accurate when he folded his arm back to take aim at a target. Boatwright sucked in a deep breath: *Bogart!*

Bogart whispered to him, "You're chickenshit." Then he shouted, at Veronica, "You can't make us go. You're our mother."

Veronica stood up. The foam re-expressed itself into breasts, thighs, hips. She killed her cigarette beneath her bare heel.

She said, "I wish you would rid yourselves of that irksome fantasy—in your best interests. It only holds you back. I am not your mother. You are obsessed—your minds are bloated with sex. No, I am not your mother." Outside, Flynn runs, crossing the path of Veronica's peripheral vision, running to go swimming.

"We have to have a mother, and you have to be it."
Boatwright was shivering a little. The sun never entered
their garage.

"I can't be your mother, because I am not. One more
time, I'm going to explain. Then I won't ever again. Now
listen: after the revolutionaries shot my parents and sib-
lings, I wandered for a while, incognito. But the revolutionaries grew suspicious of my height, of my Florentine
profile; and they quarrelled over the royal body count.
Somebody, according to some of them, was missing. I
found two baby boys beside their mother, who was dying
behind a haystack. The mother was an Irish dwarf, grateful
for a chance to die in privacy. I strapped you to my back
and continued my tortuous way. I escaped. You had grown
fond of me—fond of my backbone, I suppose. I let you
stay, even into my safety."

"That isn't what you said, last time," said Bogart."Last
time you said we were the sons of a blimp pilot whose ship
exploded in flames above the state of New Jersey—and that
you had us as a widow, by caesarean, like Caesar."

"No, that isn't what she said last time. Last time she said
we were the sons of a great Canadian revolutionary, from
Canada, the man who led the Canadian revolution to victory. 'Don't organize, mourn,' she said was our father's
dying words."

"You pays your money, you takes your choice." Soon,
she thought, I'll get in the water with Flynn. There was
something extra these days on the other side of the water.
Flynn had seen something moving where there should be
no movement. She would pay attention to it—it might
carry some smell of Daisy on it. She would exchange roles
tonight with Flynn. She would be Gertrude and the ghost.
Flynn would dance Hamlet. And Samaria would die to-

night, of Flynn's dagger. Samaria, Polonious?

"But," she continued, "I don't come without suggestions. Are you ready? Have a cigarette?"

"Oh, thank you!" Bogart took two and lighted up for both of them. "We're ready to listen. But get it straight—we can't leave. We're waiting for something, and when it comes it will only know to come here, to this place for us." They smoked, relaxed deeper into the rubber tires.

Veronica paced in front of the lighted doorway. First she was dark, then she was bright. She kept moving.

"I think what you're waiting for is about to come. And if that's what you're waiting for, then you can stay a little longer and let it come. It's not far to the other side of my lake. Can you swim?"

They understood only the question, *can you swim?* And, no, they couldn't swim. But all else she said seemed woven too strange, too full of craft, like a spell.

"No, we can't swim."

Her pacing became elliptical. She swung closer.

"So then there's my suggestion. An attractive suggestion. I'd do it myself if I were a man—great strong men like you. It means money, fame and fortune—your birthright, so to speak; your *manhood*."

"You mean women," said Boatwright.

Veronica stood still and spoke slowly, making it up as she went along. "They want you to go over Niagara Falls in twin barrels. It would be at night, beneath thousands of spotlights because night is more important. Things that happen at night are never forgotten. There will be fireworks and bombs bursting in air as you go over. There will be a beauty pageant, to elect Miss Girl of Niagara. Hundreds of Miss Girl candidates will parade past your eyes in tiny bathing suits, crossing back and forth over a bridge that is presently being built directly above the Falls—just for you. They will show themselves to you, sing and dance for you, then you will judge them. You will judge them on the basis of Beauty, Poise, Talent. I'm afraid that means, however, that you will have to fuck them, all of them. There is no other true test . . . "

"But we might die. We could drown and die."

"Famous people never die," said Veronica.

"That's right!" Boatwright urged. "Look at Elvis! Look at General MacArthur! Oh, big pictures of us everywhere, lighted up!"

"Elvis will sing and play for you day and night. You will sleep in beds made for giants, in air-conditioned motels. Cocktails, color television, ice machines, swimming pools, clean sheets, hot showers, and . . . ?"

"Girls! She means pussy, Boatwright!"

"As you go over the water, the Girl winner and her court of thirteen runnerups will follow you directly overhead. They will dangle in satin, rose-tufted swings from fourteen helicopters. They will all be wired for sound so that the millions who'll be watching—and even you, inside your barrels—can hear them singing above the roar of the falls. They will sing, 'Dancing in the Dark.' "

"Yes, it is wonderful. No one will ever forget."

Veronica smiles at them, and leaves them. She has heard thunder and smelled lightning and rain; and Samaria, slamming windows.

Besides their billygoat, Bogart and Boatwright had also owned an irritable German Shepherd dog and a small apiary. Early one summer, a bear had come at night and ravished their hives. The next night, they tied Sport near the hives to bark at the bear when it returned. The next morning, they found their dog dead of bee stings and all the hives destroyed. It puzzled them for a long time: no one had ever heard of bears before in that part of the country.

*Marina, who lived disguised as a monk in Bithynia, was
accused of fathering the child of an innkeeper's daughter.
Marina did not dispute the charges.*

Veronica runs through the rain, to meet Samaria in the
kitchen rather than swim with Flynn in the lake. She is
crazy about the rain, but hurries into the house. She does
not want to be observed enjoying the rain: she is not so
crazy as that. Flynn, in the middle of the lake, wonders if
the lightning will strike her dead, knowing that water
draws fire. She dives deep and swims underwater to keep
from drowning from the rain. Rose and Rose-lima are rum-
maging through the drawers of Flynn's desk and bureau,
hoping to find her secrets. There is nothing to find, but
they persist. For instance, Flynn has never received a letter
in her life and has, therefore, nothing to hide. Bogart and
Boatwright are too excited to take their afternoon nap.
They talk about how wonderful it will be. I am making
love to her in Rockland, Maine.

It has taken us twelve hours to get here in the car. Four
hours were lost in wrong turnoffs. Instead of watching
the road, I watched the stories she told ("I had a fist
fight on the sidewalk outside the bar, but I was so scared
of getting eighty-sixed I didn't fight good and lost. I loved
the bar. Nothing happened anyplace else. My lover was the
daughter of a Philadelphia Main Line family. She wore jod-
phurs and boots and drank her whiskey neat but never
amounted to anything.") I am like a cheap off-season holiday for her, but I don't turn out the way I should. It isn't

83

cold and rainy; the museums, the dark abbeys, the heavy dinners have all been canceled. She had intended to commit adultery with the nerve of a hippopotamus. But all at once it is hot instead of cold; and she is in the midst of breakdown. She lands on her feet in soft green grass. Her cheeks rub roses big as babies' heads. Even Greenland's icy mountains have thawed, and there is no place cold left to go. All the globe is the temperate zone, and she sweats worry.

The hotel in Rockland, Maine, is a mammoth of shabbiness and smells, and coated with grease and damp air. It is the middle of the night, but the street outside bustles with stoned teenagers who can't go home until Saturday is finished. A woman is called from behind the bar to work for me at the front desk. Her mouth moves when I tell her a double bed; but when I demand the bucket of ice, I get it. I say to her, Take a hot bath. She takes a hot bath. I say, Drink your gin. Then she lies naked on the sinking mattress and drinks the gin. She wants to fall asleep. I lie down beside her and use my fingers and mouth, beginning with the top of her head, against her wishes. Her body is silken rope. I didn't want to come, she says. I never expected to come. She goes to sleep.

On the other side of the lake is a small peninsula, curling out over the water like a sleeping dwarf's body. There is no money to be made from it. Its land is always soaking; nothing can be built on it. It is full of willows, green in season, and swamp lilies, in season. In rain storms, it seems to sink; then, it appears it will never rise and dry again. Except for Rose and Rose-lima, it serves no one. When they feel like it, the twins swim there or row a boat there. They roll in the mud; they drink a bottle of beer; they enact, within the closely packed willows, an elaborate game in which only they are the survivors of the holocaust and must perform heroically at sex so that the race may be renewed. At night, viewed from that place, the house seems no more than a crowd of quivering lights moving in and out of attendant bushes and vines. From his crouching place beside the water, what the man sees of "Scenes from *Hamlet*" makes him think he is either hallucinating or gone mad. In the afternoon he had watched Flynn swim; and that had been bad enough. Throughout the drying evening, the sound of invisible hands applauding over the still water has bothered him like the rub of molestation; and what he glimpses baffles him. Whatever is over there—if it can swim or walk on water—could catch him. He must watch out all the time, and that is like gall and wormwood. Something nasty rises in his throat and he spits it out. He can't see anymore. It makes him sick.

Two years before, he raped a nine-year-old girl and threw her over the roof of a building. When they caught him, they couldn't prove it. They cleaned his fingerprints off the pieces left of the child and buried her. In his company are two young women. Since he collected them, they have each had a baby in the back of his Volkswagen bus. The young women are stoop-shouldered and religious. They tend the babies; they fast; they compete with one another over the number and the length and breadth of visions they have been granted; they brush and braid the man's long yellow hair, and spread their legs or open their mouths at the first sign of panic in him. In tolerant communities, they have panhandled on the streets. Sometimes, so that the man can think of what to do next, they stuff their skirts into the babies' mouths and hope that everything will turn out all right. Sometimes the man, in a fit of boredom, will yank a baby from a breast so that he himself can suck it dry. For nearly two years, he has blundered through the country in a series of spasmodic crisscrossing false starts. The women have kept him fed and satisfied while he prepared for glory. He will hold up banks. He will steal cars. He will kidnap an heiress. He will hijack a jet plane. He will lay pillage to some city's gold coast and also murder the oppressor. He feasts on what will happen—diamond necklaces, bundles of banknotes, ransom payments, numbered Swiss bank accounts; himself furious and cruel.

But nothing, so far, has happened. They have landed in this terrible place because there was a turn-off from the main road. The bus is stuck in the liquid earth and daily sinks further down.

Rhipseme of Rome attracted the passions of the Emperor Diocletian, a circumstance which forced her, with her friend Gaiana, to transplant their rather large community of women to Armenia. There, unfortunately, they encountered the same trouble with King Tiridates: first Rhipseme repulsed him, then Gaiana. King Tiridates then had the entire community put to death.

Even the most paralyzed of imaginations, Veronica knows, must eventually link the separate colors of the two separate images and make of them a dimensioned one: the lake of water is also the lake of blood. Warned, she increases the erotic volume between herself and Samaria until the entire household begins involuntarily to twin her every move; to act identically. It feels safer to do so. Samaria chooses to spend more time than usual snapping arrows into her targets, splitting one arrow with the next. Veronica experiences herself as ocean, full of storms and monsters but still the containing element, and one that cannot be drunk or eaten away. Gradually, the paths across water to their immense continent become non-navigable. Veronica is a woman concentrating and therefore she and all about her become inviolable: surrounded by mountain ranges thick with glaciers, moated fortresses; dynamite-charged tunnels beneath. Flynn, Rose, Rose-lima, Samaria—energy unwinds from all of them then reunites with the source. Their atmosphere is untouchable, deadly, bright: live wires loosened by ice from telephone poles. There seems to be more women than usual in the house.

One late night, near September, Flynn dozes with her head in Samaria's lap. Samaria is counting the box office take, her hand full of green dollars. Flynn listens to Samaria whispering number after number; to paper whispering against paper. There is a chill rising up outside, rattling the French doors. The Mexican rug stirs. The English brass goes dull. Samaria touches the lamp, and the room widens. Somewhere upstairs, Veronica and the twins are as still as mice. Samaria begins to tell an aimless story, meaning to illustrate the mechanics of memory. "My mother," she says, "in the final analysis, is everything I've wound up knowing. She is *all* I know for sure. But I have been a woman without the advantages. Nevertheless . . . " Then, Mary-this and Mary-that, and Lucy. Flynn herself is half asleep; her brain, however, listens and learns. The brain decides, just before its final leap to unconsciousness, that it will not be the scalpel; it will be art that will make all the difference—but possibly will not remember the decision when Flynn herself wakes. She rubs her feet against the curved damask of the sofa arm. Her feet are cold. Her birthday is in December. Samaria is coughing. Somebody, someday, is going to die; and that will come true.

Pelagia of Tarsus was a beautiful girl unwillingly affianced to the son of the Emperor Diocletian. The young man, spurred on by Pelagia, committed suicide. Instead of choosing to punish Pelagia, Diocletian decided to have her for himself. Denied her favors, he roasted Pelagia to death inside a red-hot brazen bull.

Like all the painters in this women's group of women painters, she is engrossed in the preparation and eating of food. Mushes of lentils and Spanish onion. *Haute* Chinese. Arcane Hungarian. Elaborate; cheap. It always tastes wonderful; and Flynn, when they invite her to their long weekly dinner parties, eats the most. In her thirties, she is filling out. She has buttocks. Her breasts are wonderful.

It's beginning to turn cold, the weather just past the middle of October. It is sunny, sharp, dry. Veronica has just settled—the third time in one year—into a new apartment. More of it, and fresher, every time: which is progress. But with every move, more of the things she owns, has passionately acquired—stolen from stranger's houses, begged from friends, bought from junk shops—have been lost. Lost, or else they have refused to be budged one more time. They are big pieces of what was money, now gone for good. There is a book suddenly needed and suddenly missing. Nelly's bicycle stolen in transition. Pieces of Daisy's jewelry disintegrating on another woman's arm. She consoles her sorrow; she buys new things.

She persuades Flynn, to a certain extent, to live like a woman, in the service of love. She introduces her (she imagines) to cartwheeling orgasm. She performs, for Flynn's edification, the pretty rites of courtship. She has nearly persuaded Flynn that to live as a lover is to be brain.

Veronica leans back in her chair. They have just eaten fourteen escargot apiece. Veronica waves a fist at the waiter while Flynn packs up the empty shells to take home to her turtle tank. Veronica will pay. At Flynn's house, besides the three mud turtles in their tank, there is a stack of unread English murders. It is warm at home. In each novel, there is a young woman about to get herself murdered, but who is finally saved. She bought her books for ten cents apiece from the Salvation Army. She also owns a jar of Aunt Clara's Orange Rose Essence Marmalade, which she will share with no one. It cost one dollar and five cents. There is hot water for her bathtub, and WQXR.

Flynn parked the Valiant a block from the West Side Highway and the Hudson River. Soon it would be nothing but cold. She was already cold, and anxious about when she could eat her dinner. She would not get anything to eat until the ordeal of pleasure in Augusta's work was done. Nelly's black rubber spider swings from the Valiant's rear-view mirror. Nelly put it there so that the Valiant would not be mistaken for a tourist's car. People who suction plastic virgins to the dashboards of cars do not, according to Nelly, deserve to live in Manhattan. She is contemptuous of the ethnic devout. She pretends not to understand Spanish. She has a novel-in-progress entitled *True Facts*.

"Let's go," mutters Nelly, who never expects a place away from home to be pleasing. Flynn twirls the Black Widow just once, for good luck.

The neighborhood is in dead time. Business packed up, trucks parked and locked. The rats are rattling the sewers. It is a gangster's hideout. People who live for art in such neighborhoods are stealthy people and will someday be apprehended and committed to the electric chair. They are stealthy and nervous people, no matter what rapport they pretend with the meat packers and spice dealers, no matter how low their rent or quiet their nights or lasting their love.

The sky over the Hudson is languid and slender, like Rita Hayworth in orange and lavender chiffon. By the time she climbs the sixty steps to Augusta's studio, Flynn will see through the wide windows those colors gone and replaced by the "France" on her way to the ocean and Europe. Then she will look long at the work, while her stomach gnashes its teeth.

Like all the painters in this women's group of women painters, Augusta spends part of her space on perfecting the domestic order. There is a couch, and a rug almost Oriental, and an old oak cabinet full of food. There is a coffee grinder, a waring blender, a round dining table, a pot of shasta daisies, a giant green refrigerator beside the combination washer-dryer.

But Flynn looks first into the sectioned-off bedroom. A curtained cabinet for clothes. Inside, a thin blouse patterned with bluebirds in flight. Framed photographs of friends; framed drawings presented by friends, and a white double bed.

The wide double bed, and Veronica has at last stunned Flynn into falling in love, stunned her, perhaps, with an excess of escargots. Flynn has fallen in love with some beautiful young woman. It is a feeling like falling from a great height and never hitting the ground to die of it. Flynn, in rational moments, believes her brain has a parachute, and that even if the silk cords snap the brain will survive in free fall. Being in love is not the same as being an artist? Or being a mother? But Flynn is both. Augusta sleeps in bed with a man, like Daisy. But Augusta has dreams she tells that are in the service of Fred Astaire. She dreams she *is* Fred, and goes on Wednesday mornings to tap dancing classes. And who would know, watching him tap dance, if Fred fucks top or bottom; or at all? So perhaps not like Daisy before her—certainly there are no photos of daughters in evidence to explain why she does it at all.

Flynn makes herself have to pee, to have a look at the bathroom. On her way, she crosses Nelly's path. Nelly is lying on the rug, alternately raising and lowering her arms above her head and turning her head from side to side to flash a smile across her armpits. She is a bathing beauty. "That is Esther Williams there you're looking at on the color tv," Flynn tells her. "That is Esther Williams swimming in the moonlight." In earnest now, Flynn is unzipping her fly, to be ready. Nelly and Esther Williams switch to the Australian crawl. If Esther does a swan dive next—lengths and lengths of free fall into a lily pond—will Nelly suicide six flights to concrete, only inches from the Hudson?

The shelf beside the toilet holds economy-size talcum powder, the small-size tube of jelly, the white plastic case containing Augusta's protection, a gold rose on its lid. All of it is on view, but all of it is still a secret. What happens to a secret if just anyone taking a piss can take a look at it? The secret goes up inside the body of Augusta, hides there. They've stopped manufacturing rubber baby dolls. Every girl who ever stopped after school to see Esther Williams swim underwater—while inside the girl her insides began to widen and move (and while she bit the skin around her thumbnail)—once had a rubber baby doll with a tiny hole between its legs. The baby came with its own nippled feeding bottle. Feed the baby its ounce of water. Squeeze the baby's stomach, belly to spine. Then the baby wets, all over the palm of the hand; wets rubber-scented water. When the baby is bad and wets the palm of the hand instead of its diaper, steal a sugar ration coupon from mother's handbag and lick it and seal the baby's tiny hole shut. There's more than one way to skin a cat, Flynn's first lover told her, that first event of bed.

Augusta, and Flynn's beloved, are best friends. Flynn surprised them together, giggling on the couch. When Flynn is in love, she doesn't feel like any person she can remember. She becomes like someone sick from long illness—skin and bones to which only her beloved can give memory and intelligence and make round, like a brain. Sometimes, left alone (seduced and abandoned) she cries all night, or drinks all night, because she cannot remember who she was or when she was. Augusta is so kind and sweet to the besotted lover—a honey drop to suck on while the doctor stitches the wound. But the lover's teeth rot, but the operation was not a success, but the beloved's hair still rises away from her face into a hundred differences between that which is light and that which is voltage; and is lethal, like an electric chair. When Augusta's work is in clay or plaster, it is all little people and motion. When it is painted on paper, it is all little people and motion. Fred, when he is in love, dances on the ceiling.

They all go down to the Greek place to eat. Flynn eats the most and Nelly the least. Flynn dreams that night of how she used to be, but in daylight forgets. But the urgency to remember sometimes is so great she makes up what she cannot remember . . . . *For example:* the theatre season was almost over. The weather was stretching out, widening, reshaping, loosening, like a young girl's insides; but hot enough in daylight.

Samaria sat on the front steps, fanning herself in the noonday sun and reading her book. To anyone who crossed

92

her path she spoke of Charlotte Bronte as "autumnal." She read aloud, whether listened to or not, " 'When I first saw Ellen I did not care for her . . . she is without romance . . . but she is good; she is true; she is faithful, and I love her.' " And said of Charlotte, "She does *not* love Ellen. How could she? She is lying. Charlotte makes mistakes in her letters she does not make in her fiction."

But no one cared either way. Rose and Rose-lima, for instance, had got a brief letter from Daisy which they had let no one else read. "Her only word for you, sister, is *do your duty*," they told Flynn. They let Flynn see the envelope, but the postmark was blurred. In any case, there was no good reason for Flynn to believe they were misquoting their mother. There was nothing characteristic about Daisy but her compulsion to mate and breed more photographs of daughters to hang on the bedroom wall.

"You chew on the idea of your mother as if she were a bone," Veronica told her. "You could instead grow up— meet some nice guy and settle down. Experience unanesthetized childbirth. Forget all you have ever learned." Veronica laughed at the joke. "Will you have a Lucky?"

Veronica was not even looking at Flynn. She spoke and laughed into thin air and meanwhile never lowered the binoculars she had trained at some point on the opposite side of the lake. But it did not matter: Veronica had never spoken a serious word to Flynn in all her life. When Veronica gave advice it meant calamity to take it. There had been no return address, no word—according to the twins—of when Daisy would be finished with the husband and come home. The weather was dying. Veronica scheduled an end to the theatre season, took a new notebook, figured, wrote, and announced that everyone could hang their hopes on a time "when it gets really cold"—if anyone is left, she added.

When that was settled, she dug around in the hall closet

and emerged with a typewriter and showed it to Flynn. "We have a lot of paper. Here is the typewriter. Why don't you become a novelist? I urge you to become a novelist."

They were having Indian summer. Flynn never read books. Samaria read books. Flynn wanted only to stay in the bedroom and perfect her brain machine. "Let my grandmother do it," she told Veronica.

"Samaria is busy in her head. She hasn't time to write a novel. I'll show you how. First I'll do it, then you do it."

Veronica fixed herself a desk in the upstairs hallway. She had a stack of blue paper for her first draft, a stack of white for the second. She had not stopped talking to Flynn, so Flynn sat in the window seat to wait for her to finish. Veronica buckled a green visor around her forehead and leaned backwards in her swivel chair. The top half of her face should have resembled the green of bilious vomit or theatrical death. Instead it was the green of summer trees—a green in nature that is both a memory and a preparation for the future. Her face was like everything else about her—it said one thing but meant another.

"There is no point," said Veronica, "in trying to be a good novelist, so don't expect that from me or, eventually, from yourself. Remember that. What I want to do is win prizes and go on television. I want to be taken to lunch at the Algonquin Hotel. My novel will be what the British royal family is—*exactly what it is expected to be*. As a matter of fact, in order to provide my reader with the essential clue, I shall dedicate the book 'To Elizabeth *Regina* II and Her Sister Margaret Rose, Princess, in Memory of the Foggy Tea Time.' This is my outline. Read it aloud to me."

Veronica ripped a page from her new notebook and passed it over. "Clear your throat first," she added, as Flynn opened her mouth. "I don't want to have to wait on you once you're in the midst of it."

"*Chapter One*," Flynn read. "Rejection by Father, no good at baseball, seduction by horny rustic grandfather, gangbanged by California motorcyclists, likes it (?). *Chapter Two*. identity crisis, memory of Mother deliberately (?) parading past in black lace nightie, the march on Selma, the meeting with muscled nigger beauty who is in reality the Virgin Mary. *Chapter Three*, psychoanalysis, seduction by psychoanalyst, relationship with psychoanalyst, necessity to recover lost youth in arms of analyst's sixteen-year-old child, rejection by analyst who confesses preference for cucumbers. *Chapter Four*, alcoholism, cancer, transcendental meditation, primal scream. *Chapter Five*, grace, retreat into the wilderness, solitude (insert lines from 'The Pulley' by George Herbert), conversion to Catholicism, love, death."

"That's that," said Veronica; but all the while she had been looking through the binoculars, her elbows steadied on the back of her chair.

"Only five chapters?"

"People have better things to do than to sit up all night reading."

"It's easier than I thought."

"I told you so. It's easier than a brain machine."

"We're going to be rich."

"Yes. There's a stranger pulling up outside in a red car. There's a beautiful young woman in a red car. You'd better go see."

"I see. After you're rich, will you give me the money for the brain machine?"

"I'm losing interest in this conversation. My mind is on *no good at baseball*. Go away."

"What's the name of this book?"

"*Lover*, I told you already, *Lover*."

*Nicknamed Margarito because of the splendor of her pearls,
she was famous in Antioch for the lewd finesse she gave to
her dancing which the Bishop Nonnus at last observed.
"This girl," he said, "is a lesson to us bishops. She takes
more trouble over her beauty and her dancing than we do
about our souls and our flocks." Margarito therefore disguised herself as a man and went to live alone in a cave on
the Mount of Olives. People found this second half of her
life, into which she so abruptly departed, quite as interesting as the first; and she thereby retained notoriety until her
death, and afterwards.*

On that thin edge dividing afternoon and evening, Rose
and Rose-lima simultaneously began to menstruate; and
they told the others that the strange young woman who
had come to their house was a second cousin on their
father's side.

They said that Daisy's letter had prepared them for her
coming but that they had forgotten to mention it. They
did not introduce her. They put another chair at the table
for her.

The stranger was of medium height, thin, strong-boned.
She had tiny breasts, large hands, fluid shoulders. Her face
was both aristocratic and Jewish. Had there ever been a
Romanov Jew? Frequently her face blazed with teeth and
light. "She has what they call Russian hair," Rose-lima
said. Her hair was pale, and lethal, like an electric chair. It
spread up and away from her face into a hundred differences between that which is light and that which is voltage.

Samaria, deep inside Charlotte Bronte's grief over Ellen Nussey, assumed nothing. But she set another plate on the table and cooked extra food. Veronica was taking all her meals at her typewriter. Veronica said, "I've never seen anything so beautiful in my life. That new woman reminds me of my earliest attempts at Veronese which were naive in execution, but sold well—'Allegory of Virtue and Vice.' She reminds me of that particular one. Now at the Frick Museum. But this beautiful young woman is not."

"Time is running out," Flynn replied. "Death is just around the corner. Look at what has happened to Rose and Rose-lima. It feels like death, just around the corner."

"An interesting conceit. Not original, unfortunately, but who am I to talk?—Veronese, Botticelli, Vermeer, Franz Kline, and some anonymous Mediterranean sculpture, figurines actually. They are called *Tanagra*. When was Veronica ever an original?" Veronica pathetically asked. She pulled herself together. She stared again into her Smith-Corona. "An interesting conceit, but already over-used by the sixteenth century. An ancestress of mine was Shakespeare's mistress. She spoke of nothing, in the first flush of love, but death—but later devoted herself to nothing but work. Disguised as a boy, she was the first actor to play Queen Gertrude." Veronica began to type. She wrote, " 'Time is running out,' Flynn replied. 'Death is just around the corner.' " She was halfway through page five.

"The next thing any of you shits hear from me," Flynn yelled, "will be my fucking brain not my fucking mouth!"

"Bogart and Boatwright are bothering her car . . . "

"Fuck you, fuck car." Flynn pulled out her shirttail and wiped her eyes. Veronica noticed that Flynn's eyes, so seldom in tears, were like rainy mornings. Outside, the clouds shifted into storm formations. Inside, the stained glass Lamb of God darkened; and it was going to rain.

Flynn at once remembers the snares set in the woods for rabbits for the first simple experiments. As if they knew, three of the cats at once gathered before her, arriving from three different places. Their tails were rigid and angled over their spines. They followed Flynn outside.

" ' . . . my fucking brain and not my fucking mouth,' " Veronica wrote, then turned on her lamp. It was getting dark. It was going to rain.

But the rain was taking a long time to come. The weather heaved with thunder one moment, shone the next. The woods were dry and crackling. Flynn imagined dropping her cigarette and making a barbeque—roast Rose, grilled Rose-lima, broiled Samaria, fried Veronica; Bogart and Boatwright rotating on spits. She had caught two rabbits, both big-headed. If they could have screamed they would have been screaming—even louder at the sight of Flynn. The cats were screaming, dying to kill the rabbits. Flynn untrapped them and dropped them head first in her gunnysack; and started home. She would have time to clear the trees before she had to drop her Lucky.

The house was full of fiction and poetry. Flynn could not turn around without stumbling over stacks of the stuff. The bookcases overflowed. There was no place to sit—a broken-backed *Tess of the D'Urbervilles* would suddenly be taking up the seat in what Flynn had thought was the last free armchair. A book on the place she wanted to sit in—it sickened Flynn, as much as in insect in her soup, a snake beneath her pillow. In all of the thousands of books—she had spent a week raging through them—there was not a line written about the precious life of the brain. The books were about every part of the body—some parts over and over again in disgusting detail—but never about the part that was the brain. Sometimes an author would write, "he thought" or "she thought," but the thought would be nothing more than the substance of a tongue within a foreign mouth or of a foot lifting itself to dance. Under the whip of Samaria's authors the brain was in a bondage undreamt of by Old Black Joe. Flynn reached into the middle of *Tess* and ripped out a handful of chapter ten. Was it the brain's fault Anna Karenina had thrown herself beneath the engine? *No!* It was the . . . "I am coming to the rescue," Rose had called and galloped down the stairs. But Rose had been empty-handed. Rose-lima, coming behind, had had the goods. The book was stuffed half beneath the elastic band of her underpants, half beneath her polo shirt.

"Unless you go to a medical school—*ha, ha*—there's not another thing to be had on the goddamned subject," Rose told her; and Rose-lima gave her the book. It was a volume of the *Illustrated World Encyclopedia, IV, Bol-Can.* Literary Treasures Edition, Bobley Publishing Corp., 1959.

"That's it?" It was no fit place for information on the life and romance of the brain. It was bound in nasty maroon cardboard, slimy with dust and mildew.

"It's about all you'd be up to, sweetheart. What's the last thing you ever read in your life since Dick and Jane and Sally and Mother and Father and Spot and Puff? Huh? Except for memorizing your lines? That's it. Don't try us. We feel like the devil, we're getting ready to fall off the roof and we hate it and somebody's going to have to pay for it. We're going to kill first and ask questions later, the goddamned-cocksucking-asshole-sonuvabitch—*us, cursed!* Whoever it is is going to pay through the nose for this."

"I made myself stop," said Flynn.

"If you're so smart why ain't you rich?"

The baby-talk inside the book was as easy to memorize as Shakespeare. She walked out of the woods reciting it. The cats yowled, the bag jumped. " 'The brain is the part

99

of the body that we think with,' " Flynn said. " 'No one knows *why* it works as it does, but scientists know *how* it works. It consists of a mass of nerve fibers, in the form of thin, white strands, at the top of the head. These nerve fibers connect with other nerve fibers that stretch from the brain to all parts of our bodies. They carry messages to and from the brain in less time than it takes to bat an eyelash.

" 'Let us look at the human brain. It is shaped somewhat like cauliflower, with ripples called *convolutions*. The brain has a coating of grainy gray stuff. This is called the *cerebral cortex*, or . . . ' "

The sky opened. The rain came like rocks hurled by the mob at some scarlet impenitent. But Flynn and the rabbits were out of the trees. From there, on the path between the rhododendrons, it was uphill. The cats had used speed to disappear—wet was worse than greed-hunger. But Flynn and the rabbits got soaked and beaten; but Flynn never stopped reciting. Her mouth was full of water; she could have drowned. She saw, near the house, Samaria's arm stretched out an open window waving horizontally through the water as though it were swimming Flynn to shore.

" ' . . . or simply *gray matter*,' " Flynn shouted into the noise. " 'The gray matter is gathered into many dips and folds called *convolutions*, which give the surface of the brain a furrowed look, something like a walnut shell' " (*that goes crack between the thighs of the nutcracker,* Flynn adds silently, *and sheds its halved sphere into the ashtray, and then you eat the meat* . . .). " 'Since each dip and fold is lined with gray matter, the human brain contains more gray matter than the ape's.' " (*More than a gorilla's? More than a royal princess's?*) " 'When you use your gray matter, you are *thinking*. At this very instant, as you read . . . you are using your gray matter. With the *cerebral cortex* or gray matter of the brain we do the complex

100

things that are called perceiving, thinking, learning, and forming judgments which add up to what we call our human intelligence . . . ' "

"Yay! She made it!" Flynn's wetness worked like glue; Samaria, hugging her, could hardly tear herself apart from Flynn. The terrified bundle had rolled across the rug.

"Bloody, bloody, bloody!" the twins screamed. They lay on the floor drumming their heels, the beat as heavy as the freak hail hitting, then instantly melting against, the warm roof.

"I've made it stop," said Flynn. She stood still, her head bent, allowing Samaria to rub her hair dry. But then her head was yanked back, her jaw slung open; Samaria was pulling her hair out by the roots.

"Are you dead? Have you no heart?" Samaria was shouting Flynn's eardrum to smithereens. Samaria was the savage scalping the bewildered homesteader. Samaria was Judith decapitating Holofernes—but without the excellent, bloated look of lust satisfied. Samaria was only in pain, and clumsy; she was not like a guillotine. "You uppity little shit!" and she let go. Flynn rolled her body to the wooly red roses below and held tight to the throat of her bag. Samaria said, "Now, good God, I've had the change of life, thank God . . . " She shook her head to and fro; she spoke to the floor. " . . . but then it was seventh grade algebra, and I got up from my seat to turn in my problems and it was all over the back of my skirt and running down my legs and all the boys punched each other and grinned and the girls hissed like a nest of snakes; and, next, under my arms began to stink and breasts seemed to be growing all over me, but nothing was worse than that day, that flood. It means that you'll never be yourself again any more, not ever."

"And then what happened?"

Samaria was lost to the world. "The teacher said, Leave the room. She was mad at me. I walked, it squished inside my shoes, I had to cross the front of the room, there were long red stripes down my legs and my inside thighs were already chapped and sore from where the blood rubbed back and forth. Out in the hall it dripped on the linoleum, a trail to find me by; I couldn't move fast enough. In the toilet, I used all the paper there was on the roll, but still it wouldn't stop, still all I got was a handful of bloodsoaked paper. I'd read books about the horrors of war, the battlefield, the bull ring, and how it pumps up and out of their punctured stomachs, how it floods from the mouth and the nose; and it is not the same, and it is not so terrible. They can only die. But we are never the same again, and *that is worse.* I started to cry, because I would rather have been dead than gone forever, like I was. They came in with rags and a belt. They said, Now you are a woman. *I* had been exchanged for a *woman.*"

The twins lay quiet, watching and agreeing: "It makes me want to vomit, and it will be years and years and years of it, I'd rather grow a beard, I'd rather be stupid and big, I'd rather have junk between my legs, rather than that!"

But Samaria did not appear to be what she said she had become. Samaria was made of fine clear lines and vast open spaces. Her pigtail was sleek and well-wrought. She wore hand-stitched cowboy boots. She took her hand off Flynn's head. She put her arms around the twins, but carefully; she did not let her hands touch them below their waists.

"I know what you're thinking," she said. "You're thinking I am lying, that I was never that. The truth is I got myself back in spite of it. In spite of it, I could become a lover and could stop being a woman. What they said, *a woman.* That's why I am here, in spite of it, and not in a cage, like the rest of them, in a freak show. I am a lover, not a woman." Samaria hurried upstairs to shut windows.

Flynn asked the twins to hold her bag while she set house plants outside in the rain. It was October; it would be their last warm bath of the year. Rose and Rose-lima sat up and held the bag between them. They rubbed the harsh sacking until each had a hand on a rabbit they could squeeze, but not enough to hurt or kill. They sat with their legs wide apart. There were terrible bulges of cotton between their legs, and they held their legs wide apart.

"What we've done with each other," Rose-lima said at last, "is not what I think our grandmother means. What we do, I think, is not what a lover means, so we fell off the roof." Flynn passed back and forth above them. She was a guerrilla, using green for camouflage, outwitting the enemy, sneaking up.

" 'A green thought in a green shade,' " said Rose.

"No," said Rose-lima. "That Flynn is a killer, not a line of poetry. Though poetry is a disguise a real killer uses sometimes. She comes and goes carrying green plants, for the rain she says, but look, you can't see any part of her above her waist—she's sneaking around, a real killer."

"That's what I meant. That's what it means: 'A green thought in a green shade,' " said Rose.

"Now I see."

"Yes, and that's that. We are not what a lover is. We are not what a killer is. I hear Veronica and our grandmother in their bed at night. Their room, through the wall, sounds like a roomful of birds. Like an aviary. In an aviary, the sound of birds all together is like one single sound of a scream. But there's never the sound of breath inhaled—so it can't be like a scream. Is that what a lover is?"

"Eagles, parrots, myna birds, rooks, ravens . . . "

"Thank you, girls," said Flynn. "You talk mighty big to

103

be only twelve years old. As our mother might remark, *What are you saving for marriage?"*

"We are now thirteen. We had a birthday. *Mother* marries. She's the only one for sure."

But Flynn had already gone. But, had she heard, she would have wished them belated birthday greetings.

At the age of nine, Susanna was lured from her bed by her brothers Cythwyn and Methwyn "to see a falling star." Helpless away from her mother's side, the child was forced to submit to ravishment. Miraculously, she remained intacta *and was subsequently staked outstretched over an ant hill. She suffered a lingering uncomplaining death.*

The summons to Niagara could arrive at any moment (Veronica had told them) so they stopped modeling beach wear for each other and stopped bothering the stranger's red car and settled down to serious work so that they would finish it in time.

Bogart and Boatwright were going to make a million dollars. They couldn't remember a time when they did not have the idea: they had been born with it, they believed. The idea had arrived genetically, like their tan hair, their sex, their colorless eyes, their inability to learn a useful skill. They had not rushed it. Life was slow; they had a time to discuss it and wonder at its impressiveness and dream limitedly of what they would do with all the money. But from the first, they'd never felt comfortable with the thing in their minds. It felt weird; it did not fit—but this aspect of the idea they never discussed—there seemed no way to arrange the alphabet around the feeling and say words about it. This problem led them to refer to the ultimate materialization of their idea as a "commercial product." They could never call it what it would, in truth, be: a woman, an artificial woman.

They called it a "commercial product"—but only when they talked about it at all. Life was slow. There was plenty of time to talk, then plenty of time to do it. Even a single season, especially the long hot one and the long cold one, took forever to pass. No one they knew had ever died.

But sometimes they did talk about it—when they were fishing in the lake, when they were dressing for Saturday night. They would advertise, they agreed, with little drawings and words inside tiny boxes on the back pages of *Stag*, *True Detective*, the *Christian Science Monitor* (their product was healthful); and in certain selected comic books. They would demonstrate the product in the windows of furniture stores; they would talk about it on the radio. They would get prominent individuals—such as the Saturday night disc jockey—to try it out. They would give free samples to famous individuals like Frank Sinatra and Elvis, who would then give endorsement. They thought of Norman Vincent Peale: their item was fraught with theological overtones, and was not real and would therefore not be a sin.

They talked about it for a long time, for years. Then they bought the first hunks of foam rubber—the urge to buy, to proceed, coming at the beginning of one spring. The first experiments were heartbreaking, and hurt their enthusiasm and sent them into long depressed sleeps. In late autumn, they got a correct length. But the shapes and sizes of all the things that went between top and bottom (head and toe) went wrong. They tried fire on it. They tried knives on it. They used a power saw. Nothing about it would become round, as it should be, no matter how hard they labored.

They had a temper tantrum, wept, kicked the stubborn stuff around their floor, finally into a corner, where it became one day Veronica's chair. Then there was nothing left to do but try to talk again about what the money would buy; but the old dream of richness would not return: what they wanted to buy seemed too inseparably confused with what they had to make. The two could easily have been the same, and would not come true.

When they worked again, it was drudgery; it was hateful work, and the result was not what they had meant at all. Her left shoulder had a hump. Her right tit projected too far north. They'd made the hole too big—but they could fix that. They fixed it by lining it with layers of thin rubber (two boxes of Trojans from the congratulatory druggist) affixed to the tunnel's walls with (safe) non-toxic glue. The attachment of the electrical wires and their concealment in the body, locating the batteries deep in the head—the precision stuff—caused them the greatest grief: they thought they would never be finished. The switch to turn it on and off had to be hidden between the buttocks. They quarrelled about hair. Bogart wanted it to have a curly blonde wig. Boatwright wanted simply a suggestion of hair incised on the foam skull with a carving knife: *real* looking hair, he felt, would make it seem wrong, maybe crazy; and further (he argued) people like Japs or Negroes, might buy it. The imaginative specifics of each individual purchaser would have to be dealt with by the purchaser himself. The same went for the hair *down there*.

So it was not really right, but nothing went wrong forever; and it was comfortable, having a purpose. But then Veronica came with Niagara Falls. They were forced to hurry. If they hurried, they could have both; they could

106

have everything. There was only winter left before their spring time plunge, before fame on two fronts. Two fronts, they saw, and separate; but somehow twinned identically.

They could hardly sleep or eat anymore; and only two activities gave them rest from panic. The second was elaborating on their advertising campaign, that had become a vision of full-color slippery pages in famous magazines. The vision of Niagara had made the difference: now they could think big; the little black and white Christian Science blurs had been overwhelmed. There would be a full-length photograph of the two of them in the lower left-hand corners. They would be wearing their Niagara bathing suits. Niagara, in a blue glow, would be behind them. They would have their arms around each other's shoulders. Bogart would be gesturing with his right arm toward the center of the page where the viewer's eye would enter a partially opened bedroom door whose rosy interior would stream out into the blue of Niagara below. The doll would be within, spread on something lovely, soft, king-size. A single cocktail glass, half full, would be on the bedside table. At the bottom of the page: TWO GUYS FROM NIAGARA BRING YOU . . . A DOLL YOU CAN CALL YOUR OWN! ! ! And, just above the order coupon, a brief paragraph: " . . . a doll that other fellas cannot steal, just like the song says, just what you've always wanted, she won't say no, she won't say go, she won't stray, she won't say nay, *she only will . . .* everything! Turn her on, *she crawls all over you!* Doll has gotta happen to you!"

Rose and Rose-lima, for reasons of their own, had spent an entire afternoon compelling Bogart and Boatwright to memorize all the words to "Paper Doll." Bogart and Boatwright, despite the trouble, were grateful: afterwards, the work went much faster; the old confusions of shapes and fears vanished; they felt better. They felt businesslike.

107

Now, nothing could prevent their getting what was coming to them.

Venerated for ordinariness, plainness, and simplicity, Zaraina at last wrote a very long chronicle detailing her attainment, and ongoing preservation, of virtue; and, in so doing, roused the ire of those about her. Their anger and resentment increased when Zaraina began serving roses instead of bread from the pockets of her apron. She suffered death by the garotte *one dark night while on a spurious errand of mercy. She was twenty-three.*

Last night, I got the message that her husband, in desperation, has allowed them to confine her to the loony-bin. She is not depressed enough, so they are giving her drugs. At her last public appearance, she talked too long, loosening a galore of terror onto the audience: she did not stick to the subject. Some crept up behind her; they meant to drag her out of sight, out of mind. She said, "It only takes one of you to kill me" and she did not resist the group effort. The last time I danced with her, she did not know me; but it was not a case of mistaken identity. Her disappearing lover said to me, "Please write her a letter." Her lover promised to pray for me.

I am hoping for a quick nonfeminist death, such as mutilation, decapitation by Caribbean sharks. As soon as I have saved enough time, energy, and money, I will take a vacation in the Caribbean—providing I can find a travel agent who tells the truth (her index finger landing on a single azure spot on the map: Yes, *here* the sharks are hungry). Afterwards, my leftovers will wash ashore and the government of the country will package them in a pyramid. They will wall all my lovers, sisters, confidants in alive beside me. Cupboards lined with fresh shelf paper will be built against the walls to display the detritus of my history: gin evaporating in a water glass, mouldering mystery paperbacks, a pair of horn-rimmed spectacles, a red cardboard valentine ripped asunder to represent my broken heart.

Women from the year two thousand sixty-nine will shatter open the door with laser beams; and then they will put me and what belonged to me in the National Museum. I am their single recovery from the era of Baroque. White-robed, golden-sandaled, I will watch what happens from Heaven. She told me that *baroque* means grotesque, odd, twisted. *Barroco:* rough pearl.

Flynn could tell it was Samaria who had walked in on her. But she did not stop stuffing lettuce through the slats of the rabbits' cage; and she had never troubled herself to turn and greet someone who seemed to be sneaking up behind her.

Samaria was not aware that she was a sneak. She wanted only to satisfy her need to speak what she had to say. "Forgery," she said, "is not an act of art. It is like an act of God because, in the hands of the great masters, the forgery is no different from the real thing. Veronica is a great master, perhaps the only one left alive and she is no specialist, she has done it all. Forgery means that the art is not real but that no one, not even the forger (like in Veronica's case) can tell the difference between the first and the second . . . "

"Like twins," Flynn interrupted; "like mother, like daughter. I know that. I am busy. Veronica has done it all, from Tanagra to Snider; from Piero to Fishman. Now she is a *belles-lettrist*, she is writing a novel that is not a novel—to please you, I guess, because you like to read. She pleased herself with art. Now she will please you with literature. I am making a brain machine. The brain machine, *c'est moi.*"

"No," said Samaria. "Damn, how those rabbits stink! It was the *money* in art; it is the *money* in literature. I mean to talk about money. We have lived, since Veronica, off forgery and we have been comfortable. *Hamlet* pays for hardly anything. Although you've been clever enough to stop yourself menstruating, you must still grow up to money; we cannot afford brain machines. Rose and Rose-lima have told me you want fifteen thousand dollars in order to keep your head inside a bucket of lysol. No."

"You will be glad," Flynn answered. "It will change your lives. And if you are disguising sentiment with financial consideration I reassure you that none of you will miss me. There is no difference between me and my brain, and my brain will always be with you, in your keeping, and therefore I can never leave. I can not, like my mother, vanish with husbands. On the big round table in the parlor. You will have me morning and night. There is no difference between me and my brain. *I* can not tell the difference. Soon you will not. I want fifteen thousand dollars." She padlocked the rabbit cage; she was satisfied with what she had said.

"No! It is about money, not sentiment. Have I ever said I loved you?"

Samaria sat on the bed and looked into the palms of her hands, into lines like the canals of Mars. Flynn sighed and turned her back on the rabbits to let them eat fearlessly. The task of persuasion was a hopeless task, so she changed the subject.

"I saw a man leave here a little while ago," Flynn said.

He wore a harris tweed jacket with leather patches on the elbows. He wore scuffed moccasins, and a beard. He carried a heavy leather briefcase. Was that Veronica, the novelist?"

"Yes, on her way. Daisy is going to hate the looks of this room. It smells like a hospital. Flasks and tubes and wires all over her dainty bed. And spills on her pink carpet. Those rabbits are so frightened by the cage they are copulating."

"Such an atmosphere will make my mother feel right at home."

"My daughter will come back. You *know* that." Samaria's fingers knotted into a fist.

"You're a mother; that's what you're *supposed* to think. I'm a daughter. I want to get on with those rabbits, then a cat, then a dog, then a cow and a horse and an ape; and then me." Flynn looked at the door, wishing she could see Samaria going through it; but Samaria had shut it behind her.

"You may be a daughter, but you're no different from other grown women—you stop blood, but you can't stop feelings. Feelings in yourself, I mean; although I love you."

"You know I'm different. And from the outside how can you tell which is the real thing; I can't help it that you love me. There was the time my mother came home, so you and Veronica went away on a trip by yourselves . . . "

"We went to Puerto Rico. We swam in the Caribbean."

"I was five, and my mother was miserable. It's stopped raining, and everything smells like mildew. It is not the rabbits. All the time she was here with me, my mother's face looked like she was chewing on the inside of her mouth. She put on her black patent leather highheel shoes and took me downtown to a picture show she said was about love. She used the last of the money in the house to take us to a picture about love. She spent the money on the picture show instead of on Kotex, which she needed; she was bleeding. She used an old green dishtowel. We walked down the street to the picture show and there was a hot wind blowing my mother's dress against her. I stood no higher than her pelvis and walked a little behind her. So I could watch all the people looking at the dish towel between my mother's legs. I don't know if you understand what I mean. You should. You read books, and books are about nothing but love; and though you've stopped bleeding you used to bleed, like my mother and all the rest of the women. I am ashamed of all of you."

Flynn was trembling; her teeth were chattering. Samaria could hardly understand her.

"There's a photograph on the wall over there," said Samaria, "of you and Daisy. You were about five years old. When you were five, Veronica and I went to Puerto Rico and ate a lot of fresh sea food. After dark we gambled in the casinos and danced together in bars and drank whiskey. In the daytime, we sat beside the water and drank pina coladas and skipped lunch."

"That is a picture of Daisy taking me to ride the hobby-horses at the fair. I'm already astride, clutching the golden pole driven through the horse's brain; but nothing yet is in motion. She's bending over me, but looking out into the camera and grinning and holding on to her pocketbook. When the music started, she had to get off."

"Veronica wore dark glasses day and night and a white sharkskin suit. She sold three Vermeers to a Puerto Rican countess. Maybe she was a princess, a Puerto Rican princess. The princess wore a red flower in her black hair. Her name was the Princess Dolores Del Rio."

Flynn relaxed suddenly; and laughed. "I'm glad Veronica insisted on cash. The picture we saw about love was called *The Red Shoes*. On our way back home, her hair came loose in the wind and got tangled. She told me that when she was little—before anything ever happened—you sometimes took her to church and that when they talked about the Burning Bush, she thought they were talking about her hair. She *still* believes that. We crossed some railroad tracks; and that's when she noticed her wrist watch was missing. We stood in the middle of the railroad tracks while she yelled at me; but then I heard a train coming and we ran and she cried all the way home. I had been pulling at her arm to make her hold my hand and it was me who made the watch loosen and get lost. It was a present from the boy who was my father, she said; she said she'd never get over losing it."

"We are both too soft-hearted to convince the other of anything on earth. Neither of us will ever amount to anything. Come over here and look out the window; then I have to go fix supper. Gypsy violins and flaming crepes tonight." Samaria closed the blinds, then lifted one slat and peered out. "Look," she said, and gave her place up to Flynn. "Is that Veronica out there?"

A long, smooth blue car, a convertible with a white top, was parked beneath the trees below. Thick, final drops of rain were loosening from the leaves and heaving themselves against the white metal like worn-out rubber balls. The car had New York license plates. What appeared like a man, a man with a tiny moustache, like David Niven's, was climbing from the car, stretching his arms. His hair, from above, looked like an expertly woven toupee. He wore a rose-colored flannel suit as if it were a pair of pajamas, and black-and-white Florsheims. He swung a heavy leather brief case off the seat of the car. The huge sticker on the side of the brief case said NIAGARA OR BUST.

"I believe that's Veronica out there," Flynn said. She let

the blind drop. "That's Veronica and she's on her way to Bogart and Boatwright."

"Then I'll go and make sure there's more than enough to eat. Think about what I said. I am right."

"No, you're not," said Flynn, and turned back to her rabbits.

After having accidentally learnt reading and writing at a young age, Hester doggedly persevered throughout the misfortunes that then beset her; but eventually escaped to commit herself to a waste place near the Lake of Con stance in what is now Bulgaria. There, she was miraculously fed on honey cake and cream by a large, white bird who enjoyed her endearing modesty. It was not long, however, before a band of savages painted blue discovered her and, enraged, left no part of her body unburned. "Even her eyeballs," a contemporary wrote, "were like cinders."

When she was fifteen, her father, using both hands, broke her left arm. When she was eighteen, he threw her to the floor and used his foot to break her right shoulder. In everything she does now—lying down, sitting, walking, making love—she favors that shoulder and does not correct women when, laughing affectionately, they call her way of movement a "tough dyke act." That shoulder, since it was broken, has a mind of its own. She carries it high, hunched, rigid, under perfect control.

It took her mother three days to get the shoulder to the hospital. Her mother was afraid that the hospital would discover how it all had happened; and she herself, the one time she tried to go alone, fainted before she was past the front gate. Anyway, her mother said, he's gone with the car, working for a living. We don't have the car, so we can't go. You don't appreciate how hard he works, but I wish you would. You could tell them I fell out of a tree, she told her mother. You could call a taxi on the telephone. How would I know how to do that? her mother answered, and what would I give the taxi-man in exchange? And what would a big old girl like you be doing up a tree to fall out of? The next morning, she heard the neighbor next door getting his car out, and she shouted through the open window, Would you please wait a minute, Mr. Malone, and drop my mother and me by the hospital? But her mother had first to take a damp cloth and wash under her arms and then put on her rouge and lipstick and then wipe down her patent leather high heels with a piece of white bread; and Mr. Malone wouldn't wait that long. So it was not until the next day—the third day—that she could get her mother ready in time and catch a ride with Mr. Malone.

Her mother was afraid of the doctors, and she was right to be afraid. They shouted at her and made her cry; and no matter how much she explained to them, they never understood that her poor mother had done only what she had to do.

Macrina the Younger, a dedicated maiden, was assailed by her foes for unswerving ambition, exertion of influence, opportunism and silver-tongued wit. Suspicious rumors were also cast abroad regarding the successive untimely

115

deaths of five wealthy husbands. She endured her ene-
mies' spite, however, with cheerful forebearance and un-
flagging piety; and, in her middle age, established by the
River Iris a small but luxurious school-cum-community for
the daughters of aristocrats. Her fame as a successful edu-
catrix spread far and wide, and she died, surrounded by
her devoted students, at the age of ninty-nine.

A week after Veronica and Samaria had moved themselves and their dependents into the same house, Veronica broke through that silence with which sex had overwhelmed speech and began to talk all the time to Samaria.
From early in the morning until bedtime, she talked; the
subject was always herself. Somehow, however, her words
sounded like documentations of the past or prophecies
of the future. *Eternal passion, eternal pain,* Samaria had
learned to quote in response, as if it were a nightingale
she was learning to hear.

Listening, Samaria could hear the spell break—or a new
spell each day begin to weave: she had always wanted
someone to talk to her, she realized, as that thing began to
happen. Whatever she had wanted before, she could not
now remember. Now, she felt she had always wanted only
what she at last had. Always within range of the voice, she
spent those days fixing, painting, shaping her new home.
And memorizing all Veronica told her; and being glad at
what was new.

Veronica would begin to speak after oatmeal and her
first swallow of coffee. Her first words would swarm out
with the first burst of smoke from the first Lucky of the
day. She would begin with whatever dream she had had
just before waking.

"The dreams I have just before I wake up always start
inside some extraordinary piece of scenery—some places

116

I've visited, some I have not. The Grand Canyon, the coast of Cornwall, the canals of Venice, the Gobi Desert, the interior of a pyramid. I am always happy, but hungry; and, in an utterly unalarming manner, I am always exactly the work I am presently engaged in painting—I mean, there is no difference between me and my painting during my dream, and I am not afraid of that. This morning I was a medium-sized, late Soutine, a painting of a red side of beef. Why, I don't know. I have never made much money painting Soutines, although it is a pleasure. Such flesh . . . better than a Rubens nude."

"Maybe there is no difference," Samaria walked past her with a tomato in each hand. She was thinking of finding the sunniest sill for ripening. But Veronica made her stop and let her run her hands across her breasts. Samaria leaned into the caress but was careful to keep the tomatoes at a distance. She held her arms wide and apart above her head. Her hands held the tomatoes. She could have been diving from a great height if there had been water beneath her. But it was only that her breasts lay in the cups of Veronica's palms; and Samaria's breasts in Veronica's hands far below were the same as the tomatoes in Samaria's hands high above. There was no difference. One pleasure seemed to be causing the other; and there was no difference. Then it was over, and all was separate.

"But thinking about money was not part of the dream," Veronica continued. "I am adding that part." Samaria, released, did not move away. She stood and watched Veronica's mouth move as it talked. "And hungry. Always, at the beginning of these dreams, I am convinced that the end of my journey through the landscape—or the artifacts or the furniture, whatever it is—will take me to a delicious meal. This morning I smelled pork roast and applesauce sprinkled with fresh cinammon."

Samaria found a window sill good for tomatoes. She began to unwind a bolt of blue velvet. She was going to measure the kitchen windows and hang blue velvet for curtains.

"And endive salad, vinaigrette dressing; and brussel sprouts with cheese sauce. But as I am coming to this place where I'll be given something to eat, the dream is over—all but for the smell of the food. I never get anything to eat, and I wake up.".

"You are my darling, my darling."

"There was nothing to eat this morning but oatmeal."

Samaria closed her eyes and said it only once again: "You are my darling."

"And so this morning—throw me those matches—I was walking through 27 Rue de Fleurus, trudging in back of Gertrude Stein's coat-tails. She was being a goddamned bore—all talk and no food. But I was behaving myself because she was a client. I had, I understood, painted every picture on her walls, but all the Matisses had already been carried off by the brother. But everything else was there, and she was showing it all to me as though I were some tourist clod—room after room of it—showing me my own stuff and not a bite to eat. Miss Moneybags herself pointing out the endless virtues of her Picassos—*my* Picassos, if you know what I mean. And a Soutine, an uncooked slab of beef, coming up behind her: me.

"But then she stopped talking and started doing another thing. She started rubbing her hands and arms across the paintings and she gestured for me to follow suit; and I did. We rubbed away all the Picassos in the whole house. When we'd finished, she was covered with the Blue and Rose periods and I with all the angles of *cubisme*.

"Then she said, 'After dinner (which I hope you'll share with us) Miss Toklas and I will immediately move into the new house you've built for us." I panicked. I was covered

118

with wet paint—but I was not a forger of houses. I had no house for her. But she stood there and endlessly described all the stairways and landings and porches and dining rooms she *said* I had built! But suddenly I realized it was all a trick, the sly bastard. She knew I could not eat her food if I had not built her house. She knew that. It was all a ruse to keep me starving to death."

"Will you hold this end of the tape measure for me, darling?" Samaria's huge length of hair was held up by an ivory comb and tortoise shell pins; and she was dressed all in dark green. But Veronica was still in her flannel robe—the mornings were sharpening—and the odors of warm bed rose up out of it when she moved to the window; and other smells so poignant they made Samaria close her eyes as though she were being visited by some bright memory of a never-never girlhood. Veronica scattered her cigarette ash behind her, and she held her end of the measure; but this did not stop her from spreading her mouth, lightly, for a moment against Samaria's neck. Vampires, thought Samaria; but still she measured space and unfolded cloth.

Veronica sat down again, with more coffee. "Then," she said, "I got proof that I was right: suddenly there was Alice appearing all dim in a doorway holding a tray set with two dinners, one for each of them. For just a second it crossed my mind that maybe Alice wasn't eating with us, but I was fooling myself. Alice was eating, and I was not. Alice was already chewing."

"Then you woke up." The dark blue velvet was spreading across the red tiles.

"You know that? Yes I did. How did you know?"

"Because just then you felt my tongue and woke up. Because I was going down on you. Sleep is never so wonderful." She chose long-bladed scissors and slashed the air above the cloth. The earth turned; sun flashed all at once

119

through the window glass and blinded both of them. "And then you went back to sleep. And then what?"

"When I went back to sleep I was sitting on an onyx throne at the head of a banquet table so long I could not see to the end of it. It was covered with pots, pans, tureens, bowls, platters, dishes, saucers—and all of these were full of food. And a naked woman midway down the table's length wafting the smells to my nose with a peacock fan—*naked* but for solid gold pantaloons, a red satin turban, a pearl necklace; and her nipples and mouth painted with red rouge: Then naked women were all around me; I could hardly breathe, they were feeding me from all the food, taking turns ladling it into my mouth, caressing my head while they waited for me to chew and swallow. In each of my hands was a golden goblet—from one hand I drank red wine, from the other I drank white. I ate everything. I ate lobster their tiny fingers plucked from the shell; bits of creamy beef, partridge, one hot soup—and a cherry tart!

"Then, at the bottom of my banqueting table, there was suddenly a door, and the door opened, and a woman eleven feet tall came through it; and she was naked, too. She carried a great silver platter, and on the platter was a roast baby; it was an infant human being with an apple in its mouth, and ringed with parsley and done to a turn. The room was full of a thousand burning candles, but I woke up before I could eat the baby. It was broad daylight. That's all."

"Veronica, you are a thin person who never seems to eat enough. The seeds from everything we eat, from now on, I'm going to plant in clay pots, then transplant into the ground all around this house. I am going to make a garden for you to eat—that is what they meant when they thought of Eden—and then the seeds from that food and then the seeds from those foods. I will plant all there is to eat, and you will eat it. And I'll keep pigs, I'll cut their throats with a long knife, and you will have hams all winter long. I'll wring my chickens' necks; I will have laying hens—and when one doesn't lay I'll take her out and shoot her in front of all the others: I will terrify everything I grow into becoming food for you."

"None of that will ever happen," Veronica answered. She stood up and reached to take the bright, dangerous blades from Samaria's hand; and she began to unwind the blue cloth, thumping the bolt against the floor; and, once it was all unwound, she rewound it, this time around and around Samaria until Samaria had become a tall blue wand Veronica could bend and lift: only the face was free of the blue.

"Do you believe," Veronica said finally, "that your daughter is going to have a baby? And if we asked her, would she know if that is true?"

Veronica could not make herself care at all. "If it's true," she answered, "it won't matter whether she knows or not that it's true . . . . It grows inside you. It happens to you . . . it happens *on* you. You can't say no to it. Touch me."

Veronica dropped her robe to the floor and began to stroke her naked self against velvet Samaria. She pulled the wrapping from Samaria's head; she unfastened the comb and hairpins from Samaria's hair.

"If I called you by other names sometimes—and the names sounded real enough," she whispered, "would you answer to them?"

"I am willing to listen," said Samaria.

Called the "Wonderworker" for her ability to cause the death of new-born boys by casting a glance at their abdomens, Arabella was venerated by some and despised by others. Among the latter, her brother was prominent; and vociferous in his accusations: according to the peculiar but time-honored rule of his kingdom, he would be disinherited and deposed if he did not produce twin heirs to the throne within the first six years of his reign. No matter the extent of his measures against Arabella—even exile—son after son of his died. Arabella was said to have the power to fly invisibly through the dark and to tunnel beneath the earth like a mole. At the end of the sixth year, Arabella succeeded to the throne and lived to a ripe and lively old age, beloved by all.

"Your sisters have shaved their heads," said the stranger. "They are both entirely bald now, and I think they don't relish my company any longer."

There was no way for Flynn to escape. She had already slammed shut the door behind her, and her back was against it. And the stranger stood at the top of the stairs, blocking escape that way.

The stranger wore loose yellow trousers the color of egg yolk, and a thin purple blouse weighted to her shoulders by sprinkles of sequins. Her hair was blonde; it shone like electricity; so Flynn tried to look at no more of her than her feet. But her feet were naked and red with cold: they were devastating, like the hair.

"Well—I am famous, but I don't bite," said the stranger

bitterly. "I happen to know you don't even go to the movies, not since *The Red Shoes*—so what do you care?"

Flynn did not go to the movies, but she knew what happened in them: What happened in the movies was no different from what happened in books or in any other like places. IT BEGINS (her brain is a story book with colored pictures; is reading itself and cannot help itself) while the stranger waits. The scene is a garden, mazed with paths, bursting with fountains; it is rife with gilded pergolas, shot through with silken streams and waterfalls, populated with dainty-hoofed beasts—the zebra, the pony; the paw prints of tigers are stamped in the flower beds. And now the swimming pool, warm aquamarine surrounded with striped cabanas that are hot and secret on the inside, places where greased and streaming flesh labors into hillocks in the cup of the hand; fattens in the heat, like the tomato. Gondolas beneath the concealing willows. A bare-breasted woman behind every bush.

And Flynn is the king of it. She struts in bulging trousers; she gallops on dangerous white stallions. She lives in a castle which sometimes is a Bible lithograph of Babylon; which sometimes is all the coziness of Buckingham; which sometimes is a maniac Versailles. Her subjects are delighted and her land fruitful because Flynn fucks women. All she must do to maintain paradise is to fuck women; and she does; she fucks them behind the arras, the tuppenny stand-ups; and in the rowboats on her river; and in the swimming pool and in the grass and in the great four-posters and on fur rugs before fires huge enough to roast a cow. Face-to-face with them on horseback, she fucks them. The lustful women bounce through the air around Flynn bright as sun-lit soap bubbles which are nevertheless as tough as steel. Flynn gives them all they need; and they do not burst but multiply and Flynn increases. Eventually Flynn must

123

choose a queen, but there is plenty of time. A vagina is a long, deep swoon.

The stranger has put an arm behind Flynn and lifted the latch on the bedroom door. Flynn has no other way to go but back inside, walking backwards. The stranger holds on to Flynn with one hand; with the other she yanks the quilt from the bed and all the diagrams of generators, all the tubes and flasks and the book about the brain go flying through the air. Then she locks the door behind her.

Gemma of Camigliano desired, from the age of sixteen, nothing more than to spend her life as a Passionist, but was prevented from fully realizing her vocation because of a withered hand. Nevertheless, her fervency was continually remarked upon and many extraordinary ecstacies are attributed to her. At her death, it was discovered that her body bore several visible traces of her passion.

Back home alone from the Greek restaurant, Flynn makes coffee and receives a visitor. The visitor says to her:

"Marvelous thick ankles. Hair like gold electricity, a color *not* gold, but a color that makes the dark seem even darker, I mean, and curls inside my fingers like a nipple. I know that you're just like me—but you don't let people know it; I know you remember what the past was by what they were playing on the radio while you were driving around in a car with a buddy, throwing beer cans at road signs, listening to the d.j.—'to Susie, I'm sending this one out to Susie, from one who'll always love her, her secret love'—you remember by recalling what they were playing on the radio that summertime or that winter.

"It was 'Heartbreak Hotel'—remember?—that time at Gino's Place when Gino herself cracked your girl across the ear and then you invited Gino outside to get her cunt kicked up through her teeth. If you think back far enough, it was probably you that dropped the nickel in the box and made that particular selection. Elvis, now—he's an old man, like somebody's out-of-date invention, like trading in your old black telephone for a little pink princess that lights up in the dark. But screw all that. You pretend to be too high-class to remember Elvis. You act high-class, but I know better. I know all your stories.

"As for me—I knew it was a girl, not a boy. She was a girl in beautiful drag—a lamb in wolf's clothing, isn't it? A wolf in curly sheepskin to wrap the baby bunting in—but that was a bunny rabbit, wasn't it? However it sounds, I'm not confused—I wasn't confused then, and I'm not now. I know a girl from a boy. A boy can wear the same thing she did, but a boy is just a boy still—it's not the same—they're like they're in a uniform and there's nothing past the uniform, nothing underneath it—but the same clothes on a girl turn me on. Or is it the wolf in grandmother's nightie? You get my meaning?"

"You know I get it. Do you want anything in your coffee?"

"Hot as hell, sweet as sin, black as the black hole of Calcutta. That was her name—Calcutta—that one I already told you about. You get it?"

"I get it, you know I do. Veronica once wrote an opera by Richard Strauss—*Der Rosenkavalier*; and she made a lot of money off it. They played that on the radio, too."

"Rosen*bull*shit. I'm talking about turning on to a woman in men's clothes. I will have a little whiskey in this coffee."

The visitor put her feet up and waited for the whiskey.

"*She* was the one—*not* you; I'd forgotten, it was *her* that put the nickel in the jukebox that night and played 'Heartbreak Hotel.' But you're still the one who wanted to beat the shit outa Gino for hitting your girlfriend who deserved it."

"Ten years ago!"

"Like it was yesterday! Your type, one drink and you're drunk. You just had one drink—you're at my mercy! I could do anything I feel like to you right now. I could strap a cucumber around me and stick it up you—though God only knows why I'd want to do a thing like that. I only read that in some book or other. It was a pin-striper she was wearing. Soft cream flannel that looked like a dark pencil'd been drawn down it—your eyes could take off and follow any line they wanted and always end up at the same place; and a yellow silk necktie with little red horses' heads stamped all over it. Nice shoes, brown and white, like my father used to wear when there was a war. And cufflinks, gold horses' heads. She was the one who put the nickel in the jukebox—and before a sound was out of it, when it only was whirring, clicking like things in the grass, she was over beside me and running a finger down my arm, light as a shiver, and saying, 'Would you care to dance?' Polite, sweet—a grip of iron—I can't describe it . . . "

"It is the *rosenkavalier* . . . "

"Yes, a musketeer—that sounds right. A musketeer because before we'd danced a minute together that same finger that had tickled me had turned into a whole hand that was spread entirely across my ass—and when my ass moved, as it had to do, that hand moved with it . . . "

"There is a waltz—but the waltz is only inside the Baron's head. It isn't a real waltz, except inside the Baron's head—but we hear it!"

126

"No, it was not a waltz. It was the Fish—her leg between mine, and grind. I smelled starch in her shirt; there was a red welt across the back of her neck from where the collar rubbed. It was a woman in man's clothes. She whispered in my ear, Oh, *my heart! my dear heart!* she whispered. She talked like a valentine to me. And next we danced the Samba, and at the end of that dance she took something tiny and silver out of her pocket and hung it around my neck without letting me see what it was. She took me into the john, and I looked in the mirror, and there against my throat I saw the silver heart—but now it's lost, don't look for it. It had foreign words written on one side of it. She held me around the waist—I saw her in the mirror behind me, and then her hands moved up to hold my breasts, and I was afraid my underarms might be smelling. She told me what the words on the heart were, she said the words said, *Amor vincit omnia,* and they meant, she said, in Italian— the language of love, she said, *Will you marry me, lover?*

"I cooked her dinner, and she asked for broccoli. The first time she made love to me—and it was the next night, not the first date—she left all her clothes on. Her necktie slid up and down between my breasts, wonderful. And all the time she was with me, she never did come except the kind she did herself, against my thigh.

"On our first date, she took me to the movies. She took me to *Goldfinger* just to make me blush, but I saw most of it—there was a girl painted gold all over to make her die, and the man nearly got his prick burned off with a laser beam. I loved it to death; I nearly died from embarrassment. Then I bought myself some gold nailpolish—and *she* nearly dropped dead . . . "

"Gold and silver," Flynn crooned, dead drunk now, "Gold and silver . . . "

"You're dead drunk, Miss Whiskey. Sweet Miss Whiskey,

you're drunk and where's that cucumber of mine!"

"Ha, ha."

"It's *funny*, how things happen—she was the kind of woman my mama always wanted to settle down with—and my mama should've taken her away from me while the taking was good. But my mama of course couldn't—she was still in Georgia, where I'm from. Always *from*—but I'm still the kind of Georgia cracker lots of people want to take a bite of! There is sugar in this here cracker! But not you—you don't want no bites.

"I can't stand the way these young kids talk about their mothers, like their mothers was some kind of asshole, not the soft warm place they came out of. My mama and I had a good time together. She would stand ironing in the kitchen and I'd sit there with a coca cola after school to talk to her. It was always so hot that when her perspiration hit the iron it would sizzle—then we'd laugh! Around that time, my daddy got sent to prison, much to our relief. My daddy was the first narcotics peddler in the whole state of Georgia. And then, the day after he was arrested, his sister showed up at our door.

"Mary Theresa. She lived all the way up in North Carolina and worked there in the shipyards. She'd had to drive all night, take the day off from work, to get to us; but she was at our front door the very next day to see what she could do for us.

"Every hair on her head shone, from a wet comb through it, and every hair was in place; and her neck was raw it had been shaved so close. She carried her hat in her hand. I'll never forget the first words out of her mouth—and don't you ever forget them either: she said, 'I went to mass before I left and lit a candle for every last one of us.'

"But my mama said, 'It was good riddance.' My mama is outspoken at all times—but Mary Theresa was a relative

128

we'd not seen much of, and such bluntness, I could tell, struck her hard; she didn't know what to say next. So then my mama took her overcoat and said to me, 'Kiss your Aunt Mary Theresa hello.' But I didn't have the chance to get close to her, mama was admiring her so much, she was so outrageous shining. She was the cleanest person either of us had ever seen in all our lives. It was like she'd shown up for a wedding, or a funeral, instead of just daddy gone to jail. I can't remember now *what* made her so clean, only *how* she was so clean. I do remember her black necktie; I do remember the clean white handkerchief embroidered with a blue monogram in her breast pocket.

"Mary Theresa had a little girl too, just like my mama—but only one. I had a sister. But she'd left her home that trip with that woman she lived with named Lucy Riddle. The kid's name was Veronica. She told us, 'Next time, I'll bring Veronica, and you'll have somebody to play with while I visit.' She held me on her lap and gave me sips of her coffee, and later took us all out to eat at a barbeque place. My mama gradually got to be a changed woman—or else *not* gradually. Maybe it all happened overnight. And she stopped ironing. But just about then nylon came in, so who cared; only, my mama was a changed woman, and who can say how? It was the way people are changed at the end of the movies—when the music comes rushing up, and first it gets very bright, then it gets very dark . . . "

"The final curtain," Flynn groaned. She was slumped deep into her orange chair; the whiskey was deep in her throat. "But before the final curtain, the trio . . . but it all began in morning light, the morning light all over the bedroom . . . . That's what the *first* curtain went up on . . . "

"But every time I try to tell it, it's different. I remember it differently every time . . . "

" . . . so maybe it could be like you say. If it had

129

kept on forever, what was between them, then I could tell what would be real from what *might* be real . . . if it had kept on. But when something stops, then it begins to change.

"In the brain. It starts in the brain when it stops every other place. I should know."

"*Why* it stopped—after what I think were years and years—*that's* what I'm trying to remember now. I find a different reason for its stopping every time I remember it. This time I think it was because Mary Theresa was very devout but couldn't ever find a priest who would marry her to my mother. They would all say *no* and make her promise never to sin again and say fifteen Hail Marys. Mary Theresa begged the Blessed Virgin to please do something, but she never did. Every Friday she'd go to confession; then every Saturday morning she'd be on our doorstep, always with a present for mama—roses, a nylon nightie, candy—and always something for me—once, a bicycle; once an oboe I thought I could play, once the first book I ever owned in my life that wasn't stamped Property of Langour School System. I can't remember the name of the book, but it was good.

"Then every Sunday night I'd start crying and yelling like a baby when she'd get in her car for the long drive back, and mama would lean over her in the driver's seat to get the last kiss and get money for the week tucked in her hand—all to the tune of me yelling my head off! I exasperated mama. 'If Mary Theresa doesn't go and make a living,' she'd say, 'then what are you going to do about oboes and bicycles, girl? Answer me that!' But to keep me from crying, Mary Theresa started getting up at four on Sunday mornings—while I was still asleep—to go back home. Driving off to work before light so as not to break my heart.

"But there's another reason why it stopped—I'm remembering that reason now. Mary Theresa had a mother—Mary Agnes—who lived with her; it was Mary Theresa and Mary Agnes and always Veronica and for awhile it was Lucy Riddle and then circling way off in the distance like those billion-dollar satellites there was my mama. Mary Agnes thought my mama was too old for Mary Theresa. Mary Agnes believed Mary Theresa should have one of those little things in 'beehives' hairdos who typed at the shipyard office—but not Lucy Riddle either, who was nothing but an orphan and a bus station waitress; who Mary Agnes drove away. She wanted, I said, for Mary Theresa to have one of those girls who make you think of nothing else but lemon meringue pie when they go past you on the street; who wriggle like jelly on a plate if you so much as touch them.

"Mary Theresa told my mama and me everything: she told how she'd bring home one of those girls from the office once in a while to a big fried chicken dinner cooked by you-know-who; and then take her in the back yard and show her the flowers growing (Mary Theresa could grow anything) and pick her a bunch and wrap them in wet newspaper and keep them in the ice-box for her until morning; then spend the night with her up in her bedroom—and meanwhile, all through the night, Mary Agnes would sit and rock in the parlor hoping against hope that this would be the one.

"But not one of them was serious enough for Mary Theresa. That was the trouble—no matter how much Mary Agnes pushed and poked and tried to make it happen—not one was *serious* enough. What my mother was—that was all Mary Theresa ever wanted in the world: an outspoken woman, a woman *serious* to the touch.

"The minute my mother knew Mary Theresa wasn't ever

131

coming back again she fell fainting to the floor, then stayed sick in bed three days—and I know that for a fact; that doesn't have anything to do with what I remember or what I don't remember. But (at last) she *had* to restore her natural good humor: she was a mother and couldn't stay in bed forever. I was sixteen by that time and had got a good job, but there was my sister Augusta, who never had the sense I have—all she ever thought about was being an artist; and I believe what happened between mama and Mary Theresa and me passed her right on by. All the time she was little, Augusta thought about art—you might not believe that, but I remember *seeing* her think about nothing else; and I'm her blood kin. Then, when she got old enough, she *did* nothing else but art—and the same was true, as it turned out, about Mary Theresa's little girl, Veronica. Augusta was three years older than me, and Veronica was two years older than me.

"About the time Mary Theresa left my mama, Jenny packed her bag and left us, too, to come here to New York and be an artist, to be 'serious' she said about being an artist—though ever since I've lived here I've never been able to understand how New York City helps you be serious about anything at all. Jenny never troubled to explain it to me.

"Please listen to this I'm going to read you." The visitor unfolded an old piece of paper from her wallet, unfolded it out of countless little squares. "Listen," she said. " 'Dear Mama, It is colder up north than anybody can imagine, and the winter coat that stood me in good stead at home can't keep the wind out up here, but I don't know what to do. Could you ask Mary Theresa? Money is without consequence, because of being an artist, but I am cold. I could say I've got my love to keep me warm, but can't say that— my love is an unrequited love and my insides hurt me all day long. Sleep doesn't come anymore. But when I woke up this morning, it was two whole minutes of peace before I remembered her again. That was good. I miss you and send my love, Augusta.'

"Now I want you to just guess *who that was*—just who old *unrequited love* was!"

But Flynn was asleep; and snoring.

"Veronica, that's who. Old unrequited love, Veronica herself. What she was in New York for? Who knows. Her mother thought she'd gone to England; her grandmother thought she'd stepped outside for a pack of cigarettes. But Augusta—my sister Augusta thought she was rapping on her room door at the Y.W.C.A., the Holy Ghost itself come to call in a tuxedo with satin lapels! To call on 'kin' was her first excuse, welcoming her to the big city with a fresh white carnation in her buttonhole. Broke my sister's heart, and drove her crazy. Augusta didn't inherit—like I did—our mama's natural sense of good humor. Augusta went to men after that; I guess she's still an artist.

"These days, I'm just a lonely old woman. And my mama died last year; and it's seldom I get to meet somebody from home. For instance, I never know what to do with myself at Christmas; and these days it's hard to find a decent woman who'll ask me to her house—only nasty little younguns around now puffing on drugs and who don't know what to do with a girl once they've got her where they said they wanted her. They all look the same and talk the same, and I go in the bars less and less. They're a bunch of criminals in dirty blue jeans and making fun of me because I know how to order a drink and because I still look lovely in a nice dress and still wear the silver heart my first love gave to me, the bastards!

"I meant to say before—but forgot—that Mary Theresa didn't have Veronica because she was straight or anything before she got to be a dyke. She was always a dyke. She got pregnant and had the baby because the men at the shipyards found out after she'd been there for five years that she wasn't a man but a woman in a man's clothes and working like a man. So they raped her for that. They gang-banged her one night after the second shift. But Mary Theresa got up the next morning and went back to work; and two of those men met an accidental death shortly after that. But she was a good mother to Veronica. It wasn't her fault Veronica was a piece of shit to my sister."

Flynn woke up smiling. "How about a little something to eat?" she asked the visitor. "I'm starving."

Bartholomea Capitanio and Vincentia Gerosa met when they were, respectively, twenty-six and forty. Unabashed by the great age difference, they agreed to form a partnership whose chief aim was ministering to the spiritual and physical needs of a small community of women whom they drew around them; women who had lived formerly in a state of neglect and ignorance. Weeping crowds at their funeral (they died, in mysterious circumstances, together) testified to their great popularity and reputation for merriment.

For the first time in ten years, I can live, if I wish, absolutely alone: Nelly is going away, and I will have the entire summer to myself. I can be, if I wish, a crazy girl again, capable of outwitting any frustration—which, I have lately learned, is the point of the lesbian urge.

Tonight is the great backdrop to Nelly's leavetaking: we

134

have all gathered on Mulberry Street—Nelly (in a state of
rational calm), the woman I love, and Metro, the woman
she loves and lives with. Metro's body is tall and dark, is
rigid or muscular—or both. Her eyes seem black; her hair,
short, thick, black. She analyses the geometry of every
step she takes an instant before she takes it: she would
stop dead in her tracks if suddenly the logic of moving forward were suspended. Or would she, instead, fly? I am
helter-skelter. I am surprised she gets anywhere at all; but
she has been nearly everywhere, and successfully returned.
Whether this is true or not is inconsequential: the matter
of the truth is indistinguishable from the first fleeting impression it gives.

Metro lives with her dog, her cat, her woman. She has
plants, an electric fan, an air-conditioner, and four places
to sleep. Her floor is painted blue. Everything she owns is
encased in the noise of trucks shifting and braking, hissing
their way to the Holland Tunnel. The tumult wraps itself
around her home like a steel security net; inside is like a
bank vault. Metro wants an arrangement whereby she can
participate with me in motherhood; and Nelly is tailor-
made to such an arrangement—rambunctious, bright, tough
stuff, and the final grace note to Metro's birthright. She is
helping me, by the way, send Nelly on this trip from the
summer city to a country camp—a place my mind express-
es in fabulous images of horses and tennis balls; blue water,
white-toothed blondes. Such excellence (and Metro's invisible, soundless engineering of it) will serve to reduce whatever genetics of my past Nelly trundles about with; and the
brilliant swarm of Metro—formed by fresh food, fresh air;
by money, by skill—will rush in to close the gaps. I am
breathless with good luck.

I keep it to myself. We pack the trunk while Nelly
watches her last television show of the summer. Hours

pass. Errands are accomplished in jabbering, jittering trips in and out of traffic. Nelly practices with her new jack-knife: the cut goes bone-deep. Her arm and hand are flooded in blood; the spurt is an infant fountain. I wasn't there to see it—I was away, finding the last of the undershirts. They go to the emergency room without me; there isn't time to wait for me.

That night, we three sit around the table and, speechless, watch the thickness and whiteness of the child's new finger. We drink gin, gulping it. When we run out of ice, we drink it warm. We watch each other. My God, is all I say, over and over: otherwise, I must burst with my unspoken declarations of love; I would rant like Tristan—and Metro would know, then, that mother-guilt is no roadblock at all to the lover's progress; and she would be shocked.

Nelly is doped, and sleeps. She sleeps in Metro's work-room. I should go away, because I don't live here. But I can't (although I am the lover) because I am the real mother; and also because I will not; when Nelly was six months old and I twenty-six, we survived the East 4th Street freeze together; we lived beneath an army blanket tent I made around the gas oven, together, crazy in the two heads with fever from german measles. We are like old war buddies who've survived one jungle or another. The rest of the platoon was captured and eaten alive. In twenty years, we will meet in a hotel room, get drunk, reminisce, and talk indulgently of old so-and-so.

"I want to stay," I tell Metro. She's the one who'll decide yes or no. Because she is beloved, the beloved's opinion would be suspect.

"You want to stay." She shifts her legs, and the circle of mutual shock is broken; the adoration of the child dispelled. "You want to stay because of Nelly?" (*No! I shall scream. I want to stay so I can sneak under the covers in the night and eat her thighs apart while you soundly sleep!)*

"Of course, my God!"

(And which of us is the sort of woman who—once in her life—can undo her apron and roses, not bread, fall out? Only one of us can be the one. I pretend I am the one; but am really unconvinced of my power.)

"Then yes," she answers. "Then, all right." I should kneel and clasp her feet, weep with gratitude. That would not be inappropriate. And she would misunderstand the obeisance and believe it meant we could love one another again.

I sleep on the floor beside Nelly, who tosses and mutters with dreams on the little bed above me. The trucks don't stop for late-night, although the silences between them grow longer. In such a silence, I imagine I hear them making love in the next room. I tell myself it is only the rustle of turning in sleep; the inadvertent, the unconscious touch under the moving sheet. Or it could have been the animals, carousing through the dark, or drinking water in the dark; or leaves on house plants knocking against stems as they fold or grow. When the beloved is not with us, Metro and I watch each other with a difference. Our eyes change focus. Our pupils widen and blacken. But at the same time, in the back of my brain—when Metro can't see—I am flipping through a stack of obscene words.

In the morning, I roll to my feet, the last one to wake. In the other room, Nelly is up in the loft bed with Metro, cuddling in her arms. Metro is teaching her camp songs. Every vertebra in my back aches with floor-ache, with music. I am too damned old to rough it.

Some call the woman I love silver, and some call her gold. Before I got to be her lover, she painted a painting and presented it to me. It is entitled "One Hundred and Forty-Seven Cunts." Much of it she painted with her fingers. It is still rolled up, the three panels of it, and wrapped in plastic at the bottom of a cardboard box. I still don't have a wall of my own. The painter's frequent headaches intimidate me—I believe them a superior manifestation of cognizance of all that is horrible; they are a function of mighty brain power. Her wondrous hair sprouts from those headaches. It is like those flowers whose petals grow backwards, yearning towards the stem. Like chrysanthemums, I remember now. Except when she takes up the scissors and cuts it all off; and then none of it is any longer than a clipped fingernail all over her skull; and then there is nothing that will hide the machinery of the headache: it shows. I use the word 'love' when I speak to her, and she uses my name. I hate dancing, because someone might see me; but I will watch her dance and my watching is as much a partner in her dance as her partner; is as essential as 'the programmed code of the juke box which makes the dance start and stop. But I permitted myself to dance the Fish with her. The song was "Cisco Kid." At least, for that time, we knew what we wanted.

Meanwhile, I try to persuade her to look more closely: to *see*, be amazed: Bertha is dazzling: is irreplaceable. She should strive for vision. She should achieve bliss. She should levitate, weightless, through my intergalactic gray matter. Meanwhile, listen to this: Bertha is a still, yellow moon reflected by troubled lake water. Bertha is the one with the duelling scar across her cheekbone, who lifts absinthe with two fingers, who sits still, as unmoved as God, while the lustful riff-raff blunders by. She is that stark dark outline high above the Cliffs of Whatever poised to leap—but too pleasured by the claptrap of her swirling cape yet to make a move. You remember her—she's the one who assassinated the Princess Royal of Transylvania and caused World War Four. Meanwhile, she dresses in white trousers and gallops her stallion through the Bois every morning and does not answer letters. At nineteen, she wore drag down to her underwear, and her neckties were raw silk and her gold monogrammed ring came down to her from her godmother. She comes by everything naturally.

The question is: when is a romantic fantasy, all of it, *not* shaped to persuade a lover? The answer is: when she strikes out in some motion pertaining to walking, to moving on; while, simultaneously, her right shoulder reserves itself in stillness.

Cyrica and Julitta were daughter and mother. When, for some unknown reason, the Governor Alexander took Cyrica at the age of five from her mother, Cyrica would not be comforted but howled, struggled, and kicked; and, at last, scratched the Governor's face. Alexander, understandably enraged, threw the child down the stone steps of the Tribune, killing her outright. Far from being downcast, Julitta rejoiced in her daughter's escape and went cheerfully to torture and death.

"Well, fellas!" Veronica gave them each a firm handshake. "*Well*, fellas!"

Bogart and Boatwright stood radiantly at attention. He had come. All was well. It was real.

"Well, fellas, do we talk here or do I take you out for thick juicy steaks and a coupla martinis, whaddya say?"

"Anything you say, sir, Mr. Horoscope!"

"Then let's just *say* we did, and don't. And you can call me Harold, like in *Harold in Italy*, like when I was a poet.

I said, call me Harold."

"That's wonderful, Harold. *You're wonderful*, Harold!"

"None a that, you hear me? I don't go for that."

"Yes sir, Harold."

"You fellas swim? Did you hear what I said, I said, **Do** you fellas swim?"

"Not necessarily, sir, Harold."

"Yes or no."

"No, Harold."

"Anyway, you don't necessarily need it, swimming. But the crowds are still gonna want to see you bust open those barrels there at the end of the line (you do it by flexing your muscles) and swim the last coupla yards—get wet, show some muscle, you get my meaning? Girls scream."

"We could learn how, Harold, real quick."

"You dig nooky?"

"We dig nooky, Harold!"

"Or *cock*—like I suspected a minute ago back there."

"We dig nooky, Harold, we mean it!"

"But can you *do* nooky—like the movie stars; I mean, *really do it!*"

"Yes sir, just like the movie stars, sir!"

"What's that I see under the covers over there? That looks just like nooky to me."

"No sir, that's a secret, that's not nooky."

"Looks like nooky to me, curled up there. You don't keep secrets from your producer. Show me."

"It is a secret, sir, that doesn't have anything to do with Niagara Falls or Bust."

"That's for me to know and you to find out. Show me."

Bogart pulled aside the damp covers.

"Jesus H. Christ!" Veronica did a fast little buck-and-wing. There were taps on the heels and toes of her Florsheims. Then she held her arms above her head in a victory

140

salute. *"Idea!"* she shouted. "This's gonna be the hottest thing since Betty Grable!"

Boatwright moved closer to Bogart. Mr. Horoscope's intentions were dishonorable; he could tell. "I read our Capricorn in Jeanne Dixon today, Bogart," he whispered. "She said, *Separate friendship from commercial considerations. Remember, you'll never get out of a commitment made today.* Let's watch out!"

"You boys wanta make a million or not?"

"Yes sir, Harold."

"You boys would sell your own grandmother to make a million, wouldn't you?"

The twins looked at each other: how could they know? What grandmother? But, yes.

"Yes!"

"Or your own mother? Or your own baby sister? You boys would sell Marilyn Monroe to make a million, wouldn't ya?"

"We like Betty Grable the best, Harold."

"Betty Grable, then! You boys would sell Betty Grable for a million dollars?"

"Yes sir!"

The twins saluted, in the manner of bloodhounds finally on the right track.

"You boys'd sell Betty Grable? YOU MUST BE CRAZY!"

They didn't know what to say. After all, they were on the wrong track. Going around in circles, lost in the woods.

"Gimme that!"

They didn't know what to say, so they lifted her up and handed her to Veronica.

Veronica was whistling *Tales From The Vienna Woods.* She took Doll in her arms and began to waltz (her left hand easily guiding Doll from the waist; smiling down into

Doll's eyes). The boys were not sure they were seeing what they were seeing: they couldn't believe their own eyes. They had given Doll to Harold; but Veronica looked like she was waltzing with a living, happy woman. Veronica and Doll were circling the floor—circles so dizzying the boys had to lean against the wall. The music was terribly loud, but through it the boys could hear the rustle of silk against concrete.

Then dead silence, as though the whole planet had been switched off. The foam rubber flopped backward over Veronica's arm.

"This sweetheart comin' with us or not, fellas?"

The person seemed to be Harold Horoscope; but more silence. No answer. Then echoes from a rifle shot laving through the room.

"That comes from across the water," said Bogart.

"Then it don't have nothing to do with you," said Veronica. "It's on the other side of the water. *That* water's no concern of yours, fellas."

She began to fold the foam rubber up tight. She pulled a roll of twine from her pocket and bound Doll up into a small soft package, with a handle. It could be carried like a suitcase; it could be fastened across the shoulders like a knapsack. Veronica tucked it under her arm. "Guess who's coming along with us," she said. Boatwright and Bogart shut their mouths and locked their teeth. They stared down at the floor.

Veronica shook her parcel at them. "Is this *it* for you guys or not?" she yelled. "Are you with Mr. Horoscope—Mr. Harold Horoscope—and fame and fortune and Niagara and Elvis and nooky—or are you with some leaky jerk-off waterbed? What? It's getting later and later, and it's *up to you!*"

"What're you gonna do with our doll, Harold?" One of

142

them finally spoke. The other shuffled fearfully away. There was the sound of a second shot.

As she answered them, Veronica inched closer to them. When she had finished speaking, they were all out the door. In moments, she was roaring them away in the back seat of her car. The Doll was up front beside the driver; and Veronica was still talking: "You're asking questions to Harold Horoscope, the man who promoted the First World War. You're asking questions to Harold Horoscope, the man who promoted his own sister Loretta into the only Living Candelabra act the world has ever known and that illuminated the last dinner parties of Edward the Seventh, *you're asking questions to!*"

"You're talking to the man who invented the Irish Republican Army and was directly responsible for Rock and Roll, and you better have all the shit and stuff on you that wires this sweetheart together and makes her move—and be ready to follow me anywhere, you hear?"

Home was already a distant dream, being forgotten.

" . . . the guy who stage-managed Waterloo, the guy who picked Rasputin outa the gutter and made him a big hit, do you want to be in show business or not! Harold Horoscope invented SENTIMENT! *And that's what makes it happen!* And don't you guys know there's a war on? We gotta hurry . . . !"

After a melodramatic scene with her son in which he protested her "vehement willfulness and extraordinary conduct," Jane Patricia Rabutin took charge of an unusually large number of her son's petite amies *and organized them*

143

into a community which she called the Order of the Visitation. Although delightfully understated and thoroughly charming, Jane Patricia's group frequently evoked much tiresome criticism; and occasional raids were made on it by men from the surrounding countryside—raids which were repelled by gunfire from the windows of the House. The "gunfire" has been documented as a miracle, since to the sure knowledge of contemporaries, none of the young ladies had any skill in combat and Jane Patricia herself professed adamant pacifism. Before her death (during a visit to Ann of Austria) Jane Patricia Rabutin had founded and administered eighty such Orders.

For three days, Flynn is in bed with the stranger (who is a famous movie star). She could have stayed there for at least three more; but the telephone kept ringing—in an empty house. There seemed to be no one at home any more but Flynn.

Flynn and the movie star had been living off love and Flynn's bedroom hoard of cheese, jam, and crackers: the slip and slide of flesh through crumbs and raspberry. When Flynn at last gets up, reels across the room and out into the hall to make the telephone shut up, she notices that one rabbit is dead and the other is eating the corpse. She throws a blanket over the sight and immediately forgets it.

"Hello!" But the line has gone dead. She collapses into Veronica's swivel chair, catches her breath; then returns to bed.

She has two fingers inside the movie star's vagina, stroking the round of the cervix; and the stranger is crooning, "Oh, my dear little vagina!" when the ringing starts again.

"Cocksucking telephone bastard!" Flynn lifts her head and yells; but is out of the movie star's body in a second, rolling over the floor; is back in the hall.

144

"Speaking!" Flynn shouts.

"*Who's* speaking?"

"Nobody's home!"

"Is this Flynn? This is mama!" Flynn drops the receiver. Her hand, after all, is slippery with wet. She wipes her fingers on her thigh, retrieves the voice.

"I'd never have guessed it," Flynn replies, attempting *basso profundo*. "Long time no see."

"And you're the one I had to talk to anyway. I won't even ask how anybody else is, I know everybody must be just fine, but I had a dream and this is long distance."

"Don't worry about a thing, mama, I can get it for you wholesale, but I'm busy right now."

"I had a dream," Daisy continued, "about you. Last night, I had it again. And nobody's been answering the phone. Let me tell you this dream."

"How's married life been treating you, mama? Did you get the sterling silver Poop Scoop I sent you, the one with the quotation from Dwight David Eisenhower on one side and the profile of Martin Luther King on the other . . . ?"

"You keep on talking, Flynn, and I'll forget everything I called up to say. Thank you, I use it every minute of the day; but I had this dream and let me finish. I dreamed I was making love to you. I want you to know that husbands make love to ladies, and that's the way it is in real life; but in this dream I want you to know it was me making love to you but not like a husband does, it was with my tongue. And suddenly, in this dream, that little thing that grows at the top of a woman down there, that little bud, turned into two separate little pieces of electrical wire—two little gold electric things. And in this dream I was supposed to somehow connect the two wires together. The little bud was gone, you get it? And these two wires . . . I was supposed to connect them and fit you back together. Then the dream was over."

"That's one hell of a way to talk to your own daughter," Flynn said, after a silence.

"You have to understand it *is* long distance, and I have been drinking whiskey."

"Well, all right. Goodbye, Daisy."

Then Flynn disconnected the phone and left it behind her. When she was back in the bedroom, she locked the door behind her. She and the movie star were locked in together.

And when they staggered naked, hours later, down to the kitchen, still the house was empty. *Tess* lay broken-backed and half-finished and dusty on the table. Through the window, the movie star could see a spider's web glistening from door handle to steering wheel on her little red car.

"Rose! Rose-lima! Grandmother! Veronica!" Flynn leaned against the door jamb and croaked the names dutifully. But no answers.

Flynn and the movie star, dressed in bathrobes, each ate a steak, each drank a bottle of wine.

"My name is Lydia Somerleyton," the movie star said, when they had finished, "and I got my start tap-dancing."

"Just like in the movies," Flynn said. "And just like in the movies there is no other way to say this: I am in love with you."

Attracta, an Irishwoman of the sixth century, after fleeing home for sound reasons, began to excite, shortly after-

146

wards, considerable attention; and several very surprising miracles are attributed to her, some of them having to do with a precious oil which exuded from her lips and fingertips.

I am spending this summer alone in a two-room air-conditioned apartment on Grand Street, beneath which powerful waters flow and flood basements and sidewalks. Some mornings I look out and see that I am a body of land entirely surrounded by water.

Before this time, (counting backwards) I lived in Chinatown; on Star Route 1; on Spring Street; on Timberwolf Drive; in Caesar's Forge Complex; beside the Tar River on Willow Street; behind the University library; on West 82nd Street; on East 4th Street; on West 15th Street; in Brooklyn Heights above my mistress Hudson; on Jane Street.

The center of my home is wherever I most frequently choose to flatten my behind. Here, it is a wicker chair set before a plywood table. On the table is carved the telephone number of the first precinct; and the table holds a Lettera 32, a red and gold Martinson coffee can containing a steak knife, three pencils, spare car keys, a stack of yellow paper, a blue pen, a page of dread-inspiring telephone numbers, an orange accordian envelope enfolding one thousand student papers on either "The Tragedy of Sylvia Plath" or "Why I Cannot Relate to Virginia Woolf;" a Marlboro box, half full; a glass ash tray supporting the one I'm always smoking.

There are shelves above the desk, three of them, on which: a roll of scotch tape, some curling blue Boston Tea Party commemoratives, white envelopes, unpaid bills, art postcards, an ex-lover's expired pass to the Museum of Modern Art, three Manhattan telephone directories; and some books: *Orlando, Slang Today and Yesterday, Earthly*

Paradise, S.C.U.M. Manifesto, Mystery and Manners, Epilo-gomena to the Greek Religion; but it is the avid Miss Jane Marple and the fastidious Monsieur Hercule Poirot who caretake my sanity. At my feet, a basket full of ashes and butts. Behind me—and to my right—a round oak table, a homemade couch covered with an India print, striped curtains at two windows, an orange armchair where my landlady when she is in residence (but not I) takes her ease, a radio inside a metal box. There is a fireplace which will be lighted long after I am gone.

In the kitchen, beneath the sink, there is a box where three cats shit and piss. There are black waterbugs bred in the torrent below, brown cockroaches, three cats. A shower, a toilet, the bedroom with a double bed and a mirror which shifts against the wall every time a certain kind of footstep jars the floor; and a television set painted silver because once it was caught in a fire.

Last night, I said to one of them—it was at the Firehouse—"You're looking like a little piece of sugar pie; but then I'm a little drunk."

And she said to me, "It surprises me I still look like sugar pie, because I got raped last night."

A dog, whose name is Evans (Evans, Mary Ann) runs her nose up and down my pants leg, then shunts off sideways taking my cat smells with her.

There is no way on earth any of them could ever rape me—but that is my secret, the secret of how a sudden landslide can block the entrance to the tunnel that leads to the treasure; or the mystery of how my female body can, under threat of ravishment, miraculously sprout thick coats of hair or turn into a beast whose head is coiled in hissing snakes.

"I was coming home from work. It wasn't even dark yet ... "

148

Who asked her? The next time I piss I will piss a spray of sulphuric acid. I will shit hand grenades; but who asked her, anyway?

"He stepped out of a doorway. He grabbed my arm. He held a gun to my head. He said, Keep walking, I'm going to rape you, but if you make a sound I'll kill you first then rape you . . . . Nothing was more horrible to me than the thought of my dead body being raped. He pushed me down some steps into an alley. He made me lie down. He made me pull down my underpants. He pushed my dress up. He took it out. He stuffed it inside me. *It took him twenty minutes to come.* The whole time I watched the luminous dial on my wristwatch . . . "

Who said I gave a good goddamn? Sometimes, when I am drunk, it can take me thirty minutes to come; but the woman between my legs adores her own fantastic energy.

" . . . then he went away and then I got up and went to the hospital. The hospital said, What were you wearing? Do you wear little dresses like this one all the time? Do you know this man, we mean personally, when was the last time you had sexual intercourse before this man, did this man have an orgasm, did you have an orgasm, junkies don't, you know, did you have an orgasm, undress, put your feet in the stirrups, we don't see no evidence of nothing. I think I might have to get an abortion."

What can I say: I'm sorry? Shall I make love to her, make it all go away? But now, all the time, I am too tired. I invite her to go to the Frick Museum with me next Saturday. She thinks the Frick is a funny name, and says so: but that's only her way of flirting with me a little bit. "A little funny, that Frick," she says, "also a little sexy." "To see the William Blake watercolors," I add. "They're hilarious. They're crazy." "You're so sweet," she answers. "You ever been to California?" she asks.

Back on Grand Street, I dial WNCN. Dennis Brain plays the Mozart Horn Concerti, but not entirely for the purpose of making pretty music; but to cover the screams of anguish, the gasps of terminal speech, which will shortly be emanating from my rooms. I don't want the neighbors to come rushing up to see if I'm in any trouble. Since Kitty Genovese bit the dust, neighbors occasionally feel obliged to interfere; and this novel undertaking I am structuring would make them feel strange, and I like them—they put dimes in the parking meter for me.

I have invited eight men, chosen at random, to Grand Street. They turn out to be fathers, brothers, sons, and grandfathers to each other; a surprising coincidence. With some difficulty, I have got my hands on a Sten gun. I am a little concerned about the trouble of fitting such a crowd into such a little space. I have locked the cats in the closet, with a bowl of fresh water; and, for a wonder, they don't howl but sleep. I want as little as possible to clean up and renew afterwards: I don't want to have to give the cats baths.

The men arrive, all in one bunch, and therefore experience problems of protocol: who shall precede whom through my narrow doorway. Some of them stub their toes and cry out. I lock the door behind them. I take the gun from its hiding place behind the hippopotamus-patterned shower curtain, demand that they line up against the wall with their hands up, and clear my throat. I tell them what they are going to do: I say, "Listen, fellas, I got this thing. I'm a little kinky. I want you to fuck each other up the ass, while I watch—and then we'll *all* have a party." (I smile encouragingly.) "Then I'll let you go. Just do that for me, and I promise I won't hurt you. Just do that, and you're home free, fellas. This gun is real, but it's really just a joke. You fellas know I wouldn't hurt you, not for

150

nothin'!"

One of them turns to another. "This is just like in the movies—or it's gonna be just like in the movies, if she makes us do it."

"I'm making you do it. Hurry up and do it."

"Whatcha mean, the movies? What movie?"

"*You know* . . . Marlon!" (The exasperated grandson is a Harvard graduate.)

"Oh, yeah, Marlon. Marlon *liked* it even when he was the girl!"

"Fags like it too, and of course, Pop, your ideas on sex are utterly out of date—one can do anything at all, if there is *feeling, warmth, tenderness, passion*—but I am absolutely *not* going to be the girl!"

All of them say that they are not going to be the girl. One of them is a little apart from the others, so I shoot him. I pull the trigger, his body leaps, there is a flash of blood and brain. They realize I am serious. They begin to beg, variously, for butter and/or vaseline.

"No vaseline. No butter."

"*Please!*"

"No vaseline. And all of you have to take turns being the girl. Hurry up. Fuck each other up the ass and then I'll let you go."

They do it, sobbing, wailing, gnashing their teeth. They drop their trousers and do it. But I can't wait for each of them to take turns being the girl: as the first of them appear to be reaching orgasm, I pull the trigger many times and kill them all.

My beloved sits on the floor in front of a hundred women, all of whom want to be painters and workers. My beloved says that sometimes it makes her vomit, even thinking of approaching her work. Her large hands, full of silver

151

rings, move in arcs, angles, circles, showing silver as she talks.

After her husband's untimely death, Cornelia rebuked all suitors, refusing remarriage on the grounds that she found herself far too irritable for domesticity. She then devoted her life to instilling in her daughters a desire for fame and glory.

Veronica says, "*Mio figlio vende quadri con fondo d'oro a ricchi Inglesi ed Americani,*" as she unpacks from her collection all that has (so far) gone unsold. "What fools these mortals be and all that—loosely translated, sweetheart."

They have been in the house for six months, and Veronica is at last bored with her own dreams. There is a squalling infant upstairs, and a new mother already so sick at the sight of it she does nothing but lie in bed and herself cry like a little child. "But I am only fifteen!" are her only words. "It isn't fair!"

Downstairs, Veronica and Samaria can hardly hear a sound. Oak timber, thick plaster, floorboards, tight as a tick, insulate them; and anybody—no matter how young—who can scream that loudly will surely live. But one or another of them regularly rocks Flynn. It was Veronica who bought the rocker. And one or another also rocks Daisy, every night, so that she too can sleep at last.

Samaria looked at the paintings, amazed: shine and gold and woodworm holes, the oldest things she'd ever seen. But Veronica, whose skin looked new as morning, said she'd made them all herself, and all within the last five years. Portraits of sharp-nosed, high-bosomed ladies; madonnas; merchants in purple. Diptychs, triptychs; wood and muslin.

"I have the Southwest territory," said Veronica. "Texas. Texas is crazy for Italian, and the more cracks the better. These are all Siennese, fifteenth century, and easy as rolling off a log. They're starving for what's real in Texas, and baby or no baby this shipment has got to get out of here. And then immediately I must move on to languishing youths—there, I can use Daisy. It will become her interest in life. I prophesy that the Texan interest in sacred motherhood will soon be on the wane. The heat will be on for melancholia. My names are presently Piero, Oriolo, Bartolo di Fredi." Veronica sat back, smoked her cigarette, watched the late afternoon light skim the profile of a ravishing beauty.

Samaria tilted her head to one side and crossed her long-fingered hands on her breast.

"A *pieta*. Do you want to be a *pieta*, my love, and little Daisy a Christ?"

"I can't stand ever to lose sight of these pictures," said Samaria. "Veronica, I couldn't stand that!"

"There will be more."

"*How* can there be more?"

"Just wait and see."

"And all of *us* will become all of *them*?"

"Even the baby, especially baby Flynn. Gesso and gilding, then all scratched off. A patina that will spread like a century of dust. Fly-spots achieved with a pointed stick. Baking, refrigeration, and the new cracks filled with soot from last night's fire. Icilio Federico Joni—but I am as good as Joni. All hail to Joni!"

The paintings were beginning to darken. The sun was quitting the room.

"They are only fakes, Samaria. They are not the real thing, Samaria. Do you understand?"

"They are real. I see them. I will be glad to become them, do you understand?"

"The forgery *sans* original. The fakery of the unheard of . . . " Veronica laughed, delighted. "I am to invent origins. And then fake them. With you, my dear, I will plunder my own virtue. Now it is time for a drink."

She said, "I dreamed I was trying to pass my final law exams. I am full of despair. There is only one correct answer for every question, and I don't have the answers. Because of this, the rest of my life will be only what is wrong. I am seated with the other candidates inside a huge oblong classroom—full of chalk dust, along with all the other ordinary details of hell. They pass the questions out. The questions consist of wooden boxes the size of foot lockers. One box to each candidate. The outside of my box is smooth, sandpapered and planed down, empty of clues. We all open our boxes when the proctor claps his hands. Inside my box there is a set of men's clothing—a dark, three-piece suit and a tweed jacket, three neckties, some white shirts, and a pair of good leather shoes.

"From all this, I must construct both the real question and then the real answer to it. I am terrified, and stumble from the classroom. I cannot even begin. Nothing I can remember has prepared me for this. Outside, I see a long fishing pier extending into the ocean. The water is calm and green, and I hear the soft noise it makes as it brushes against the timber pilings. I run to the end of the pier, and there I see a famous blonde movie star waiting for me. She seems a little distraught, withdrawn; but she is waiting nevertheless, with her back to the sea. For a moment I stand still and watch her breasts rise and fall, then I say to her,

154

Help me or I'll fail.

"She doesn't speak—she makes some gesture which I must accept as the only response she'll give. I don't understand; I'm still baffled. But I turn, and run back to the classroom. My box is still waiting on the desk. I look inside again, but nothing has changed; and I still can't arrange the clothes into the real question and the real answer. For hours and hours, I run back and forth—exhausted and panicked—between the box of clothes and the movie star. But nothing changes. There is no enlightenment. Then the day grows dark, very suddenly, like a curtain dropped. The warm becomes cold, the ocean stormy and harsh.

"The movie star does the same—she turns, like the weather, from fair and undulous to shivering and ravaged and gray. At last, I put both my hands on her, just as the ocean is leaping and drenching us. When I have my hands on her, she speaks to me for the first time. She says, 'You touched me.' Then I lead her inside, and begin to write the examination. I feel exhausted, and disappointed. Then I woke up."

"I started out as the baby Jesus," Flynn replies, "and in my adolescence, was changed into a languishing youth dangling a single rose from nerveless fingers; eyes swimming with frustrated lust. This face of mine—this face you see before you—is synonymous, in the museums and private collections of the Southwest, with romantic love. But when I *did* become a *lover*—Veronica stopped painting me—because my face did not seem real anymore: they stopped buying me. How do you like that?"

"All I know is what I like," Flynn's friend answered.

"Exactly," said Flynn; and pulled the shades and locked the door.

155

A young woman named Mary was sitting alone one day stitching herself a new blue dress when a white bird flew through the window and attempted to commit an abomination on her body. Mary, however, thinking fast, pierced its beady eye with her embroidery needle and that night ate the bird for dinner. Although Mary was brought to trial under the Commission of Unnatural Acts with Animals and Fowls Law, she was acquitted and spent the rest of her long life in self-satisfied spinsterhood.

"This is Lydia Somerleyton," Flynn told Veronica, Samaria, Rose, Rose-lima when finally they all came home. "I am going to marry her. She is the daughter of one of England's richest and noblest lords and resides at Black Swan Hall, in England."

"For God's sake," said Rose-lima, "give us a chance to catch our breaths and get our shoes off."

Lydia Somerleyton, in yellow silk, lay stretched upon the gray velvet chaise, one bare muscular foot, still red with cold, dangling in midair. She was sucking on her blue glass beads. Her extraordinary hair nestled against a bunch of creweled cushions.

"I thought I would get used to that hair," said Samaria, "but I think it's the sort of thing one never grows accustomed to. It's *still* a knock-out. It could stand in for the electric chair, and I believe in capital punishment for capital crime."

"She's a movie star," said Flynn.

"She told me she was a Jew from Philadelphia," said

156

Samaria. "And *all* of us saw her first."

"That's true," said Rose, "and we do not have our periods anymore. We stopped forever up at Niagara Falls. Don't you want to find out what happened?"

"You said Niagara Falls," said Flynn and smiled goofily at Lydia Somerleyton.

"It's so charming to have you here," said Lydia Somerleyton. Her beads—like the Pearls of Wisdom—fell one by one from her lips. "But I hope you will not try to come between Flynn and I—except with great tact and delicacy of maneuver, of course."

"She is naked under that bathrobe. It reminds me that I am starving and exhausted," said Rose-lima. "You mean Flynn and *me*."

"I was under the expression that *I* was the first for Flynn," said Lydia Somerleyton; "and anyway, *you* and Flynn would be against the law, what they call *insight*."

"That's what I would call it, too," said Samaria. "I'm going now to scramble eggs. I cannot recall a single scrambled egg in all of Virginia Woolf."

Although everyone but Flynn was starving, it was Lydia Somerleyton who grabbed most of the eggs—because she ate the fastest and was not under the constraint of stream-of-consciousness. She ate six eggs. She came to the table quick-changed into faded denim—jeans and a workshirt, with "Harold" embroidered in red over a pocket; and still with cold, bare feet. Samaria had to make more eggs; and, immediately after eating all she could hold, Lydia Somerleyton retired to the parlor, stretched out full length on the carpet and instantly slept. Flynn, after eating two bites, followed her, to watch her sleep. They were both in the dark and it was cold in there.

Rose spread a large spoonful of apricot jam on toast, at last getting enough to eat. "It's my impression," she said, with a great grin of sticky self-appeasement, "she's on the lam from the feds."

"You are blessed with a romantic imagination," said her twin. "I am pleased it chose you to beset instead of me." Rose-lima was irritable. She wanted thick steak, not eggs.

"There is nothing criminal about the young woman that immediately strikes one between the eyes—like a lion cur- tailed by Mr. Hemingway," said Samaria. "It was *my* im- pression, however, that she was the daughter of a rich and noble English lord and a movie star and a Jew from Phila- delphia."

"*And* on the lam from the feds," said Rose.

"You can believe anything you please," said Rose-lima, "and not be far wrong. For instance, Veronica always said that *she* was the last of the Romanovs—and Flynn, to my knowledge, has never acted like a love-besotted jackass over Veronica."

"Don't kid yourself," said Rose, mysteriously. "She has yet to ask us why we disappeared to Niagara Falls for four days. It's a shame, but she doesn't seem to give a damn."

"We could wake her up and ask questions," said Sam- aria, "if neither of you is too exhausted."

"We are never too exhausted for that—for one thing."

On the way to the parlor, Samaria asked, "By the way, how did you meet her?"

"She came to buy one of Veronica's Gozzoli's—'Saint Ursula with Angels and Donor.' "

"Then she knows it was one of *Veronica's* Gozzoli's."

"Yes, and she prefers it that way. She is also rich. She prefers to be rich also."

"She's already awake. She's already talking."

A soft voice, rising up and falling down between sips of brandy; a breathless voice, very soft and very clear but speaking (although spectacularly) the usual: the story of my life. Flynn waited nearby with the brandy, like a butler on call for more, intent upon the call for more. The scene was revealed to those entering it. Samaria, moving swiftly, seeing in the dark, switching on three lamps, then sitting back, unlaced her boots and let Rose and Rose-lima each have a knee to lean back on.

"Sometimes a sponge, sometimes a blotter—that's the way I was thinking about myself. But I didn't always think about myself that way—only after I got rich and famous. Then I did what everybody else does these days when they've got something extra after they pay the rent and buy the groceries—I decided there must be something wrong with me. That's what happens to you when you have a little free time and start recollecting about your mother and things like that—you decide something's gone wrong with you. And what the hell were you going to do with all that money anyway, besides a Cadillac and a ride in a gondola? You give it to a psychiatrist, just like everybody else.

"So it was the shrinker who got me started thinking about myself as a sponge lady and a blotter lady. Three grand dropped on Freak Alley (that's anywhere, my dears, below Harlem and above 72nd Street) for that information—it makes you weep, my dears. I could've bought myself a Vermeer to go with the Gozzoli. But that was before I knew any better."

Lydia Somerleyton rolled over on her stomach and clenched her fists. Flynn poured Lydia Somerleyton another drink. She took one herself, straight from the bottle; and passed the bottle on. The room was getting colder, the night later. A big wind was rushing up against the house. She could build a fire. She imagined the cherry-pink and siennese gold of Lydia Somerleyton all naked before a fire and nearly fainted. She quickly crossed her thighs.

"I'll have you know," said Rose-lima, "that we went to

Niagara Falls and saw the two B's go over it in twin barrels. The barrels were painted blue, for boys."

"Hush," said Samaria. "It is neither wise nor proper to speak ill of the dead—they might sneak out of their graves some night and come back and eat you up." Rose-lima burped.

"They did not survive?" Flynn asked irritably: Lydia Somerleyton, all pink and gold, spreading her legs, letting the fire inside.

"Oh, they survived that part all right," Rose said.

"Understand," said Lydia, happy again, "a sponge soaks up anything. That is the chief characteristic of a sponge. I was wet all the time, soaking up any and every woman I came near—any woman I fell in love with, or was envious of, or admired, or hated, or went to bed with—and then I talked like that woman, walked like her, dressed like her. If she switched from gin to vodka, well, so did I."

"If you ask me," Rose muttered, "sponge is just old-fashioned foam rubber."

"It was not necessary to remark on that aspect of the lady's character," said Samaria sternly.

"Although it is true," said Flynn.

"That's probably what makes her such a dynamite movie star. I've seen her on the silver screen—she can do anybody."

"And she can sing and dance just beautifully!" Rose-lima added.

"I'm glad you like me a lot," said Lydia Somerleyton. "My psychiatrist told me I was crazy—but of course I was paying him to tell me that."

(I will eat her from the toes up, thought Flynn; all up.)

"Won't you tell us some more?" Samaria asked politely. "It is all very interesting and reminds me of that opera by Richard Strauss Veronica composed."

160

"So we like you a lot," said Flynn. (First, she would suck every toe, from cold to hot.)

"The usual humble beginnings," Lydia Somerleyton sighed. "*Moderne Screene* told the absolute truth. We lived on Amsterdam Avenue in a five-room railroad. The old man lived in the front of the apartment and me and my mama—Loretta Horoscope is her stage name—in the back of it. I had just dropped off to sleep. And the last thing I remembered from the real world was that beautiful little yellow radio light that shows the stations in the dark. Then, *bang*, I was wide awake again and colder than you've ever dreamed of—like you don't own your hands and feet anymore—they've been frozen to death and cut off with a knife. You can't get any colder than that, can you?"

"I guess not," said Samaria, uncomfortably swallowing a yawn.

"Well, that's a lie. You *can* get colder than that, yes, you can! That apartment we lived in, let me tell you, most of the time was like living in the belly of a glacier—never any heat except the free kind they send up in June, July, August, September . . . "

"*Ah sweah Ah'll nevah go cowold agayun! sayed Mizz Scahlett,*" said Rose-lima.

"You can laugh all you want to," said Lydia Somerleyton, and held out her glass to Flynn, "but I haven't even got to the good part yet."

The twins agreed with her; they nodded their heads. Some fur was returning to their shaven scalps. Their heads looked like something pale and prickly dredged by mistake from the floor of the sea. The windows began to rattle.

"I was cold—I woke up cold with a *bang* . . . " (and clapped her hands!) " . . . because my mama was looking before she leapt! She'd thrown back the covers and in that couple of seconds before she got in bed with me and cov-

161

ered us both up, I'd had a dream about being a mastadon frozen deep inside a glacier for a million years. I was thirteen and we were doing mastadons in school."

"I thought we were getting to the good part," Rose said. "I'm exhausted."

"And Bogart and Boatwright dead in Niagara Falls, the American side," Rose-lima added. "And who knows what's happened to Veronica?"

"My mother, Loretta Horoscope, was daring and dashing and beautiful in her youth. I come by it all quite naturally. She could sit on her hair; and they liked them fatter in those days. There're studio portraits of her—the kind you prop up on top of old radios, the kind that're signed in gold by the photographer—wearing skintight black boots and skintight pink tights. And a tight corset. You've never seen such ass and tits your whole life long! And roses in her hair! It's funny you mention Niagara Falls. One of the first things she did to make herself famous was to walk across Niagara Falls, smiling, on a tight rope and exactly as I've described her except for the boots. There's even a jerky little movie of her doing it, from Canada to America.

"But when I'd grown up enough to know her, she was nothing like that anymore. She reminded me of two vegetables I hated—a carrot in the summer, tough and skinny and crunchy. And in winter a cauliflower—dead white and bloated."

But all at once Flynn is struck nearly unconscious by a hammer-blow of memory; and all else was slammed aside; and it was past midnight and the clock was chiming the quarter hour. It was her lost brain machine come back inside her head, and there it was, all resplendent plexiglass and fresh and pretty as an ice cube and her own darling brain inside muttering and pumping and—should it care to do so—revealing all knowledge. It was showing itself to her

162

one last time before it disappeared forever. YOU COULD HAVE BEEN A BRAIN MACHINE! said the words writ in fire across her vision. I could have been anything, Flynn grieved. Her mouth moved uncontrollably. The tears fell. It felt so horrible it could have been the loss of love that hurt her.

She thought of Hera, born from a brain. Then Hera was gone and replaced by *The Dance of Salome* by Benozzo Gozzolli. Daisy, Flynn remembers, looks like Salome; and Daisy looks like the angel in Lippi's *Tobias and the Angel.* And it was Tobias who exorcised the demon from Sara. And it was Sara's demon who had murdered Sara's seven husbands on their seven wedding nights. Hera gleamed, returning as a wet gray muscle. Salome twisted and shivered, waiting for her mother to tell her what to do. Sara pretended to rant and rave with possession. Seven had died. Flynn's eyes were dry—memory was gone.

And she seemed to have missed nothing of Lydia Somerleyton's girlhood. She heard the final chime of the quarter hour. She heard Lydia talking.

" . . . and in winter, all day long, she sat by the little oil stove with her skirts up, feet up, reading the ladies' magazines, eating, listening to the radio. I'll never forget 'Our Gal Sunday—Can a girl from a Little Mining Town in the West Find Happiness with One of England's Richest, Most Noble Lords?' Who knows! Who cares! The next morning I got up and went to school. Then I came home and there she was, just as usual—but she shot me a glance. It was a glance entirely devoid of significance. I had ratted, however, to the school guidance counselor . . . "

"They waste a lot of taxpayers' money on things like a school guidance counselor," said Samaria. "I know that."

" . . . so I said, Listen, Loretta Somerleyton—if that's who you really are—child molestation is a serious offence.

163

People get sent to jail. And she said, 'I should hope so!' And that was the end of that!"

"She skipped the good part," said Rose. "I knew she would." But her twin was asleep, snoring; her head thrown back. There was nothing left to drink but gin, so Flynn began to drink it.

"But my mother had a reputation . . ." Lydia Somerleyton could go on forever. "My mother had a reputation. The neighborhood we lived in was Irish and Puerto Rican. She had a reputation in that neighborhood for having no memory of anything at all. Let me give you an example: she would go down to the *bodega* for bread, pay for the bread, and then forget that she'd added a can of tuna fish to her bag on her way out the door. And she would use the toilet at the corner bar and then forget to flush it because—and God knows why!—she wanted the barmaid to see what she'd left in the bowl. But the guy behind the counter at the *bodega* really *believed* my mother had no memory. But I knew better than that, and the barmaid knew better than that. And I knew she remembered *the night before*! But, anyway, she took me to the movies nearly every afternoon, and that's how I learned how to tap dance and sing—when we got back home, I'd do the whole movie over again, and she'd feed me the cues and hum the music.

"And she had the nerve to just sit there and say, *I should hope so!* And then ask me to warm up the coffee for her. Which I did; and she put a little whiskey in hers, and I put a lot of milk in mine so it'd be warm as mother's milk, like they say. Not hot, just warm. When I brought the coffee out, she slapped shut the *Ladies' Home Companion* and sat on it. We drank and ate, and she said, 'Listen, my dear, I've been reading "Can This Marriage Be Saved?" and this time it's about some lady's hubby who's committed the worst crime a man can do and get away with—this particular hubby had molested (that's the word) a close female relative of his, not his wife. There's a lot of that going around. That's why they did an article on it. The marriage counselor thinks that if the lady would give up her job at the telephone company (which the lady thinks of as her career. *I* had a career!) and stays home and takes care of her personal appearance, then the hubby would stop molesting this close female relation. Now what I want to say to you is do you remember that time you were four years old and that gorilla I'm married to sat you on his lap and went bouncy! bouncy! ride-a-cock-horse? I want you to know that that's what child molesting is! All I want you to do is know what it is, what the real thing is,' she said . . . "

"Obb-vious!" Flynn sighed. She sighed; and then swallowed the last of the gin. "Obvious, you poor little thing. My darling!" Everybody else in the room was asleep.

Lydia Somerleyton got up from the floor and went to Flynn's lap. Then both were warm.

"My mother," she said at last, "was crazy, you got to understand." She twisted Flynn's curls around her finger. "Listen, killer, my mother was crrraazy." She kissed Flynn. "My gin-Flynn, but no gin for poor me!" Flynn held her tighter; she did not want Lydia up and looking for drink. "But she was like me, she had two kinds of ideas about herself. With me it's sponge lady and blotter lady. For her it was Wonder Woman and Billie Holiday. She was the only grownup in the whole world, I know it, who had a subscription—a *subscription*—to *Wonder Woman*—and had every record Billie ever cut, I mean it!"

"It's understandable, understandable . . . " (Flynn currying favor), "I mean, you got to do something with yourself when you can't be Loretta Horoscope walking across Niagara anymore!"

"*You understand!*" And she curled like a yellow butter-ball (despite the blue denim) all the more closely to Flynn. Flynn could have spread her on warm toast and drenched her with honey; Flynn could have tucked her inside a hot biscuit and swallowed her whole.

Flynn licked the inner coils of Lydia's (shell-pink) ear; but Lydia talked about Loretta, and now all the cats were coming home: the flip-flop of their cat door in the kitchen, their processional entrance into the parlor. They took the velvet chaise and began to clean each other vigorously, and the whole room shook; and it was the cats, not the wind outside, causing the room to shake. Samaria, in her sleep, shook the twins off her knees, but the twins slept on, collapsed one on top of the other against the rosy wool; and they snored and gasped further into the dark.

" . . . wore her Wonder Woman suit in broad daylight, in public. She made it herself—but not really so extraordinary when you consider it wasn't that different, except for the colors, from the sex outfits she had when she was Loretta Horoscope . . . "

"That gold band around the forehead, too?"

"Certainly, yes, indeed!"

"Like being married to your own brain!" And Flynn laughed, delighted at the brilliance that had flashed up so unexpectedly from her mouth. What a wonderful idea!

"Blue-black hair, and a circle of gold, just like the pictures in the comics, and in public. You wouldn't know about the upper West side—but if you *knew* the upper West side, you would know you can be as upfront weird there as you want to be and no butterfly nets. I mean sex-change operations, for instance, managing sixty-nine-cent-discounts and old ladies identifying themselves as the Lion of Judah . . . anything anybody wants . . . "

"Bearded Jewish neurotics carrying bags from Zabar's and *The New York Review of Books*," Flynn added. "And the communist party and library cards from Columbia University . . . "

"Flynn? You *have* been around. I hate it."

"Finish about your mother." (Her right hand sweet against the sweet right buttock).

"Her favorite act was to go to the matinee at Loew's with . . . "

"Low-eeease!"

" . . . with her true Wonder identity concealed by an old black velvet cape from her Loretta Somerleyton days. She'd watch all of the movie, then hang out in the lobby beside the gilded nymphs and wait for the high school drop-outs and the Golden Age clubbers to show up. Then they'd get there. Then she'd just ease up to one or two—like she was going to ask the time or something—AND FLASH! She'd reveal her true colors!

"The person would stand there scared shitless. And then while she had him in shock, mama would grab him by the arm and say, right in the face, *Well, tell me—who do I remind you of, schmuck? Who do you think I am, sonny?*—or, *old man?*—whatever—and she would never give him a chance to think. Right off, she'd yell, *WONDER WOMAN!* at the top of her lungs—*WONDER WOMAN, you stupid bastard!* or *WONDER WOMAN! You criminal little jerk-off!* And sometimes—if they didn't try to run or hit her or scream or anything—she'd show them the muscle in her arm, flex her biceps, you know, and tell them what she was going to do to them if they didn't clear right away off her turf . . . "

The cats all purred, revving like expensive sports car motors. It was a noisy middle-of-the-night.

"Charles Atlas graduates kicking sand . . . " said Flynn.

"That stuff was on the *back* page of the comic book, but I know what you mean. I asked her one time, I said, Mama, how'd you get that muscle—slinging the old gorilla from the floor to the bed, is that how? And she'd say, *Hell, no! From crossing Niagara!*

"Our favorite movie was 'Singing in the Rain.' I could do Nina Foch, Gene Kelly and, also—but with difficulty—Leslie Caron. We saw it about sixteen times. After that movie—I wish you could've seen her flexing her biceps! Arms like giant clenched L's—but people started throwing popcorn at her. They had all got used to her, so they treated her with contempt, you know. The Golden Age Club started throwing the popcorn. *Desiccated old assholes,* she'd yell at them. I'd be hiding in the ladies' room."

Outside, rain falling down, rattling like silver in a dishpan. The murderer across the water would be getting drenched and angry. How would anyone know what his women were feeling? Nothing, perhaps; or just a little cold. Tomorrow, because of the weather, Samaria would predictably serve up a *Pickwick Papers* meal; and no one would feel hungry for days afterwards.

" . . . and my old man, when he worked at all, did day wages at the fish market, corner of 89th and Amsterdam. He pried open clams, shoveled ice, cleaned shrimp . . . that kind of thing. Sometimes, when she was Billie Holiday, she'd walk up that far, but only when he was working there . . . "

"Humming under her breath or singing out loud? Billie Holiday—I thought she was a black woman. Your mother, Loretta Horoscope—from the looks of you—had to be white."

"In blackface, of course! She *had* to—what would a white gardenia look like against a *white* face, I ask you? Death! is the answer. And wore a purple sequinned dress

168

and carried an oversize silver mesh handbag with a bottle of tabasco in it—to go with the butterfly shrimp she was going to take from the fish store. And forget to pay for. She'd sing the songs out loud sometimes, and sometimes she'd hum. It would depend on the weather conditions, like for everybody."

"I understand. Nobody feels like singing in the rain, for instance."

"Right. You sing out loud when the sun's shining on you. Have you ever known a soul who really did sing in the shower?"

"We just have bathtubs. I was born here, as far as I know."

"She didn't really walk that far just for the shrimp. The shrimp was a bonus. She went because the fish store had a big sign she loved out front. It was painted white with little blue waves at the top and bottom; and it said, WE SELL EVERYTHING THAT SWIMS.

The sleepers, the cats and the people, shifted and creaked and sighed: Lydia Somerleyton had shouted the sign.

"She'd get there always at one of the busiest times of the day—when all the faggots and the so-called career girls were picking up stuff for their tacky little dinner parties— the liquor store was right next to the fish store—and she'd stand around until everybody noticed that she was Billie Holiday in blackface (the gardenia, by the way, was artificial, but real silk); and then she'd grab the old man (who was pretending he didn't see her) and yell, *Hey, buster, I see you got everything that swims here! Is that right?* And the old man—helpless in her iron grip, and I mean it— would mutter, Yeah, go home.

"But she'd just yell again, *Hey, fatso! I didn't hear you! You say you sell everything that swims?* and Yes, Ma'am,

169

my old man would finally answer. *THEN GIVE ME A COUPLA SLICES OF ESTHER WILLIAMS!* And then start laughing her ass off and slap him on the back so hard that once he puked his guts out in the clam basket; and then she'd strut on off down the street."

"Did she get the shrimp? You were poor then, I guess." Flynn thought of Veronica's thousands; of Lydia's movie-millions; the little red car, the paintings in the Frick Museum, the solid gold hair.

"First thing, of course, she got the shrimp." And Lydia fell asleep. All in the twinkling of an eye. Flynn saw it happen; and after it had happened, it was as if Lydia Somerleyton had never been there at all.

The wind, too. It had raked the weather and left, in the twinkling of an eye. But the rain had left behind it a flood; the lake would swell and put all it could underwater. Flynn knew what was on the other side of the lake; she could always tell safety from danger, as easily as though one were a woman and the other, a man. It was that easy for her. She had known from the beginning of it. She thought, drunkenly, of the babies; she thought of herself swimming with a rifle in her jaws. But she would drown in the rain; but nothing she did would bring back the brain machine, nor the immemorial feel of it.

In love with Lydia Somerleyton, she had found out a new thing about herself: that she had no sense of direction. She could not, especially, tell north from south. And then she thought of another new thing: she knew that Lizzie Borden had done it. Forty whacks. She gave her mother forty whacks. And when she saw what she had done, she gave her father forty-one. It was as if Lizzie herself lay in her arms and told her the truth; as if Lizzie had rolled up her sleeves, clenched her arms into giant L's to show how strong she had had to be to do it.

But then the electricity first wavered, next struggled; next gave up to the dark, all power gone. A new wind began, lifting noises never there before out of the house. Flynn realized that, with darkness, she had shut her eyes; but why had Loretta Somerleyton left the tightrope, the high wire, the tumbles in thin air—her career!—for the fish market, for Lydia, for blackface and the red, white, and blue?

She lifted Lydia and shook her. "Why?" she asked, urgently.

"Because she was nearly burned to death in her last professional appearance," Lydia answered promptly. "How it all happened—well, it was this way. From one thing and another, she'd lost a lot of weight and Harold began to think she was too skinny for public appeal, for the music halls; and that only people with private means could now afford what Loretta Somerleyton had become. He thought and thought; and one day just looked at her and *realized* the Living Candelabra Girl—for them who could afford it. Sort of like the girl-out-of-the-cake number but high class . . . " Lydia was asleep again, her heavy head ever weightier on Flynn's shoulder.

It didn't matter; the picture was clear. Skinny Loretta with just enough flesh left in the proper places, hustled through the back hall, past the lesser Gobelin woodwork ("There's *some* money to be got out of Gobelin," Veronica had once yawned) and then tucked into a small but well-appointed (red? pink and white?) boudoir. (Gilt swan bed; with chamber pot; with flickering gas light. It was a royal hunting lodge.) Harold gives her a supportive pat on the behind, a tweak of the cheek, and disappears with the props, which are:

A human-sized, wooden X, decorated—every inch of it— by an expensive German pornographic wood-carver (a

Catherine wheel); a *Loretta* wheel, custom-carpentered to Loretta's new size and engineered with silver hooks and chains to twirl her slowly (her weight the trigger) above the banquet table; and twenty white candles (and five spares); and twenty holders all especially carved to fit a specific curve of her: the forehead, the breasts, the belly, the outstretched arms and knees and feet (knees, thighs, biceps, clenched fists). But one candle singularly different—thicker, longer, and elaborated into roses at its base. Now where would that candle go?

She would be naked, but modesty achieved with shadow is no laughing matter. The gents would have to stand on their chairs to get a really good look. Maybe over the port.

Before dinner, the anonymous Mr. X (terrifying to imagine who he really was; but Harold *knew*) would bring Loretta, with his own hands, a glass of something to quiet her tremulous nerves: a soft rap at the door, a view of handlebar moustaches, the charming smile impossible to disrupt: "My dear . . .'" Loretta had been doing her hair, and smudging a little rouge here and there to deceive the eye into believing that flat was round—from a distance. Did she stand to drop a curtsey (still in her dressing gown)? Or, forecasting Wonder Woman, glare, clench, demand that he tell her who she reminded him of . . . ?

A twelve-course banquet for fathers, sons, grandfathers. It was cognac they poured onto Loretta's pubic bush, the burning bush—only what they had at hand. " . . . And only your kiss can put out the fire!" Is that any way to run a railroad?

"You shoulda seen her down there—all scarred and dead white, and could never feel a thing no matter what I did . . . " Lydia muttered.

Pale scars I loved beside the Shal-i-mar! To look at something in the dark, do not look directly at it. Look to the right of Samaria, or a little to the left; then you'll see her. Flynn did that, but still could not see. They had all crept up to bed, the cats with them.

The storm was rumbling across the county line, away from there. But the rain had returned and would not stop all the night long, and there would be mould and mildew in the bookcases—as if she cared. She turned her palm and slid it beneath Lydia's shirt, bumping it down the vertebrae to the tailbone, feeling for something round to hold. But the hand was too cold, and Lydia shivered and complained. And Lydia's skin, too, was like ice. They gave up and stumbled to bed, to sleep. Nothing else was going to happen.

It took until nearly noon for the sun to reach through the curtains of the Grand Street windows. When it did, Flynn woke up. The visitor from the night before was crashing the parts of the percolator together and running water. The Martinson can thudded to its side, rolled across the tiled formica; there came the grainy spill of coffee onto the floor. Flynn rolled over for an extra doze. Waste not, want not. A bird in the mouth is worth two across town. There is no intimacy between woman and woman which is not preceded by a long narrative of the mother; and "Motherfuck!" shouted her visitor to the water boiling over, scalding her hand.

Placidia, attempting to cross a river, nearly drowned attempting to tame a lion, was nearly eaten; attempting flight, shattered her arms and legs; attempting love, broke

173

her heart. But she survived all vicissitudes until, at the age of thirty-six, she was captured, ordered to be burnt: "And the flames made a sort of arch, like a ship's sail filled with the wind, and they were like a wall round Placidia's body; and she looked, not like burning flesh, but like bread in the oven or gold and silver being refined in a furnace."

He sat all by himself in the van, colder (his mind chattered) than a nun's cunt. He was reasonably certain that exposure would finish off the babies.

With his rifle, he had killed one of the women outright; but had only wounded the other—seriously, from the sound of her cries—but there were no more bullets left to make her finally die. He sat behind the driver's seat, looking only to his left. If he looked in any other direction, he would see them, or the pieces of them; and a piece was as bad as the whole to see. He could slog on foot out of here, going back the way he had driven in, but maybe there was quicksand, maybe snakes. He would not, either, abandon the van. It had been hard work getting hold of this van. If he ever got out of here, he promised, he would become a gospel singer and make a lot of money and they would love him again. But the back of his guitar had cracked, unglued, in the damp and water; but somehow he would find another. He could find a chick and take her guitar away from her. I am God Fuck, he said out loud.

He should be hungry, but he didn't feel hungry at all. They were beginning to smell bad. *Something* smelled bad. If they caught him, they would put him in prison, which would be wrong and wicked of them. He thought, If I could swim, then I would abandon the van; then I would swim to that house over there and kill all the people in it and live there forever. The two little girls who used to come there, suck cunt, climb willows, eat raw tomatoes,

174

could swim like fish. He closed his eyes; he experienced a few seconds of dream: two little girls were pulling him by ropes through the water, as though he were a boat.

He opened his eyes. The water was so terrible it had waves, and the van's running board was sunk down in the mud. The wheels had disappeared yesterday. If they didn't help him soon, he would die here; he knew that. Anger made him so hot; he was suddenly sweating he was so hot; when were they going to come and help him? *Why* didn't they come and help? He would kill them for this. It was raining again, the kind that lasted forever; and the left front of the van sank suddenly a foot further; and now he had to sit on a slant, lean, and it hurt his stomach. To calm himself (he had begun to weep) he planned what it would be like when it was all new for him again. He would have five new girls, and two of them would be the little cunt-suckers from across the water. He gave them names: Sweet, Sour, Mother, Daddy, Baby. And he promised he would .not use guns any more, but piano wire to kill people, but he would have to practice first with piano wire. They would all live in the great outdoors, in real man's country, how about Arizona? When each girl got to be sixteen, she would bear him a son. When that girl was seventeen, he would make the others kill her and roast her and eat her. That would be the religion part. He would get some boys, too, to be his right hands; but he would always be the best and first. He would give himself a new name. His new name might be Lotsa Luck, and nothing would ever go wrong again. Bayonets, guns, wire-cutters, movies, broads, everything I want.

Bogart and Boatwright had argued for a little while, but that was because they were shy and a little excited. Rose and Rose-lima, after all, could not—probably—be wrong;

they had, after all, taught them the words to "Paper Doll."
Who knew? The girls might have made all the difference
between poor and rich, between knowing and not knowing. It was the little things that counted; but they wanted
to wait until morning. The middle of the night, especially
after Niagara, was a terrible time for anything.

"We can wait until morning."

"Somebody might see you then. Do you want somebody to see you in women's clothes?"

"We don't want that." "I don't *think* we want that."

"Look at the dresses, aren't they pretty?"

"They're very pretty, they're very soft."

"And the pretty underpants are pink." "No, you can't
touch them until you're putting them on."

"It doesn't matter anyway. We could never wear wom-
en's clothes. We won't do it."

"So you don't want to know? So you don't want to be
rich?" "We promise you that Doll will be nothing but a
sham; Doll will be nothing but a piece of shit—*she will not
sell*—until you know all about women that you don't know
now."

"Do you believe them, Boatwright? Do you believe
women get together in the dark and do things that men
never know about?" "It could be. There is nothing else I
can think of to explain what they are—do you remember
Harold dancing with Doll, but then Harold was Veronica?"

"We have long flowing golden hair for you. We have
soft, long dresses of the finest linen for you."

"We would be ashamed. They would know and laugh at
us." "But, Bogart, they say the women will *kill* us if they
know we are men." "And men have disappeared mysteriously before and never been heard of since—you never hear
of that happening to women."

"It all adds up, doesn't it, fellas?"

176

"How could those women be there across the lake—
doing that—night after night all our lives and we never
knew?" "Bogart, you idiot, because they are a secret! We
would be the first to know, and then we will have Doll perfect—she will be no different from the real thing." "Boatwright, she *would* be the real thing!"

"We will row you across. We will steer a little to the left,
to the willows nearest the water. When you get out of the
boat, hold your skirts up carefully and climb the trees. If
you are detected, what you are doing will only seem right
and natural."

"I'm sorry we haven't been nicer to them. They are so
sweet and generous." "It's their nature, don't worry."

"Of course, fellas. And—*what is noble every heart loves
best*": Veronica had, one summer, produced *The Bacchae*
instead of *Hamlet*. Rose and Rose-lima still knew all the
lines.

So that when they come back in the dark, making noise
to wake him, they were bloodthirsty ghosts, all in white,
come for revenge and sailing through the air; and at first he
sat tight and trembled and moaned; but then with all his
strength he ran to them, furious that they should try to
spoil everything, and pulled them one by one out of the
air by their ankles and when he had them on the ground he
took his knife and killed them again at the throat and then
knew more than anyone else ever had, that ghosts shed real
blood. Or they could have been lions, with long golden
manes, who had no right to be there.

Euphrosyne of Polotsk, a twelfth century recluse, from early age refused to leave her room. Much later, after many adventures, she was accused of immodesty and several fruitless attempts were made to force her to perform useful work. With sweet patience, she rode out the storm.

Flynn sat down in the hot dust of Veronica's workshop and waited for the twins to come and get her. They had promised her "a finale, before winter really comes." She twisted Lydia Somerleyton's letters in her fingers and hoped that Lydia Somerleyton was therefore choking to death.

She had waked that morning into Indian summer; and it was two days before Hallowe'en. She had waked to cats pressing against her thighs and had rolled over to press her front against Lydia Somerleyton's back (already, the habit formed and pronounced); but Lydia Somerleyton had been replaced by cold linen space. And there had been no noises from the bathroom; and there had been no breathless voice rising in conversation up through the weakening floorboards.

Instead, there were fifteen glossy still photographs and three envelopes full of letters on the pillow—which should have been collapsed beneath that hair. The pictures curled at the edges; the envelopes were numbered one, two, three. But Flynn got up to piss first, and to know for sure what she suspected—that her knees would knock, when she walked, like the jaw of the *Hamlet* skull.

As soon as she sat, someone banged on the door. The

wide-awake voice of Rose calling, "Don't take it so hard, Flynn, there's always more where that came from." "Get away from here!" Flynn croaked; and wiped, waited, at last heard the bare feet, heel-first, pound away.

The typewriter out in the hall began to clatter. Veronica had come home.

All the photographs were signed with the same inscription: "Best of luck to a sweet kid. With fond memory, Lydia Somerleyton."

She must have been up by dawn; she must have worked through the middle of the night to accomplish so much. In dark blue ink, with a real fountain pen. She opened the envelopes; the pictures were still no more than shining blurs. *Number one:* "My darling, try to think of it this way—as if you were George Gordon, Lord Byron, and I were the beloved Annabella. Four days only! And world-famous! Them, then us. Love forever, Lydia." *Number two:* "I will think of you always. Never forget. Love Always, Lydia." *Number three:* "I want to be alone. L."

Three pieces of paper, each folded into three parts. Flynn let them go. They ruffled across the sheet and the cats rearranged themselves to lie on top of them.

Three sheets of paper, each folded into three parts. And now it was hot again, as if the cold days had never happened, or would never return. The typewriter ran ahead. Outside, Samaria striking the target at perfectly coordinated intervals. Life as usual. Flynn had buried the rabbits, splintered their cage; had destroyed the fifty pages of notes and dumped all the expensive plastic, glass, wire into the garbage—all at top speed to hurry back to Lydia Somerleyton. There was now a silver-framed photograph of Veronica with the two Little Princesses propped up on the parlor table—the same table where her brain had once meant to live. She began to go through the Lydia pictures,

179

her numb fingers looking for some secret message which would cancel the mistaken letters.

They were in chronological order, but Flynn could not help but mix them up as she threw them one by one over the side of the bed where, on the floor, a third cat met each and began to lick whatever delicious coating held the image to the paper. She was about five years old and in a starched white pinafore and sausage curls. One dainty hand lifted the hem of her skirt; the other held to the white-gloved paw of some Bojangles brute. They were tap dancing. And there was a line of chorus girls, all kicking their left legs up, at the edge of the painted steamship backdrop. Then she was about fourteen, in a Sears-Roebuck plaid dress with peter pan collar; girl scout shoes; hair tortured into plaits, tied with red bows; and staring premenstrually moody through a tenement window, smiling wistfully at a big-city tree. And then she was hugging a horse around its neck. And then she was jitterbugging in bobby-sox, her skirt twirled so high her underpants showed. And she was in antebellum ruffles racing across an antebellum porch; and something large and antebellum seemed to be burning on the distant horizon. And she was on a beach, in the tiniest of bikinis, holding a striped ball against her hip. (Much larger in the bosom, Flynn observed, on paper than she had been in flesh. Either the camera or Flynn was lying.) In a Carmelite habit, pale hands flickering (like two white doves) above some brown and ragged kiddies. In a slit skirt, ankle-strap high heels, much dark lipstick. In lacy satin, the color of her pink Caucasian flesh, being lifted into bed. In existentialist Paris: black leotard, ballet slippers. "Love forever, Lydia."

On one of the four famous days, Lydia had tried to make Flynn get inside the little red car and be driven to the ocean. "The ocean is nearly three hundred miles away,"

Flynn had said; and Flynn could think of better ways to spend their time. But in the next hour Lydia had refused to do anything but talk about all the oceans of the world and herself buoyed in them, herself beside them, herself swimming and sailing them, Pacific, Atlantic, Caribbean, the Red Sea of Israel.

Lydia had said, "On Cape Cod one night I sat out on a deck above the bay. There was a quarter-moon shining down on the black water, and the water was chopping the moon up into pieces of gold. It was the Stairway to Paradise, and there was me tap dancing up and down it, from moon to water and back again."

When Lydia had finished talking, they had gone on to do other things together. Now Flynn was remembering that she had never *refused* the invitation to the ocean. She had not said yes or no. She had only pointed out that the ocean was three hundred miles away.

Highest motives were attributed to Bathild's and Anne's attitude of resignation—their unwillingness to repel injustice to themselves by force and violence. They were, therefore, reverenced as "passion-bearers," or voluntary sufferers.

If she came to my door this moment, I swear I would turn her away. I would say, "Oh my goodness, I wish you had called first—I'm busy: working, taking a bath, playing poker, shoeing my horse, perfecting the detonator which will blow Eastern Standard Time to smithereens."

Besides, I am in no mood to be a lover. Two terrible things have happened to me today. So I feed the cat, I feed

Nelly. I pull the bedspread over me and lie down. I get up and take the phone off the hook, then I crawl in bed again. But my mystery is on the bathroom floor, and if I don't get up again, I'll never know who the murderer is. And while I'm up I have to find Nelly's galoshes, then find her door keys, then recite all the things she'd better not do: do not stay out past dark, do not speak to strangers, do not shoot smack but bring it home to mama. An ice-blue river is running through that space between my eyeballs and my brain, and that's where I daily shoot the rapids as I leave home to go be a schoolteacher with my shopping bag of paperbacks. Two terrible things happened today.

I have sixteen students in my class. I used to have seventeen; but number seventeen—Minnie—was last week forcibly removed. Minnie could get too excitable—everything that happened excited her; and then she would pick up her aluminum and plastic desk and bang it rhythmically against the floor; and she would talk, louder and louder every day, to some unseen Mr. Interlocutor, stopping only to inquire when she could expect the test.

Today, six days later, she returned; but did not come inside. She stood outside and kicked the door to the class hard and loud. But that wasn't so bad—it gave me and the sixteen time to scratch, stretch, light cigarettes. It was one more thing we could get used to. But then she stopped the kicking and began to beat with her fists, using them like sledge hammers: the long swing back, then bang. It was as though she'd been locked inside some place that wouldn't let her out. But our door was not locked—she could have turned the handle and come in. The sixteen stared at the door, then at me: I could tell they were expecting to hear, *"Let me out of here!"* coming from one throat or another. Minnie did shout, but not that. Between beats, she shouted, "Filthy woman, sexy woman, filthy woman, sexy

182

woman!" It came through the wood sounding like some highly specialized Caribbean calypso. Indeed, I caught one of the sixteen beginning to tap her toe. But what I heard was grief-filled, raving, like the last of the Late Quartets: Sunday afternoon at the Frick. Our soloist will follow with three Mozart arias from *The Abduction from the Seraglio.*

"Keep your seats and shut your mouths!" I order. Then I open the door myself, braced for Minnie to fling herself into my arms. Surprisingly, she keeps her balance; and keeps on beating with her fists, now at nothing but the thin air between us.

So I shut the door and return to my chair. But I have got a good look; and now the door is shut again and she can begin to kill again when she's ready. One of the sixteen makes bold: *Well, what did she look like?* I answer, Well she's skinnier than ever. Her legs and arms are like knotted cord. She's dyed her hair red. Her lipstick is thick, nearly black. Her blouse is nylon and pink, and has ruffles at the neck and wrists. She's wearing a plastic miniskirt with a belt made of what looks like Canadian pennies. Her stockings are twisted; and just below her left knee there's a scrap of toilet paper stuck to congealing blood. On her feet, white, sling-back sandals with high heels. As a matter of fact, there are straps everywhere. Her hair is strapped into curls. Her mouth is strapped into a smile—yes, indeed! She was smiling all the time, and her teeth were white and clean. There are long purple nails strapped to the ends of her fingers, and her ear lobes are strapped to rhinestone clips."

The sixteen nod their heads up and down, concentrating, memorizing, in case they are examined on the subject of Minnie; but, as a matter of fact, none of them matters anymore: any minute now I am going crazy; but it won't be my fault. Since it is spring, floods will happen I cannot

183

stop. The reservoir dam is cracking wide apart, the blue water rising and bursting into falls. Forty janitors with forty mops are hurrying, as fast as they can, slursh, bang. I could open the door again and fight her, here and now, challenge her to the death. Choose the weapon, pistol, shiv, sword. I could break her in half with my bare hands; could grab her when her back's turned, in the ladies' room, in the elevator.

In this school, all the secretaries are women and all the teachers are queers. Minnie wants one of those secretaries: she's been grabbing at a blonde prize who sits behind the office Royal. This morning, Minnie, making haste, knocked the Royal on the floor. *And* she spilled the vase of jonquils the secretary's mama had put there.

The resident shrink has whispered to me. The shrink has whispered to the secretary. The shrink talks out loud to Minnie, and says, *Trust me.* Minnie replies, I'll trust you if you'll *drink me*—but I don't mean anything dirty by that, it's what I read in a book. You grow up or down.

Again, the shrink catches up with me (padding up on little buffalo feet). He says, She doesn't comprehend how you can have a daughter out of your own body and also do the things you do to the bodies of women? You, he says, are driving her nuts. Winks. *He* comprehends. He says, Everytime I take my wife to a party, there's some lesbian there who puts the make on her. His blue movie unreels and casts itself flicker-glitter against my face; whereupon the dyke springs a leak.

Sitting on the toilet in the Algonquin Hotel, I am reading an article entitled, "Organic Farming in Nebraska: 'Wonderful to Farm That Way Again.' " *Organic Gardening*, August, 1974. I stole it from a table on my way out of the fullsome lobby.

184

Daisy is twenty minutes late; and it was her idea to meet me here, not mine. I can't afford it; but she will expect me to pay. I'd rather be home, safe in bed, figuring out new ways to persuade that woman to love me back. A blizzard is predicted; and I'd rather be home in bed. Crop rotation, chemicals, and $10-$12 an acre. Outside my stall, someone is shuffling from foot to foot before the mirror; she's whipping a brush down long straight hair. It sounds like brown hair.

I take my time. I memorize the part I like best. It will be something to discuss with Daisy, in case she has nothing to say. If I get back to the lobby and she's still not there, I will have to order martini number two; and she'll never have time to catch up with me. I clear my throat and first speak the title: "*Garbage Worms in the Planting Row?*" then forge right ahead: "A word of warning should be inserted here"—(my voice is only moderately loud)—"the worms that you raise in your garbage pit—the Red Wiggler or *Eisenia foetida*—will do a splendid job of turning your garbage into castings whose nitrogen content is almost fabulous—five times that of good soil. But he almost certainly will not live in your plant row unless you keep feeding him compost there—as you did in the box or pit. The fellow who is good for your garden—the *geophilous* or soil-loving worm—is bluish instead of reddish and he prefers literally to eat his way through the soil rather than through your garbage pail or compost pile. The Red Wigglers you put out in the garden row will, when they die, fertilize the soil with their bodies. But there are better and less expensive ways of enriching the earth. Of course this does not apply to the castings which are an excellent fertilizer and highly recommended for all plants as a side—or top—dressing."

I leave out the last sentence. The writer has overextended himself; and when I had raised my voice to declare "feeding the compost" had driven away the hairbrusher. Her departure had been a swish, a moan, a clatter.

I flushed, I dropped *Organic Gardening* to the floor, I did not wash my hands.

As bright and shiny as a mint-condition buffalo nickel, Daisy was seated upright in the Elizabethan-tapestry chair, her knees crossed, her hand banging the bell for a second martini. I would have to hurry to catch up with her. Her feet were hidden by bunches of snappy shopping bags from Lord & Taylor's; she appeared amputated from the calves down. Her hair, now, was long, straight—and brown; but it had been red and frizzy in her youth.

"It's so *gooood* to see you!" I shout; and bend to dash a kiss against her cheek, but am ensnarled by shopping bags and, instead of kissing, knock her momentarily unconscious (my head is full of rocks). When she recovers, the waiter is there with two more drinks. The waiter tries to pretend that he has seen it all before, but I know for a fact he has never before seen me on the lap of an unconscious woman.

I arise, trailing clouds of tinted tissue paper, and sit properly on that which is genuine leather.

"So," Daisy says (as if nothing had happened), "let me tell you this joke I just heard while we have these drinks."

"Okay." I resign myself to speechlessness and pop peanuts, like spitballs, to the back of my throat.

"This farmer out in Iowa one day decides to get himself a zebra for his farm, so he gets the zebra and the zebra is from Africa and has never seen a single farm animal in her whole life, and on her first day at the farm she goes around to meet all these farm animals she's never seen before, and first she goes to see the pig. She says to the pig, 'What kind of animal are you, dear madam, and what do you do around here?' And the pig says, 'Oh, I'm a pig. And when

186

I get big and fat and the weather turns cold, they will kill me and turn me into pork chops and sausage.' 'Uh-*huh*,' says the zebra and moves on. Then she goes up to the cow and says to the cow, 'Excuse me, my dear, but what kind of animal are you and what do you do around here?' And the cow says, 'Oh, I'm a cow. And every day at the crack of dawn, I give milk to the farmer, and someday he will kill me and turn me into steak and hamburger.' 'Uh-*huh*,' says the zebra and moves on. Then she goes up to a chicken and says to the chicken, 'Listen, sweetie, what kind of animal are you and what do you do around here?' And the chicken says, 'Oh, I'm a chicken, and I lay eggs for the farmer, and someday he'll kill me and turn me into fried chicken.' 'Good God!' says the zebra and moves on. Then she comes to the horse. She says, 'I must be crazy to ask, but would you mind telling me what kind of animal you are and what you do around here?' And the stallion answers, 'Honey, I'm a stallion! AND IF YOU JUST SLIP OUT OF THOSE SEXY LITTLE STRIPED PAJAMAS YOU'RE WEARING, I'LL *SHOW* YOU WHAT I DO AROUND HERE!' "

A hush falls on the lobby of the Algonquin. A prominent Southern novelist falls gasping to the floor. Daisy and I have three more drinks each, then I go home. I was drunk, I was scared of getting mugged on the subway, I was scared of breaking my legs in the snow. But I made it. Those two terrible things happened to me today, and if she came to my door this minute, I swear I would turn her away.

Minnie is still loose, they can't catch her. Minnie is at large; and I never found out what Daisy wanted from me. She had been tan as toast, a little burnt around the edges. She had been wearing white linen beneath Emba mink; and gold had been hanging from parts of her body. I don't know what she was wearing on her feet. Once I was sitting in the lobby of the Plaza Hotel, giving myself two minutes to be late for an appointment with a widow on the ninth floor. In a great commotion, suddenly several High School of Music and Art types came bounding through the revolving doors, turning and twisting to snap cameras at the approach of Lana Turner. It was Lana Turner, the movie star. A gold anklet twinkled above her right foot. Her dark mink brushed the anklet. She strode purposefully forward as the hotel staff beat the boys aside. I reached the elevator before Lana Turner did, and waited inside for her. Alone together, we ascended. We got off on the same floor.

When there is nothing left to eat and the tea is all gone, the fire goes out: that is how Grandmother Bert described Kilkenny weather.

Romaine, who gives her name to that which is fragrant, green and edible, was entrusted to one Serena whose duty it was to teach Romaine a foreign tongue. Serena, in addition, converted Romaine and in consequence was killed by Romaine's father. Romaine fled from home and settled with a companion named Gilda on the Isle of Jersey. After fifteen years, they were murdered by a band of sea-rovers.

Maryann, Honor, Grandview, and Daisy leave the country house about once a month and go to the city so that Maryann can be recognized as a famous dyke. One day they will leave and never return—or, if they return, they won't be able to get back inside their house. New people will be living inside the house; and, even from the outside, they will hardly be able to recognize the place. A little red car will be parked outside. The garden will be hugely planted. The neighboring wife will have recovered from brain cancer and gone off to live with her mother-in-law.

They will stand on the other side of the lake, unable to get across to where home once was. The day will be wet and gray. The willows will sag. "Somebody call a taxi," Maryann will mutter. But the others will already have turned, to slog through the mud, back to the road where they left the van.

They go to the city so that Maryann can be recognized as a famous dyke. That's not hard. Maryann is taller than most women, and when she moves hurricane conditions follow in her wake. And her face is as stamped on the public consciousness as eagles, as Abraham Lincoln. It is a face by Norman Rockwell; about fifteen years old, both innocent and knowing, cute and freckled with a snazzy grin: it pouts in the Kansas barber's chair getting its first professional haircut; it snoozes by the old fishing hole; it sails above the red Schwinn bike, a paperboy arm aiming the *Morning Star* directly at the briar patch. Maryann Evans after George Eliot, who admired this woman's grandmother.

They go to the city, then they go to a bar. It has a box loud with pelvic rumble-bumble; it has a sneering, incompetent bartender (martinis so wet Florence Chadwick has mistaken them for the English Channel) who tries through pedantry to achieve glory; and through eccentric pederasty (they must be club-footed). He keeps a stained, broken-backed Bartlett's *Quotations* beneath the bar. He shoves the dripping glasses at the waiting waiter and snarls, " 'Who ran to help me when I fell,/ And would some pretty story tell,/ Or kiss the place to make it well?/My mother.' Ann Taylor, *Original Poems for Infant Minds*, stanza six."

" 'I like little pussy, her coat is so warm;/ And if I don't hurt her she'll do me no harm.' Jane Taylor, *I Like Little Pussy*, stanza one." The waiter's response was contemptuous; it was aristocratic. His tray balanced on the tips of his fingers. All smiles, he presented the tray to Bogart and Boatwright; but Bogart and Boatwright were concluding a business arrangement with two types from Canal Street and it was one of these who snarled, "Just siddum down, just bug off!" The waiter arranged the glasses in a semicircle around the jar of vaseline on the table. The businessman's hands, feeling for quality, passed around a hunk of foam rubber.

There are desperate. characters racing up the stairs to pant into the telephones. There are girls making warlike noises with their platform shoes.

Honor returns from the toilet waving her graceful wrists to and fro. "Somebody in the Ladies'," she calls, "is spraying herself with vaginal deodorant."

"Did you tell her to stop it?"

"I told her to stop it. She wanted to know why."

"Did you tell her why?"

"Mr. Bones? Mr. Interlocutor?" Daisy adds.

"I told her why. I told her about the one who tasted like the rose of Sharon. Maybe it was lilies of the valley. I told her what I don't like." Honor is wearing the most distinguished items from her collection of denim. Her smiling Irish eyes are like a morning spring. She shoots her cuffs and tickles Maryann's left breast. Daisy and Grandview agree to get up and insult the bartender, to demand a Tanqueray.

Maryann slips a hand slick with salad oil down the front of Honor's shirt. Someone recognizes her.

"We just recognized you." Bogart and Boatwright's business associates take the empty chairs and smile approvingly at the hand down the shirt.

"We have a business proposition for this famous lady Maryann Evans," the stouter, richer individual says.

"Speak up!" Maryann inadvertently spits some salad green onto his brow, but still she glows. She is harvesting what she has sown.

"You, Miss Maryann Evans, in a suggestive pose with our all-American, girl-next-door, hundred per cent Baby Doll foam rubber and latex vaselined interiors wired for sound (*oooh, ahhh, o honey*) when you pull the string, and wired to move the way you, big boy, want her to move. Personally yours. Ready when you are. Available in your choice of three skin colors, black, brown, flesh-pink. Later model than that with a French accent. The perfect gift for a loved one. $99.98, no extras to buy. Accessories available."

Honor can't help herself: "What are the accessories?"

"They don't concern this famous lady here. They don't appear in the nation-wide campaign. But if you want to know for curiosity it's net stockings, black simulated-leather bra, black spike heels—accessory group number one. Accessory group number two is mink-trim bikini briefs, a black lace nightie trimmed in cherries. Doll comes with a cherry, too. In all the big magazines, on tv—the famous lady in a suggestive but not dirty pose with the product. We got the message: what the boys dig, the ladies dig too. Especially since the vote—whatever—happened. I mean it. We want this famous lady here to tell the ladies of America how they will sincerely dig this product."

"How much?" Maryann unfolds her sunglasses and puts them on.

"Let's shake on that. A lot. You know something? You're one a' the most wholesome-looking ladies I ever set eyes on. You're wholesome, that means Doll's wholesome.

191

Look over there—our inventors are waving at you. They *know!*"

Maryann graciously returns the bows. The inventors have fresh drinks delivered—this time, Beefeater's, and done to a perfect turn. The great stillness of perfect amity dissolves the noise around and about them. Maryann strokes the sample of foam rubber. She takes a taste of the vaseline. She says—although she is speaking only to herself—"I used to steal vaseline to eat when I was a kid. I used to love the taste of it."

Maryann decides that no one will go dancing after dinner: she must be fresh-faced for the early morning session with the photographer.

Three weeks later they all try to go home again, but can't get inside. They stand under the dripping willows, their toes at the edge of the water between them and home. If they squint, they can just barely see, through the tiny distant windows, Veronica telling dreams at the kitchen table, Samaria measuring.

In full living color: Doll on the bottom, Maryann on top; black satin sheets by Gentile of Hollywood. Doll on top, Maryann on bottom, on a billiards table in the basement-turned-rumpus room. Doll and Maryann side by side, dreamy before a roaring fire. In a field of clover. In outer space. On the kitchen floor.

At their trial, Tibia Perpetua and Felicity were condemned to death by wild beasts. Returned to their cell, Perpetua had two dreams which present problems of interpretation

(Felicity, being a slave-girl, did not dream); and, upon wa-
king, had a vision of herself wrestling with and overthrow-
ing "something evil" disguised as an Egyptian. On the day
of their death, they entered the arena "with gay and gal-
lant looks" and proclaimed themselves, in loud tones, "the
darlings of God." After encountering a leopard, a bear, and
a cow, they were each killed by a sword through the throat
but only after they had kissed each other so that their
death "might be perfected." Upon their arrival in Heaven,
they were told to "Go and play."

Rose and Rose-lima enter Veronica's workshop, but are
in no hurry to get started.

"Flynn," they say, "you have a face on you like Heath-
cliff yelling *Cathy Cathy.* My stomach turns."

"I'm not anything you say I am, but you won't have to
worry about me much longer, poor old Flynn is leaving,
then you can be glad. I'm moving into the garage. I'm going to spend the rest of my life alone in the garage."

"Probably not. Bogart and Boatwright might come back.
Besides, the bed leaks."

"They can't come back. They're dead and drowned and
gone forever."

"But maybe not. For instance, there's a Bogart and a
Boatwright making a million dollars this very moment with
something called Doll. And Maryann Evans is helping them
and an ice hockey champion is helping them."

"So I guess they did good at Niagara. They are rich, famous; they have friends and helpers. What do I care? The
summer turns to winter, my heart to stone."

"And the brain to mush. Take Niagara Falls, for example. How do you know it happened? I mean, it *happened*, but if nobody *knows* it happened then it might as
well not have happened. *The New York Times* was not

there. The *Village Voice* was not there—you name it, it wasn't there. Even *The Furies*, from D. C., *Majority Report*, from New York weren't there. *You* weren't there. Honeymooners were there with Instamatics. And us, with a fucking Brownie."

"And," Rose-lima continued, "the barrels went over the falls, they floated to shore, Harold Horoscope unpacked them, and out popped the dear familiar faces, dead white, and dragging a waterlogged hunk of foam rubber behind them. The boys wore tigerskin trunks, the foam rubber wore tigerskin bra and panties. Then the twelve-piece Holy Agony high school band struck up the only tune they appeared to know: *Ave Maria* by Humperdinck. They played it twelve times without cease. Then it was over and everybody went back to bed or whatever. It was cold and rainy."

"I don't believe a word of it," Flynn said.

"How could you?" Rose asked. "It hardly seems real to us and *we* were there. But it *will* seem real . . . when?"

"About this time next year," said Rose-lima. "Metro-Goldwyn-Mayer is making a movie of it. Guess who's the female lead!"

Flynn put her head between her knees and began to sob.

"I think you're wrong," said Rose. "I think it's Twentieth Century Fox. It is the one with the lion roaring through a bright circle."

"That's right. Twentieth Century Fox."

Flynn wiped her nose back and forth against her knee. "This story is taking so long to tell. It must be the heat. This heat is all wrong. It should be cold by now. This heat is wrong."

"The mysteries of the Gulf Stream are revealing themselves," said Rose-lima. "The story of the event always takes longer than the truth of the matter. Look at *Lover*.

Look at how long Veronica's novel takes. The story makes the truth seem like a dream—something that happens in the middle of the night, fast and forgettable."

"You are wrong, Flynn, about the female lead. Don't cry. The movie will star the great Loretta Horoscope in the greatest come-back of all time. You've heard of resurrection? We had breakfast with her. We met Loretta Horoscope."

"She is charming," said Rose-lima. "She has up-dated herself. She has changed her name from Loretta to Daisy."

"That sounds charming," Flynn sniffled.

"But her name in the movie will be the Blessed Virgin Mary."

"But I feel sick on my stomach," Flynn added.

"A broken heart gets drunk and stays drunk until it is cured. And when it wakes up it is like it never happened."

Rose-lima was mean; she said, "*I* saw those old movie stills, and they were *not* pictures of Lydia Somerleyton— whoever she is. They were pictures of *The Good Ship Lollipop*, of *National Velvet, A Tree Grows in Brooklyn, Casablanca, Gone With the Wind, Camille*—stuff like that."

"Shirley Temple, Elizabeth Taylor, Peggy Ann Garner, Vivien Leigh, Greta Garbo, Marlene Dietrich—stuff like that," Rose said.

"You sure have been around, Flynn," said Rose-lima. "Now that's what I call experience!"

Flynn drew a deep breath and sneezed. Goldenrod in full bloom surrounded the workshop. In the glare of the sneeze came a vision of Greta draped over her arms; of her hand against the thigh of Dietrich.

"Let's have a drink," said Flynn, smiling bravely. "Let's have a drink to celebrate: anybody who would buy a fake *Saint Ursula with Angels and Donor* must have been a figment of my imagination."

"Your fevered, sex-starved imagination!" Rose-lima produced the workshop vodka. "We don't need ice; just pass it around." But the twins only pretended to take drinks.

"Just in time," said Flynn. "I'm getting cold. It's getting cold all around. The sun has moved."

When its big double doors were wide open, the workshop had only three sides. With the sun out of it, its floor instantly cooled. Flynn's bare feet rubbed the dust, shunting the vodka down to her grateful toes. Inside now, it was a time like waiting in a darkening theatre for the play, brilliant from above and below, to begin: a Marshallin with a girl who is Rosenkavalier singing together on a bed, like the first wonder of the world.

"We have a letter from the Pope of Rome expressing his delight in this script's encouraging view of the Virgin. Entire convents will be taken in buses to see the matinees."

Rose explained: "It goes like this. Two young girls living in a lonely countryside wake one morning and find gallons of blood pouring from their bodies—out of you-know-where. Their families, everybody, turn away from them in horror. *They* turn from themselves in horror; from each other, too. They are condemned as witches: cows and horses and crops are dying; waters are rising and flooding the land. The night before they are to be burned, they escape and travel a hard, dangerous route through wilderness. They are beset by wild animals and besotted cowboys; and a posse from back home is hot on the trail of their bloodstains. They live on wildcats they have caught and strangled with their bare hands. Now they become evil and grow to enormous size and strength. The people cower, whispering tales of twenty-foot women from outer space. They steal baby girls, and the babies are never seen again."

"We see their big bunioned feet stomping down on town and village, demolishing little red cars with their big toes, inciting tidal waves when they squat to rest. Behind them now flows a river of blood: the whole world is going to drown in it. Soldiers and presidents of republics begin to commit suicide; a great religious leader builds an ark. Then people begin to notice that there are *more than two of these dreadful women . . . !*"

"The little baby girls they stole have grown up!"

"And have become just like the dreadful women!"

"Four, five, six, fifteen of these twenty-foot women bleeding all over the world, glory hallelujah!"

"Bloody rampage," Flynn murmurs, smiling, deeply satisfied. "Murder, murder, murder!"

"So far you like it?"

"So far. When is Daisy's part?"

"Not yet. First, small-town America happens—a wonderful stampeding of New England Congregationalists. Then, big-city highlights—for instance, when one of the original bleeding women snatches Loretta Young from the path of a crazed construction crew and lifts her to safety at the top of the Empire State Building."

"Loretta *Young*, not Loretta Horoscope."

"Correct. All the big stars are getting cameo roles."

"Oh, Flynn! The excitement! It is going to change your life."

"I said already that I liked it. Don't entice me or I will hate it. But I don't understand what it has to do with Bogart and Boatwright going over Niagara. I don't understand about Daisy being the star. She is *not* twenty-feet tall. Explain that. See if you can find me another bottle."

"Here is another bottle, my sister. You don't understand because you've been drinking. Here, drink some more."

"Answer this question, then you will understand," said Rose-lima. She crouched against Flynn and stroked her

197

hair. "The question is, would anybody in their right minds make a movie about Bogart and Boatwright and Niagara Falls? Answer me, would they?"

Flynn rubbed her head back against the sweet pressure. "No, I guess not. But I don't ever get to the picture show. And, after all, they did sleep on a water bed. They did drive a fast car."

The rubbing stopped; in stopping, it left hurt. "Answer me: *no*. That's the correct answer."

"NO," said Flynn; and slumped all the way to the floor. She lay flat against the floor, and it felt like a hard furry beast of burden pressing up against her; powdery sand, or something Veronica used for faking.

"Good girl. First of all, the movie is about me and Rose-lima. Not about Bogart and Boatwright. About us, your sisters. We are the original twenty-foot women."

Flynn shook her head. The faraway ceiling, its criss-crosses of rafters and beams spun like a wheel. "You're here, though. Here in this place. Not in Hollywood, California, where they make movies. You're shorter than I am."

"Forget about short and tall. If you understood life, if you had experience, you'd know it's all done with mirrors—just like everything else. The tidal wave happens in something the size of a swimming pool. All with mirrors. Open your eyes and look at your sisters: now, *answer me*: wouldn't anybody in their right minds want to make a movie about us? Look at us."

Flynn looked. She saw the memory of them creeping naked and gold-faced across the floor to frighten her out of fever. She saw how they could go bald the instant they left her sight. She saw how they knew all the words to "Paper Doll" and could turn men into women, then into murder victims, and herself into a wild beast. She understood

198

that everything was done with mirrors, that a thing—if performed—is its own duplicate.

"I see," said Flynn. The things, in space above her, lay still in space. "Will you go falling over Niagara?"

"Not us. With us, safety first. Our *doppelgangers* will perform at the Falls. Also born Siamese. They will pretend to be Rose and Rose-lima falling over Niagara. Maybe they *are* us—I can't tell."

"*They* will be us, and they will go over Niagara Falls and it will be the Blessed Virgin Mary who makes them do it," said Rose. "Stick to the script."

"How will Daisy look? How will she seem?"

"Typical Blessed Virgin Mary. No confusing experiments with style—like the time you insisted on playing Hamlet in a pin-striped suit and made the audience miserable. People want the real thing."

"You mean all blue and white? You mean thin rays of gold blazing from the palms of her outstretched hands?"

"Yes. The real thing."

"And here's how it all happens. One night, Rose and Rose-lima and their gang are sleeping in the forests of Canada. And Daisy appears to them in a dream and says to them, '*Thou art light.*' Just like that. In a trance, they rise and follow the vision—through trees, through a haze of silver moonlight, through swirling fogs . . . "

"And a sound of singing coming from nowhere . . . " The twins stood and moved like zombies up and down the workshop, demonstrating. The workshop was becoming a freezing place to be.

" . . . until they come to the roaring falls." Flynn opened her eyes again. The two above her appeared a swarm. They were a swarm of wormholed gargoyles unfixed, free-floating.

"On location?" Flynn asked. "In a swimming pool?"

The gargoyle stuck out its long pointy tongue. "Let me remind you, Flynn," said Rose-lima. "Let me remind you that the human nervous system can hardly tell the difference between its acts of imagination and its acts of reality."

"Remind me? I never knew that before."

"I could persuade you that I was holding a burning candle against the sole of your foot, but in fact I would be pressing an ice cube against you there. But you would feel your flesh begin to burn. You would *smell* your own flesh burning. There might even be a blister left as proof."

"I should have gone to school, like you did, like Rose did . . ."

"It wouldn't have made a bit of difference, the way things are working out. Would it, Rose-lima? English poets, then chemistry, then dissection of the frog—would any of that be making any difference here and now? One rabbit would still have eaten the other. Lydia Somerleyton would still have come here to buy St. Ursula. Isn't that true, Rose-lima?"

"The Blessed Virgin guides them to the falls," said Rose-lima, "on location. And our *doppelgangers* are multi-skilled—they ride bareback, they drive motorcycles through flaming hoops, they leap one hundred feet into a tub of water. They tame lions. They belong to a Russian circus. Our *doppelgangers* will *do it*—in *actual* Niagara."

"So there is Daisy against a background of sunrise and sparkling spray. A pause, a silence. Then she unfolds her cloak and out roll two huge transparent bubbles. Without a word, Rose and Rose-lima enter the bubbles and then the Virgin lifts both up with her fingertips and holds them high above her head. We reflect blinding light. All is radiance."

"And a sound of singing coming from nowhere."

"But what about the blood?" The ceiling has begun to spin again. Flynn takes another drink. "All that blood inside the precious glass balls . . ."

"The glass balls are filling with blood. Will they drown in their own blood? What will happen next? the audience will wonder. I will tell *you*—but just keep remembering that it takes longer to tell a thing than to do it. Look first at the gang of grown baby girls who by this time have wakened, followed the trail, and watch mesmerized at what is happening to the only mothers they can remember. And, remember, they too still bleed—the great river is becoming a blood-bath . . . "

"But the moment of sanctity is short-lived—hot on their trail come their pursuers, the entire Panzer division, the French Foreign Legion—and, as they arrive, see the miracle and fall to their knees . . . "

"Then above them, out of the sun it seems, comes the 82nd Airborne prepared to bomb—but they see the miracle: they crash-land over Ontario. Bursts of smoke and fire are now added to the melee . . . "

"Whereupon the Virgin, Daisy, begins to twirl the balls on her fingertips, faster and faster. And the sun is now her nimbus, and now all we see are three furious balls of red, their center a cone of blue. Then the balls fly from her hands. Over the falls, down into water, weightless, buoyed up by the spume."

"Rose and Rose-lima, by now, have drowned in their own blood. I didn't expect that," said Flynn.

"No! Listen to me, Flynn—you are looking for more than you're given to see. All you see is light, water, blood."

"They crash against the rocks. Glass flies like glitter in all directions. There is no difference now between glass and water; and water has become a river of blood. Those on shore leap—they dive like the famous Esther Williams—

201

and swim to Rose and Rose-lima. Using all their arms, they lift us up."

"Everyone ascends into Heaven then."

"There are a few details to be ironed out."

"But the ending?" Flynn asked. Since Lydia Somerleyton there was nothing more interesting to her than endings. But the brain, she recalled, was sometimes the heaviest part of the body. If you lay unconscious—perhaps dead drunk—perhaps hit on the back of the skull with a hammer—and someone came along to pick you up, that person would have to lift the head first. Take care of the brain, and the rest takes care of itself—flesh, the ball-and-chain comes tumbling after. Isn't that what she had done?

"It ends with Justice being done," said Rose.

"Isn't that nice?" said Rose-lima.

But Flynn was silent, half-asleep in the cold. As her eyelids closed, the stage beyond the open doors narrowed, darkened; lights burned out, the farce complete; mistaken identity unmasked; true lovers united. Pure and simple Justice accomplished, as if she had every right to expect such a thing.

It was only, then, the middle of the afternoon—still, it was that dead space of day, that post-meridian threeish, fourish—too late to begin something new; and what is being done will never be finished in time. Besides, Flynn was asleep, struck unconscious by combat with movie stars, by a glimpse of the future; and Flynn was drunk.

Veronica, the twins heard, could work like the devil. The rings and rattlings of the typewriter faintly falling from the top of the house never seemed to stop except for those pauses in which they knew a match was being struck, the first drag from the Lucky being taken. When Veronica painted, she was silent. The twins shuffled through the cooling grass, worn out to the bone, never noticing the absence of the noise that should have been there. That time of day the noise belonged to, always—the snap of arrows into the target: the sound indistinguishable from the time it took Samaria to make it. But Samaria was gone, to do something else.

He had taken those ghosts by surprise, and he had slaughtered them. They were dead again. But still he didn't know what to do. He couldn't think of anything to do. He would have to think of something or something else would have to happen to make things change.

Little toy women sometimes moved across the yellowing grass over there. He could lift his hand above them and smash them, a fly swatter against flies. Then he would go inside their house and break it, he would break it. Then he would drink water, now the last of his water was gone. He would drink the good water that comes out of a faucet. In a minute, he would have to get out of the van and kneel by the water that was the lake because he would die from thirst if he did not. But he had already done that in the night, and with the water some terrible thing had come into his mouth where it had fluttered and beat its wings until he swallowed; and then he had choked and vomited, so again he was thirsty.

And it was hell-hot in the van now, baking him like fruit in a crust, and now that it was hot—although they were half-covered with clay—they all stank and stank; and the stink poured past his closed windows like water, forcing him to remember water. He should move back in the direction he had come from, if he could remember that direction. Then he would be on the highway and then he would hitch a ride and rob and kill the driver and then he would have a car again, and money, and things would be all right again. But there would be that dreadful, dreadful time between leaving this place and getting into the car that would stop for him; and it was that dreadful time to come that stopped him dead where he was. He would, in that time, be on foot and so he would be ugly. He imagined himself ugly and on foot, trudging, waiting for a stranger's grace; the begging thumb. He nearly, once more, vomited. He would put it off until night. When it was dark, he would *feel* how terrible it was to be on foot but he would not see it; then he would not be ugly. But if he smashed them down, a swatter against flies, then they would stink too. Would that be worse or better than watching them move like little colored spotlights there across the water? He would jerk off, to kill time. Thinking of how it used to be, there, that was good; but then it stank. But then it would not stand up in his fist; he tried and tried, but it would not. So he shut it up again all in the dark, and he hit it and hit it because it was bad.

Samaria stood upright in the boat and poled it across the lake. Full of gin and canned food and hardbound works of fiction, it was too heavy to row.

She would live in the boathouse and not come out, and nothing and no one could force her out until it was all over. It was hard and hot work; and the water lilies were a snarl of bloom, leaf, root chewing at her progress to the upper western bank. She had to circle around; she had to zig-zag. If she got stuck, she would have to stand there and yell for help; or get out and walk home across the water. But she was doing reasonably well; but the urgency to get there and to get there fast was unreasonable; and reason could not assuage it. Someday, when it was all over, she would dynamite the fucking lilies to death. But once in the boathouse she would be all right. To distract herself, she tried to pretend she was the boatman of the Charon and her books dead souls; but then it was not the work of moving the boat that was killing her: killing her was the work of drawing yet another breath: if Flynn had not fallen in love with the stranger, then she would never have fallen in love with Flynn, would never have noticed, walking in the door that night, how Flynn's ankle so certainly arrived at Flynn's heel; and how that heel became instep; how she had suddenly known that what she saw, (and what seeing it made of her) was the meaning of everything Veronica had said, ever, of art. So her eye had stopped there. The rest of the foot, the rest of the flesh, was a darkness, then a spilling of after images (as though after bright light) from beneath her eyelids. There was nothing, before blindness, but that one thing to see; and it rammed against the chair rung supporting world-without-end above: and all above, the illuminating *rest*.

It had been sensible to pack the boat with food, despite the sweating labor. It is always sensible, when withdrawing from the world, to have a lot to eat: lima beans, pie, cake, cans of corned beef hash, sacks of coffee, candy bars. The orphanage had been a withdrawal from the world which meant endless oatmeal, the cold grits fried for lunch. Withdrawal from love—and experience had taught her love was the world—meant, oddly, the same (but different) persecuting concentration on what there would be to eat; and the same inability to imagine swallowing any of it. There were three bottles of gin in the boat: there had been none at the orphanage. This time, if she chose, she could drink herself to death.

She had clenched her teeth (preventing trembling) choosing the books to take: although they meant nothing now, she knew that quite soon they would mean everything: there would be nothing else to have. She was sure she had *Wuthering Heights* ("Ellen, I *am* Heathcliffe!") but the rest had been snatched at desperate random—those footsteps, she had thought, were approaching to catch her out, but it had not been *those* footsteps. She was laughable: Flynn was old; she was young. There were things-as-they-are to consider: what would Veronica think? What would Veronica believe to be true, or false? Such questions were like signals from a distant planet—certainly to be considered; mostly impertinent to things at hand, making not the slightest impression on the torture of the real which was herself in love with her granddaughter, Flynn.

Before dissolving, her brain had performed its last bit of cleverness, realizing the cause behind Flynn's transformation from grandchild to beloved: it had been Flynn's lapse from custom: "Eccentric, with Brain Machine" into "Lover;" and Flynn was no longer recognizable except as lover. She had fallen in love with the lover. From some place other than in her body she perceived she was starving, exhausted and too old with years of comfort to confound exertion; but it didn't matter because she had landed and was there. She had rammed into land.

She waded to the shore and tied up the boat. She would rest, draw the next breath; then draw the next breath, then proceed. But pulling in the boat, wrapping the rope around the nearest stump, her toes tangled in the hair of a human head. When she looked and saw what she saw, she praised the distraction as though it were miracle and she a saint discovering not roses but bread in her apron pocket. Gazing on a severed head was ease; it was rest. It took on the light of her working concentration: watching, she sighed. Something had happened, then she—like work—had begun to happen to the first thing. Without noticing the change in herself, she had begun to breathe in peace again.

The story of Veronica goes: inspired by a suffering face, she held a cloth to it; and on the cloth was left an image of the face she had wiped. No one knows for sure, however. Some imagine her to be that woman who had "an issue of blood." Others point out that the English word "vernicle" means true image.

"So it is left up to me," Veronica wrote, "to be the one to tell the truth—and the truth being that this fiction, like all before it, ends with the lovers being pulled in horse-drawn carriages down springtime roads, with the moon at full, with the air sweet, with a sound of singing coming from nowhere. Not even the aging Marschallin is left alone, to be in peace: the curtains dip, blot out the light, rejoin at center; and she is met by roses in her dressing room—red roses from the florist shop: the silver one is gone for good, back to the box in the properties room.

"One thing leads to another: when the novelist falls in love with the painter, then her novel becomes a forgery of paintings—she is hoping to screen her quick-change acts behind a confusion of forms, and ever deny them change. This is true love; and its course runs true, though not smooth. All that really happened is that the lover won the beloved, and became the beloved; and the nature of all kinds of rapture, including this, is that it must clothe itself in disguise—the god in swan's feathers, the mother in sheaves of wheat; the act of love a magic-lantern show, a proliferation of forgeries: which, taken all in all, seem real enough. There is no ending that is, eventually, not happy: it is a comedy for music in three acts . . . "

Veronica stops typing, deeply breathes the sudden silence, lights a Lucky. She stands to stretch and look out at the rose garden in its final act of flowering. Both smoke and breath cloud the window pane. She wipes it with her hand, looks again, clouds it again.

The garden is rich, curved, secluded; full of hours of care. It is approached by paths made through the pine tree grove. It has been mathematically terraced to seat the summer audiences, who bring their own cushions; and to let the audiences in and out without letting them near the flowers. The stage is a circle of bare ground, dead center among the roses. The audience sits above and behind the roses; the audience must look over the roses to see what is happening in the little arena. It occurs to Veronica that the performances are over for good; then, that she and all the rest are going away soon, all in separate directions. She sings, absentmindedly, tonelessly, "Yet in my flesh shall I see God . . . ;" but stops mid-song. She sees something through the glass that is neither rose nor thorn. She *thinks* she has seen something, but once more the glass clouds. She does not wipe it clean; she does not make certain. She snaps the curtains together, then makes a peephole; through it, she inhales and exhales and the scene appears and disappears.

First she sees Daisy—or some woman like Daisy, who reminds her of Daisy. It is probably Daisy, Veronica thinks. Daisy's hair is as meticulously stacked into curls as it ever was. Daisy is as fat as before, even fatter (but when Veronica inhales, clearing the glass a little, Daisy is thinner;

208

in fact bone-thin). Exhaling, Veronica sees Daisy wearing something that could be a ball gown voluminous with skirts and shimmery with damp or light. Inhaling, she sees the exact opposite: Daisy in flannel trousers and jacket, a necktie with a glint of stickpin.

Veronica holds her breath. Daisy has appeared at the edge of the pine tree grove, and she is dragging something behind her. About to descend the terraces, she stops and looks behind her, moving her mouth, speaking. It is Rose and Rose-lima behind her; they have entered from the trees, carrying the other end of the bundle between them. Veronica exhales; the twins disappear. The twins are still too far away. But then (Veronica inhales) the twins are much closer, closer to her than Daisy: they have dropped the bundle. They are running down the terraces. They are naked, are holding themselves, keeping the cold off. Drops of water fly from their hair. Daisy comes behind now, bumping the bundle downhill; and quickly all are gone, fragmented among the roses.

Veronica is breathing too fast; she discerns nothing but quaking blots of color—yellow, pink, red, orange, lavender: the Nellie Melba, the Mrs. Andrew Elton-King, the Abraham Lincoln, the Miss Muffet: then holds her breath: they are stage-center, unwrapping the bundle. They are unwrapping a human body, what seems to be a tall male Caucasian, blond-headed, black-bearded. What seems to be a man—but Flynn has worn beards, has been Gertrude wearing a beard. Then, Veronica can't be sure if it is a feather-tipped arrow jutting up from the body's chest. Her eyes could be deceiving her, or her breath—it could be a thorned branch. Neither is she sure if what Daisy holds in her hand is a gun. When the bearded person is entirely revealed, Daisy, Rose, and Rose-lima stand up still and straight and look down at what they have brought home. After a while, when nothing else happens, Veronica drops the curtain and returns to her desk. "By the way," she wrote, "the person was wet with water and drenched in blood."

Although Veronica had not looked yet at her, Veronica could tell that Daisy was smiling. Then Daisy touched her on the arm, then Veronica looked up, but still frightened by what she might see—the real Daisy or the one who was not Daisy. Flynn had once said, in a fever, "My mother copulates on top. She rides men like horses, to keep her hair neat." Veronica took her hands off the typewriter and smiled back at Daisy.

"I didn't want to say anything until I was sure you were finished. I didn't want to startle you—I *am* a sudden appearance."

"I'm almost finished, but not quite. Have you come back to live here again?"

"If you're almost finished, that may be impossible."

"That's true. For a start, I'll go to New York. There's a little apartment on Grand Street I can have."

"But on the other hand, I just got back. I've already seen my mother and two of my daughters. Either my mother or I have recently killed someone. I thought the man was attacking my mother, so I shot him. My mother says, 'I thought the man was attacking my daughter, so I sent an arrow into him.' We both happened to him at exactly the same time. No one can ever know which of us got there first. He was between the two of us. He couldn't decide which of us to take. In the first place, I was only there to commit suicide. I had come home to do that. I was going to shoot myself through the mouth. I was going to lean over the water, then shoot. I had hoped you'd find my body floating in the water lilies. I heard a noise—the

210

way a cat hisses before it bites. He was stumbling between me and my mother, confused with a knife in his hand. One of us, or both of us, then killed him.

"My mother is in love and is going to live in the boathouse now unless somebody stops her. I have been married again—of course you know that. But this time it didn't work—no daughter for all my trouble. So late yesterday the thought of suicide caught my fancy—and what a lucky thing! I saved my mother from certain death."

Veronica began to type again. "Will you speak more slowly," she said. "I want to make sure I write it the way you say it. It's terribly hard working from the real thing." But she stopped writing and only looked at Daisy.

"Such a beauty you are, Veronica! I always thought so. I assure you I'll speak more slowly. Go ahead and write some more."

"I stopped because it struck me you just said you saved your mother's life."

"I said—no. No, I said I saved my mother from certain death."

"That isn't my point. Certainly I know that one person is dead. I saw that. I see that one person is alive—you. And you *say* that Samaria is alive, and in love, and suffering, at the boathouse. But I say *Samaria*, and you say *my mother*—so I am confused—perhaps the way the killer you killed was confused. How do I know which is the mother and which is the daughter? How can I know that for sure? Two grown women—which is which?"

"Now how can I answer that!" Daisy laughed. "Search your memory! Use your brain! Find something to remind you of something else—perhaps a snapshot of me in a little woolen bathing suit, a bathing suit with a duck on it, and I'm standing at the edge of a lake with my feet in the water. Or you can remember how I was—*I* remember how I was! A young girl in a porch swing on Valentine's Day eating candy hearts from a paper sack—*Be Mine, Thine Alone, I Love You*. And so forth."

Daisy leaned forward a little, her smile coming and going. Veronica believed that Daisy meant to tease her. Veronica said, "It could be Samaria in that picture, not you. I might be remembering another girl in a porch swing, not you. I wonder who the real one is. It might be me. Like everything else, one is real, the other a forgery."

"Which is the mother, which the forgery? My goodness, Veronica." Daisy shook her head. A curl loosened and fell against the middle of her forehead. "Forget it. I helped my mother into the boathouse with all her things. Then I went back to where we had left the killed man and saw the twins swimming the lake, coming to get me. We used my mother's blanket to wrap it in—she'll need a new one. We used the boat; we rowed it home."

"I know all that. Don't sit so close by me, Daisy. I want you to tell me about how you and Samaria discovered the half-buried torsos, the severed heads, the remnants of arms and legs. Eyeballs gouged from skulls."

"I don't remember anything like that. You're making that up."

"Rose and Rose-lima will say that what I've said is so."

"It sounds like the petrified things in Pompeii, those things you faked and put there. Will we find necklaces of hammered gold, too, across the lake? And clay shards painted with wavy blue lines to suggest that the pieces were water jugs, once upon a time?"

"It's not a bad idea, Daisy." Veronica wrote it all down.

"I saw my mother. Then I saw my daughters Rose and Rose-lima. They told me they menstruate now, and I cried a little. They are old enough now to go alone to Hollywood, and that's where they say they're going. Then I saw my daughter Flynn. Flynn was in your workshop. She was crouched high up on the rafters waiting for the nerve to walk across to the other side. She is learning how to be a rope-dancer, she told me. She told me that she will be a rope-dancer thousands of feet up in the air for the rest of her life."

Veronica wrote it all down. "Was she excited to see you? Did she fall?"

"She was excited about learning rope-dancing. She would not look down, not even to look at me. Thousands of feet up, in thin air, my daughter."

"So one more time, which is the mother and which the daughter?"

"If I say it, it is true. Believe me, Veronica."

"You are patronizing me, like a child or an old woman—while your daughter walks through thin air."

"My mother grows more and more to look like my daughter Flynn."

"There's frost predicted for tonight. You're just in time for a last look at the roses. Flynn will freeze to death rope-dancing tonight."

"She will think of something."

Suddenly it is dark, so Flynn inches back down to the ground and switches on all lights. She aims the lamps at the ceiling, but the ceiling is too far away; the light reveals nothing but mazes of criss-crossing shadows. But that is enough for Flynn. She goes back up, ready, nerveless, her arms her only balancing pole. She puts one foot out, readies the second. Beneath her, is lamplight and space; and smells of old wood, turpentine, colors. Before she moves, she breathes. It is as if she breathes the colors—

213

yellow to blue, brown to green to purple. Then she is into the light and gone, nearly across before she has even begun, Veronica wrote, the end.